A PENGUIN MYSTERY

The Gigolo Murder

MEHMET MURAT SOMER was born in Ankara in 1959. After graduating from Middle East Technical University (ODTÜ) School of Industrial Engineering, he worked for a short time as an engineer, and for an extended period as a banker. Since 1994, he has been a management consultant, conducting corporate seminars on management skills and personal development. Somer has written a number of made-to-order scenarios for feature films and television series, as well as classical music critiques for various newspapers and magazines. He currently lives in Istanbul.

KENNETH JAMES DAKAN was born in Salt Lake City in 1964. After spending a year in New Zealand as a Rotary Youth Exchange Student, he attended New York University's Mass Communications Department. On January 1, 1988, he set off on an around-the-world trip. He has not yet returned. Currently, he resides in Istanbul, where he works freelance, translating, writing a morning news bulletin, contributing to travel guides, editing, and doing voice-over interviews for industrial films.

The Gigolo Murder

· MEHMET MURAT SOMER ·

PENGUIN BOOKS

PENGUIN BOOKS
Published by the Penguin Group
Penguin Group (USA) Inc., 375 Hudson Street, New York, New York 10014, U.S.A. • Penguin
Group (Canada), 90 Eglinton Avenue East, Suite 700, Toronto, Ontario, Canada M4P 2Y3 (a di-
vision of Pearson Penguin Canada Inc.) • Penguin Books Ltd, 80 Strand, London WC2R 0RL,
England • Penguin Ireland, 25 St Stephen's Green, Dublin 2, Ireland (a division of Penguin
Books Ltd) • Penguin Group (Australia), 250 Camberwell Road, Camberwell, Victoria 3124,
Australia (a division of Pearson Australia Group Pty Ltd) • Penguin Books India Pvt Ltd, 11
Community Centre, Panchsheel Park, New Delhi – 110 017, India • Penguin Group (NZ), 67
Apollo Drive, Rosedale, North Shore 0632, New Zealand (a division of Pearson New Zealand
Ltd) • Penguin Books (South Africa) (Pty) Ltd, 24 Sturdee Avenue, Rosebank, Johannesburg
2196, South Africa

Penguin Books Ltd, Registered Offices:
80 Strand, London WC2R 0RL, England

First published in Penguin Books 2009

1   3   5   7   9   10   8   6   4   2

Copyright © Mehmet Murat Somer, 2003
Translation copyright © Kenneth James Dakan, 2009
All rights reserved

Originally published in Turkish under the title *Jigolo Cinayeti*.

PUBLISHER'S NOTE
This is a work of fiction. Names, characters, places, and incidents either are the product of the
author's imagination or are used fictitiously, and any resemblance to actual persons, living or
dead, business establishments, events, or locales is entirely coincidental.

LIBRARY OF CONGRESS CATALOGING-IN-PUBLICATION DATA
Somer, Mehmet Murat, 1959–
[Jogolo cinayeti. English]
The gigolo murder / Mehmet Murat Somer ; [translated by Kenneth Dakan].
p. cm.—(A Penguin mystery)
ISBN 978-0-14-311629-5
I. Dakan, Kenneth. II. Title.
PL248.S557J6413 2009
894'.3534—dc22   2009029659

Printed in the United States of America
Set in Dante MT • Designed by Elke Sigal

Cast of Characters

Ali   Money-counter Ali; freelance computing employer
Ponpon   Drag queen, close friend
Sofya   Former mentor, current archenemy
Hüseyin   Taxi driver, admirer
Kemal Barutçu (Cihad2000)   Fellow hacker, confined to wheelchair
Selçuk Taylanç   Police bureau chief
Refik Altın   Gay poet
Cüneyt   Club bodyguard
Hasan   Club waiter
Osman   Club DJ
Şükrü   Club bartender
Volkan Sarıdoğan   The late gigolo
Okan Sarıdoğan   Volkan's brother, a junkie
Ziya Göktaş   Volkan's uncle and former lover
Haluk Pekerdem   Handsome lawyer
Canan Hanoğlu Pekerdem   Haluk's wife
Faruk Hanoğlu   Loan shark, Canan's stepbrother
Nimet Hanoğlu   Faruk's wife
Sami   Faruk's business partner

The Girls at the Club
Afet
Aylin
Dump Truck Beyza

Çişe
Hairy Demet
Blackbrow Lulu
Mehtap
Melisa
Nalan
Shrewish Pamir
Bearded Barbie
Sırma

Glossary

abi elder brother

abla elder sister

aman oh! ah! mercy! for goodness sake!

ayol/ay exclamation favoured by women; well!

ayran drink made of yogurt and water

bey sir; used with first name, Mr.

börek a flaky, filled pastry

dolma cooked stuffed vegetables

dürüm sandwich wrap

efendi gentleman, master

efendim Yes. (answer to call). I beg your pardon?

estağfurallah phrase used in reply to an expression of thanks, exaggerated praise, or self-criticism

fatiha the opening chapter of the Quran

geçmiş olsun expression of sympathy for a person who has had or is having an illness or misfortune

hacı hadji, pilgrim to Mecca

hanım lady; used with first name, Mrs., Miss.

hoca hodja, Muslim teacher

ibne faggot (derogatory)

inşallah if God wills; hopefully

kandil one of four Islamic feast nights

kilim flat-weave carpet

lokum Turkish delight

maşallah   what wonders God has willed; used to express
    admiration

mevlit   a religious meeting held in memory of a dead person

meyhane   Turkish taverna

meze   appetizers, traditionally accompany drinking

namaz   ritual worship, prayer

oglancı   pederast, not necessarily considered "gay" in Western
    sense

peştemal   waist cloth worn at a Turkish bath

poğaça   flaky pastry

rakı   raki, an anise-flavored spirit

sen   you, second person singular; used in familiar address

siz   you, second person plural; used in formal address

teyze   aunt; used to address older women

vallahi   by God; I swear it is so

When I'm good, I'm very good.
But when I'm bad, I'm better.

——MAE WEST

I believe in censorship.
After all, I have made a fortune out of it.

——MAE WEST

The Gigolo Murder

Chapter 1

Superhandsome Haluk was pale when he returned. Even in the dimly lit room, it was clear the color had drained from his face.

"That was Faruk on the phone. He's been arrested for murder."

We both looked at him in astonishment.

"I don't understand," gasped his wife, Canan, who was dressed as a stylish Nişantaşı girl.

"On suspicion of killing a minibus driver."

He looked at me apologetically as he spoke, sorry for having ruined what had promised to be a pleasant evening with this news.

That's how it all started. While my dear friend Ponpon was onstage, putting on a sensational show at one of the trendiest, hippest, and priciest nightclubs in Istanbul, yet another murder fell right into my lap. My passion for amateur sleuthing was suddenly inflamed, my stomach full of butterflies.

Naturally, the beginning to this story has a prelude. I was smack in the middle of one of the most depressive periods of my life. If I had to describe it as a color, it'd be violet. I was imprisoned in a chunk of amethyst.

It had been ages since I'd left the house. Days since I'd shaved. I'd occasionally catch glimpses in the mirror of a strange presence: a cross between a cadaver and a ghost. It couldn't be me. I was down in the dumps and unable to surface. Of course it wasn't the first time I'd been jilted. But this time was different.

I'd hoped for a serious relationship, even indulged in foolish fantasies about the future. I'd imagined us growing old, shaving side by side in the morning, dozing in front of the TV, taking a long cruise together. I hadn't envisioned the slightest friction of any kind, with the possible exception of those classic tugs-of-war for the morning newspaper, or scenes over who forgot to put the cap back on the toothpaste.

I loved waking up to his scent, nestled in the glistening golden hairs of his chest. I'd even begun going less often to my nightclub and made an effort to be at home when he returned in the evening. His routine was the opposite of mine, off in the morning, back in the evening, the reverse of the rhythm of my life. I'd normally leave just before midnight and return home at dawn. But what I really wanted was to spend evenings with him, next to him, just talking. His appreciation for my skills in the kitchen drove me wild, the way he'd come up behind me while I was cooking, throw his arms around me and kiss me, make love to me on the kitchen table, Jack Nicholson to my Jessica Lange in the *The Postman Always Rings Twice*.

Our affair was as trouble-free as any relationship between two men could be. He wasn't ashamed of me, introduced me to his friends and even to his children. He wasn't fussed by my choice of social identity, by what I wore, by whether I dressed as a woman or a man when we went out. He said he loved me for who I was, as I was, and didn't try to change me.

Our relationship had not yet turned into a power struggle; there was no jockeying for the upper hand.

He'd explained to me why it had to end, but I still didn't get it. I ran through everything from every possible angle, repeatedly analyzing each word of every sentence I could remember. But I couldn't find the answer to that one-word question: Why?

It's said that within every story there's a vacuum just waiting to be filled with fantasies and fabrications. Wherever this vacuum had been in our relationship, I couldn't find it. Were I to locate it, to fill it somehow, I would find peace. But I couldn't. Either my powers of imagination were lacking or my brain wasn't working.

I discovered for the first time the full physical effects of sorrow and heartbreak. And painkillers didn't help.

The phone was unplugged. Visitors were turned away, politely at first, then harshly, with no regard for their feelings. I couldn't have cared less about the number of friends I'd lost. For I was as alone as I would ever be. Abandoned. In the final equation, what difference would the addition of a friend, or the subtraction of two, make? Forsaken and alone, that was me.

In the old days, my pain would turn to rage. Perhaps that's what was so difficult now. I couldn't cry, couldn't get angry. I just sat there.

I was too weak to shake myself out of it. If I could just shake myself out of it, I'd pull through somehow, I knew that. I'd never seen anyone in such a state, hadn't heard of it, hadn't read about it in books, hadn't even seen it in films. It was something else entirely. Interminable and unrelenting. The rain would never end, the sky would remain shrouded in lead, forever dull, and I'd grow thinner and thinner, even though I ate only junk food, shivering always, trembling inside as I wasted away to nothing. Yes, my case was something else entirely.

Seeking relief for the pangs in my stomach, I rummaged through the kitchen cupboards. There wasn't much there. I returned to bed with half a package of stale potato chips. The sheets were still warm.

The doorbell rang. There was no way I'd open the door. Whoever it was, they could ring and ring, get bored, and eventually go away. Ignoring the sound, I continued sipping coffee as I watched a music video on TV.

There was pounding on the door.

"I know you're home. Open up, or I'll break down the door."

It was Ponpon. My loyal, devoted, ever cheerful friend Ponpon.

At that moment, her numerous admirable qualities only made her that much more annoying.

She wouldn't be able to break down a steel door. I brushed her from my mind, turning up the volume on the TV to mask the racket. Ponpon raised her voice to a shout. The voice lessons she'd taken many years earlier enabled her now, at my house, to produce a soulless screeching reminiscent of Sertab Erener in top form. Fortunately, her cries conveyed more emotion than Erener, who belts out each song with the same utter lack of feeling. There was something threatening about Ponpon's cries; she was bullying me openly. And by now there wasn't a soul in the apartment building who didn't know it.

"If you don't open up I'll get the police to smash the door down. I mean it. Open up this instant!"

She meant it. Like the other girls, Ponpon doesn't know where to stop. I waited until the clip for R.E.M.'s "Losing My Religion" had ended, deciding once again that it was my all-time favorite and that it accompanies full-blown depression beautifully.

Ponpon clearly had no intention of leaving. The screeching was intermittent, but the pounding nonstop. I decided to open the door. I'd make up some excuse to get rid of her; failing that, I'd tell her off and send her on her way.

When I opened the door a crack, she pushed her way in.

"Look here, girlfriend, if you're trying to make me worry myself to death, give it up already. I'll wring your neck first!"

Ponpon was at least as tall as me, but nearly twice the weight. The threat was not an idle one, as she grabbed me by the arm and propelled me inside. I was in no shape to defend myself with either Thai boxing or aikido.

"Leave me alone," I said.

Her grip on my arm hurt.

"Don't even think about it," she barked. "I came here to get you to snap out of it. What's with this depression, sweetie? Enough already. It's been weeks. You're acting like there aren't any other men around. For a dish like you? They're everywhere!"

Bug-eyed, she droned on and on, as though that was the only problem.

"Cut the long face! I'm not going anywhere until you're better."

"Enough Ponpon! Please . . . . go. Leave me alone!"

"You're a real nutcase! I came here under my own steam, and I'll leave when I'm good and ready. I'm not taking orders from you. Humph!"

I was unable to lift a finger. Ponpon's persistence is well-known. Once she's made up her mind, that's it.

She turned on the lights and threw open the curtains. I couldn't understand why she bothered. It was dark outside.

"It's so stuffy in here," she scolded, opening the windows. A damp chill filled the room. Istanbul was suffering one of its raw, blustery winters.

"Ponpon, you heard me. Go!" I said, surprised by the vigor in my voice.

"Don't be ridiculous, *ayol*. You're not thinking straight. You're not yourself . . ."

"Go, I said! Get lost, *ayol*!"

"See, you said '*ayol*.' You're coming around. And your eyes are positively shining."

"Shining daggers, you mean," I corrected her.

"Well, shining nonetheless," she shot back.

"Ponpon, my nerves are shattered. Don't push me. I'm in no shape to fight. Just go straight to the door, and leave."

"*Ayol*, who do you think you're trying to order around? Getting on your nerves, am I? Yes, sir! I've gotta laugh at that one. *Ayol*, you're the one who's been getting on *my* nerves—for a long time now!"

"This is my house," I pointed out. "It's my home, and I don't want you here. That's final."

"You know not what you say. First we'll get you bathed, then a shave and some makeup. Then you'll be ready to chat."

She radiated energy, positively glowing in the most meaningless and futile way.

Ponpon raked me over with her eyes. She was probably calculating exactly how much weight I'd lost. With my beard stubble and the rings under my eyes, I must have been a sight indeed.

"Ay!" she screeched shrilly, demonstrating once again those hours of formal voice lessons. "Just what is it with you? You're skin and bones. I'm not leaving you like this. And your clothes stink. Now march! Straight to the shower!"

I was dragged to the bathroom and thrust inside. I didn't have the strength to put up a fight. Like a helpless child, I surrendered.

"Are you going to wash yourself, or shall I?"

"I'll wash myself," I said, bowing my head.

"Good," she replied briskly, but didn't forget to take the key with her as she left. "Leave the door open . . ."

She must have been afraid I'd try something stupid. I hadn't even considered such drastic measures. At most, I'd have locked myself inside and waited until she left. But Ponpon wasn't going to be outdone in a waiting game or test of wills. She'd invariably come out ahead.

Ponpon had been around the block. She knew it all, and had a strong opinion on every subject and a solution to every problem. She spoke mysteriously of numerous adventures, had supposedly savored every conceivable flavor of love and screwed in every possible position. I'd never known her to be involved with anyone, though; just had a series of one-sided crushes.

She claimed to have become a transvestite solely to spite her family. She also claimed that she'd never worked the streets, that she'd always been too "refined" for that sort of thing. She'd been working at the same nightclub for years, taking to the stage in Bodrum in the summer. She was certainly consistent. The doyenne of our little circle, the Yıldız Kenter, even the Bedia Muvahhit, of our glittery stage. Ponpon paints on heart-shaped lips and vaudeville makeup, just like Bedia, and has us in stitches with the same subtle, cutting wit.

When I turned on the hair dryer, she poked her head in.

"Good for you," she said. "See how much better you look. Fresh as a daisy."

She studied my naked body, from head to toe. Clearly she didn't think much of what she saw.

"When was the last time you ate? You look like one of those Ethiopians."

"I eat," I protested guiltily.

"Don't lie to me. The kitchen's bare. I checked the rubbish bin, too. Empty."

I wasn't pleased that she'd gone so far as to rummage through my garbage. But, on the other hand, her interest pleased me, gave me a sense of pride.

"I just had some potato chips."

She screwed up her face, as aghast as any health nut.

"That doesn't count. Junk doesn't replace real food!"

Ponpon is one of those who believe there is a direct link between a balanced diet and health, and between a healthy appetite and happiness.

"Your legs are getting all stubbly, too, but we'll sort that out another time," she said. "Now why don't you give yourself a good shave. I'll be waiting."

Shaving was more difficult than I'd expected. With shaky hands I set about doing something I used to do effortlessly twice a day. Now I was afraid of cutting my face. Fear! Yes, a sense of fear. So, somewhere deep inside, there was still a spark of self-interest. Not all my feelings had dried up and died. I was able to feel fear.

"How's it going?"

I turned my face, half-covered with shaving cream, and looked at her with empty eyes.

"You're about to die of hunger, God forbid. I should have realized the second I set eyes on you."

She walked over to my side and popped a piece of hard candy into my mouth. I had no idea where she'd found it.

"It'll do you good, give you energy."

Winking, she added, "For now at least."

She was sucking on one as well, her scarlet lips pursed into a button as she spoke. Cinnamon flavor.

When I emerged from the bathroom Ponpon sat me down across from her, chattering all the while about who had done what with whom, as she applied a thick coat of makeup in the over-the-top style that was all she knew: for my face, a dusting of powder over layer after layer of foundation; for my eyelids, at least four different shades of eye shadow; and for my mouth, lilac lipstick and a dark shade of purple penciled along my lip line.

When I turned to look at myself in the mirror, I couldn't help smiling in amusement. I looked like something out of Kabuki theater, a stylized, plastic version of myself.

Ponpon misinterpreted my smile.

"You like it, don't you?" she said. "You look great. Baby's back and it's all thanks to me."

"You don't think it's a bit much?" I ventured timidly.

"No, not at all. It's perfect for a fresh-faced young thing like you. I know how much you adore pastels."

It's true that she'd thoughtfully chosen pastels, my favorite, but there were enough of them to paint at least three more faces. It would take me at least half an hour to scrape it all off.

I managed a smile, an appreciative one this time. It didn't work. There's no point in trying to fake it when Ponpon's around. Her face fell when she realized I wasn't completely thrilled by her artistry.

Every article of clothing selected from the wardrobe was too big for me. The Audrey Hepburn figure I'd struggled to maintain all these years was gone, swiftly replaced by Twiggy's—and suffering from chronic wasting disease, no less.

"You're a mess," Ponpon confirmed. "At this rate we'll have to choose your clothes in the children's department."

We finally decided on a bright red jacket and miniskirt ensemble that I rarely wear. I think Audrey Hepburn wore the same outfit in *Charade*, only hers was pale pink.

As I held the jacket up in front of me, I studied myself in the mirror. I'd hoped that smiling would make me feel better.

"That won't do; you'll need another lipstick," Ponpon observed through narrowed eyes. She seemed to think that my only problem was that lilac and red don't match.

The outfit was clearly too big, and the legs sticking out below it were spindly and unshaven.

"It doesn't fit," I said.

Lips pursed, a single eyebrow raised, Ponpon looked me up and down.

"You're right," she agreed. "It doesn't."

Taking off the skirt and jacket, I dejectedly sank down onto a corner of the bed. She came and sat down next to me, putting an arm around my shoulders and pulling me close. I leaned my head against her.

We wordlessly studied ourselves for a moment in the full-length mirror opposite. She sat erect, her ample bosom glorious in its generosity. Shoulders collapsed, I huddled against her dejectedly. Like a child in need of protection. A skinny, weak child with frightened eyes, my ribs sticking out. The garish makeup only heightened the effect: a clownish hussy face and an emaciated, hairy body.

She gently stroked my shoulders and leaned over to kiss the top of my head. Then she pulled me tight. She was watching me in the mirror.

I wanted to cry. To break down completely and sob on that sturdy, warm shoulder. To sniffle and drool. But I couldn't do it. Ponpon cried for me silently.

"My mascara's going to run," she said with a weak laugh.

But she kept crying. Perhaps she was remembering a long ago adventure, one of those great love affairs she always talked about, the ones that inevitably ended in heartbreak, the ones that had left her numb and hard. Or perhaps she cried hoping I'd join in.

But I didn't. I couldn't.

Chapter 2

The place where Ponpon took me to "have fun" after we'd eaten was none other than the club where she worked. It was nearly time for her to go onstage and, not wanting to leave me alone, she'd dragged me along. I hadn't seen her new show. Nor was I even faintly interested in doing so. After all, I'd watched her perform for years. How much different would this one be?

The second we entered, she gave the headwaiter a quick rundown of my situation. She wanted to make sure they treated me well. That is, she wanted to make sure I was pitied!

A callous, hard-bitten old thing, the headwaiter nodded his head sympathetically. Compressing his thin lips, he studied me. I suppose he imagined the pose expressed understanding and an appreciation for how much I'd suffered.

The two of them kept talking. Like any true artist, Ponpon was casing the joint, gathering information about the crowd. Beaming, she turned to me.

"Two dear friends of mine have turned up. I'll make certain you're seated at their table. You'll love them. They're so refined. And there'll be a man for you to check out, to boot."

"Perhaps I could sit on my own? Somewhere in the back?"

"I won't hear such nonsense! You can even watch me from the wings if you like. Really, sweetie!"

I was overcome with drowsiness from the food Ponpon had practically forced down my throat and didn't have the energy to respond, let alone argue. Back home, all I'd wanted to do was sink back into bed. But the B$_{12}$ she'd given me at dinner was beginning to take effect. Yes, I was definitely perking up.

We followed the headwaiter to the table with Ponpon's esteemed guests. They were sitting right in front of the stage.

Ponpon kissed each of them on both cheeks, singing out greetings as she did so. I made a point of hanging back. Although I hadn't even seen their faces yet, I was already recoiling from the couple's confident chuckles and throaty coos. But fate had assigned me to Ponpon's care, and the unavoidable inevitably happened: She turned around and introduced me.

Canan Hanoğlu Pekerdem was the personification of what they call a "true lady": beautiful, imperious, elegant, and icy. Naturally, she didn't rise, merely extended a hand for me to clasp, palm turned slightly toward the floor so I wouldn't miss the large diamond ring. She also displayed a French manicure on that exquisitely shaped hand.

Her hair was styled in the latest fashion, her makeup deceptively simple—and oh so preferable to what I was wearing—her clothing screamed "label," her jewels were few in number but no doubt insured, and around her floated the summery scent of Vera Wang. In other words, I was green with envy.

Her deep green eyes told me she was as calculating as she was clever.

I turned to the husband, who knew how to treat a lady and had risen to his feet. When I shifted my gaze from the seated wife to the standing husband, I got my first jolt: What a dish!

"My name's Haluk Pekerdem," he murmured, enfolding my hand in his. I went weak at the knees. "We'd be so pleased if you joined us tonight."

Yes, and so would I. I felt myself blush, but was confident Ponpon's handiwork with the trowel would mask the glow spreading across my face.

Having surrendered me to her friends, Ponpon headed for her dressing room.

Haluk Pekerdem was a well-known attorney who handled sensational corporate lawsuits and the occasional libel suit brought against the press. Any self-respecting businessman made a point of carrying his card. I could only guess at the number of court scribes and junior partners whose hearts he'd set aflutter. He was even better looking in person than the glimpses I remembered having of him in newspapers, magazines, and on the occasional news program. While previously he had caught my attention as someone worth a second look, he was certainly proof that not everyone is photogenic. Yes, his was one of those fabulous faces to which a photographer can't begin to do justice.

I was immediately assigned the role of conversation piece: Canan monopolized the conversation with Haluk on the pretense that she was drawing him out for my benefit. She talked about every subject under the sun.

I sat there, silent and deeply ashamed, in a shapeless outfit and painted face, supposedly nursing an unhealed wound but all atingle for the unattainable man so close by. I was embarrassed by the whole situation. Still, I smiled at all they said and responded with the briefest possible replies.

Canan, who had taken pains to enunciate in bell-like tones each syllable of the Hanoğlu surname she'd inherited from her father, was not a lady of leisure, as I'd expect of someone of her class, but took an active interest in the family's yarn business. They had connections overseas. She mentioned, in passing of course, that she was often forced to pop over to England.

I prayed that Ponpon would soon appear onstage, that for the rest of the night I'd be free to look elsewhere, that I'd no longer have to politely meet their eyes; or rather, that I wouldn't have to refrain from simply staring into Haluk's. My heart still aching from abandonment, my soul as black as night, there was most certainly no point in falling for someone oozing heterosexuality from every pore, particularly while he sat across from me and next to his doting wife. Sometimes one thing can lead to another, and a cautious overture is not necessarily ill-advised, but I wasn't up to it. I was terrified that another blow to my fragile, bruised self-esteem could well push me over the edge.

Although I struggled to avoid his eyes, the table at which the three of us were seated was tiny. Even when I kept my eyes demurely downcast, I saw those hands, one holding a glass of whiskey, the other occasionally reaching for a nut, well-groomed, vein-filled hands that had grown strong and large playing elite sports but had remained entirely free of calluses. His nails were wide and curved at the edges, not trimmed too short. He was wearing a wedding ring, the only blemish on those perfect hands. I'm not a hand fetishist, but those paws were to die for. I'd have allowed them to travel the length and breadth of my body. In fact . . .

Ponpon took the stage in the nick of time.

Her new show had a Latin theme, from the melodic rhythms of *sevillanas* to the driving eroticism of the tango: samba, flamenco, castanets, multilayered skirts . . . After the frilly skirt had done its duty in a flamenco dance number, off it went, revealing a skin-tight skirt with hip-high slashes and fishnet stockings, and the entrance of a slightly mincing but tall and muscular tango partner.

As the simpering tyrant jealously guarded his submissive Ponpon, who was sweating buckets by now (and had thrown her considerable weight into his arms, as though for dear life), Haluk answered his cell phone. He was far too well bred to allow his phone to ring during a performance, so he must have felt its warning vibration. Looking at me and his wife apologetically, he listened for a moment. Whatever it was he heard over the Latin racket, his expression changed completely. Canan and I both looked at him, alarmed.

"Excuse me, I won't be a minute," he said, as he rose and walked to the door, cell phone still pressed to his ear.

Not missing a beat, hips thrusting and feet kicking, Ponpon was watching us out of the corner of her eye, no doubt wondering why Haluk had left so abruptly. She's such a pro, I'm sure I'm the only one who noticed.

"It must be one of his clients," Canan explained. "They ring at the most inconvenient times. Representing tycoons does have its drawbacks, I suppose."

"I'm certain it does," I murmured agreeably.

"They think that the fee he commands entitles them to pick up the phone whenever they please."

"I'm sure they pay for the privilege," I observed, even more agreeably.

She settled for a wan smile, then turned her face toward the stage to indicate that our little exchange had been terminated. The curve of her lip on the side of the face that she presented me with suggested that although events outside her world meant little to her, she was absolutely certain that no offense would be taken.

I wasn't jealous. Not yet. But were I to become so—and it happens fairly often—it would be toward someone like Canan. The fact that she shares a bed with Haluk would have been sufficient grounds. But even if she didn't, her feminine graces would have provoked envy at the least.

Haluk was noticeably pale when he returned to our table. Even in the dimly lit room, it was clear the color had drained from his face.

"That was Faruk on the phone," he said.

That information was directed at Canan. After all, the name Faruk meant nothing to me.

"He's been arrested for murder."

I wasn't the only person at the table to be stunned. But I was the only one content to gaze on worshipfully at Haluk. *She* insisted on speaking.

"I don't understand."

"On suspicion of killing a minibus driver."

He glanced at me apologetically as he spoke; his eyes were deep and riveting. I wanted to dive into them, to surrender myself completely.

Canan was not about to allow me to do any diving.

"He had a traffic accident?"

"Dear, you know they don't detain anyone right away for a traffic accident."

When Ponpon, who had just begun her grand finale, realized that the attentions of her guests of honor, sitting at the VIP table no less, were focused on one another rather than on her spectacle, she resorted to a catcall from the stage.

"Sir, would you mind bargaining with the ladies *after* the show?"

With three sets of outraged eyes suddenly trained on her, Ponpon realized she'd committed a major faux pas. She froze for a split second.

"I'm afraid I have to leave immediately," Haluk said.

"I'm coming, too."

"But that would be rude to our guest."

That he would think of me at a time like this, refer to me as their "guest" even though Ponpon had forced me on them, filled with me pride and allowed me to be gracious.

"I really must insist you leave now. Don't trouble yourself by thinking of me at a time like this. You have urgent business. And Ponpon is a dear friend, so I won't be left alone for long. I'll pass along your regrets. Now please, do go."

"This has all been most unfortunate," said Haluk, a gentleman to the end. But they proceeded to leave me there anyway, each of them handing me a business card as they wished me a good night and assured me they wished to meet again as soon as possible. Ponpon's astonished eyes on their backs, they left the club.

I couldn't help looking at their departing backs as well. What a pair they were! My eyes had strayed to Haluk's bottom. He'd thrust his hands into his trouser pockets, causing his jacket to ride up. Straining against the fine fabric of the seat of his pants—a silk blend, surely—was a magnificently muscular pair of buttocks, two thrusting halves of a crisp apple, the wondrous dancing motions of which were visible even from where I sat, riveted, until they'd swaggered right out the door.

That was how the murder fell straight into my lap, sucking me deep into a swirling vortex of events.

Chapter 3

On the way back to my place I told Ponpon everything that had happened. So relieved was she to learn that they hadn't merely walked out on her show that she began chattering on about everything she knew concerning both Canan and Haluk.

Canan came from money. Her prosperous central Anatolian family had settled in Istanbul shortly after World War II and quickly, in less than a decade, their small fortune had blossomed into a large one. The result of her father's second, and final, marriage, she was an only child, although patriarch Hanoğlu had also fathered two sons with his first wife. Canan enjoyed all the advantages rich parents can buy, including nannies, private tutors, and a Swiss education. Her family did all they could to spoil her, and she was the apple of her doting father's eye.

Ponpon couldn't remember exactly where Haluk was from, but she knew it was somewhere in the Aegean region. He'd arrived in Istanbul to study at the university, after which he went on to earn a master's degree abroad. Although handsome Haluk could have had his pick of any nubile girl from a good family, it was no surprise when he settled on Canan. In fact, the marriage was approvingly considered a match made in heaven.

As far as his law practice, it was unlikely he'd been entirely on the straight and narrow: No scrupulously honest lawyer could have grown so rich so fast.

Ponpon naturally spent the night, sending me off to bed once

I'd downed a glass of warm milk mixed with a spoonful of *pekmez* molasses and a handful of vitamins, under her watchful eye.

I awoke the following morning to the smell of toast, extremely hungry, perhaps as a result of all those vitamins. Sniffing greedily, I detected various other heavenly breakfast aromas mixed in with the toast. I couldn't stand it anymore and jumped out of bed.

Sunlight flooded into my bedroom as I opened the curtains. The first sunlight in days! It had to be a sign: resurrection!

Hearing I was awake, Ponpon sang out a cheery good morning.

"Well, goodness me! Look who's up. If it isn't our own sleeping beauty."

"Good morning," I shouted, keeping it short.

Bursting in on me, Ponpon was dressed in one of her signature embroidered kimonos, an impish smile on her face, to which she'd already applied what only she would deem "staying-home *maquillage.*"

"Go and your wash your face," she ordered. "Breakfast is ready!"

"I know. The smell woke me up. Goodness knows what you've prepared."

Ponpon is an absolute whiz at all things domestic. In a spare hour or so, she'll have whipped up stuffed cabbage rolls dressed with olive oil, mouth-watering Circassian chicken salad with a dusting of ground walnuts, and spinach *börek* with hand-rolled, nearly translucent layers of mille-feuille. Her refrigerator is always full, and her hands usually nimbly at work on a bit of embroidery or delicate lace. "We simply must keep alive the traditions of the sultanas," she'll mumble through a mouthful of pins while hand sewing a bewildering array of beads, sequins, and spangles onto the performance costumes she designs. In a home overflowing with tacky gimcracks, gewgaws, and bibelots of all descriptions, Ponpon busies herself polishing silver candlesticks, ironing doilies, dusting the fake crystal dangling off velvet lampshades, and affixing "life-affirming" handmade chiffon butterflies to the drapes. Her store of knowledge in the domestic arts could fill a series of cookbooks and a complete encyclopedia of domestic instruction for the ambitious homemaker.

The breakfast she'd prepared was top-notch, a veritable open buffet worthy of any five-star hotel.

"How'd you manage all this?" I asked. "The cupboards are empty."

"The last thing I expected from you was a silly question like that," she admonished. "The numbers of the local market and corner shop are written down in your address book."

She had a point, but much of the lavish spread she'd placed before me couldn't have been found at the overpriced *bakkal* on the corner.

"But our shop doesn't stock bacon . . ."

Yes, she'd even fried up a dozen rashers of bacon. Nice and crispy, just the way I like it.

"It was just a simple question of going online, and presto, two bags of groceries delivered right to your door in half an hour."

"You used my computer?"

Oblivious to my tone, her answer implied she'd simply exercised her most fundamental right:

"Uh-huh."

"But how did you open it? I've got a password."

"As if that'd be a problem. How many times have you typed in your password right in front of me? I know it by heart: Audrey!"

That I'd chosen the first name of my idol as my password was no surprise. But Ponpon's ability to determine my password from the movement of my fingers on the keyboard—since it was impossible for her to have read it on the screen—was a bonus point for her, a demerit for me.

"Oh, before I forget. I charged it all to your credit card . . . Your handbag was here in the kitchen."

"That's fine," I said. "No problem."

"I just thought I'd let you know."

Breakfast was every bit as magnificent as it'd smelled and looked. I savored each mouthful.

Although I'd finished a healthy serving, I ate another plateful at Ponpon's insistence. Strangely, I even relished it.

"I phoned Fatoş. She'll be round this evening," I was informed.

Fatoş Abla is a girl getting on in years who makes house calls to our little circle of drag queens, trannies, and she-males. "Geriatric wolves are the laughingstock of newborn lambs," she'd announced one day, rather incongruously and signally with a well-worn Anatolian maxim, her retirement from the business. That is to say, once she'd hit forty and discovered that her list of clients, her "circle of gentleman admirers," was fast diminishing, she'd exchanged prostitution for a career of waxing, depilatories, eyebrow plucking, arm-hair bleaching, hair coloring, and the like. Her personal life was stormy, punctuated by noisy public scenes during which she cast out a seemingly endless stream of shiftless young lovers. She was said to spend all her earnings on them, for which reason she remained virtually penniless. Nevertheless, her pride was intact, her bearing as regal as Queen Elizabeth's as she deftly tore a tuft of pubic hair from between some girl's legs. Except for Ponpon, we all addressed her as "*abla*," and gave her the respect any elder sister would traditionally expect in Turkey.

"What time is it now?" I asked.

"It's coming on three."

"I must have slept in."

"You need it, sweetie. It's just what your body requires."

I decided to read the newspaper until Fatoş Abla showed up to subject me to the tortuous beautification rituals required of any self-respecting she-male. The news was on page three.

HIGH SOCIETY SENSATION! screamed the headline.

Prominent financial consultant Faruk Hanoğlu had been arrested on suspicion of murder, accused of killing twenty-four-year-old minibus driver Volkan Sarıdoğan.

Displayed side by side were an identity card snapshot of Volkan Sarıdoğan and a posed photograph, obviously taken by a professional, of Faruk Hanoğlu in his office. I called out to Ponpon: "Isn't Faruk Hanoğlu Canan's brother?"

"Uh-huh," Ponpon confirmed. Then, a few seconds later: "Why do you ask?"

"Have you seen the paper? He's been arrested . . ."

"I know. What are you getting at?

There was one question we couldn't get our minds around that morning, one no doubt shared by members of Istanbul high society: Why on earth would this wealthy family man and "personal financial consultant" (read "loan shark") murder a minibus driver?

I reread the article, which was decidedly short on detail. The dated photograph of a young Volkan Sarıdoğan looked out at me with dreamy eyes, handsome even in a cheap instant snapshot. Next to him, in the other picture, Faruk Hanoğlu ostentatiously rested a hand on his desk. He must have taken after his mother; he looked nothing like his half sister, Canan. But then again, the proud, cool smile was the same.

"I met Faruk Bey once," said Ponpon, "at a party Canan was giving at her home. He seemed like a gentleman, not at all the type I'd have pegged for a murderer. He was quite flirty, and very talkative. But there was something strange, something unpleasant, about him. Like he was looking down his nose at everyone."

"In what way?" I asked.

"You know . . . like he wants it, but doesn't want it. One of those who are desperate to give it up but don't bend over when the time comes—and despise those who do. Do you see what I mean?"

I had no idea what she meant. If even Ponpon, who was as eloquent as they come, couldn't find the words to express what she was talking about, it must be difficult indeed to explain.

"You know, there are some people who want something, crave it even, but they're too proud to admit it, even to themselves. Then they despise, or belittle, or harm whatever it is. Almost as though mocking the object of their desire will stop them from wanting it. Do you get what I mean, sweetie?"

"Like the fable about the fox and the sour grapes?"

"No, not exactly . . . *Ay*, enough already! Forget it."

As expected, Haluk Pekerdem was representing his brother-in-law. His name was mentioned in the article, but there was no photograph, or any further details.

"Snap out of it, sweetie. You're all spaced out."

Ponpon was right.

"Penny for your thoughts." She winked.

No amount of money would have persuaded me to admit I'd been lost in a reverie over Haluk Pekerdem.

Chapter 4

In Ponpon's words, I was "back in business" and "good as new." She left me no choice but to allow the world to come crashing in and to respond civilly as it did so. There was no point in putting it off.

"Make sure to smile when you speak; you'll sound friendlier," she instructed. Then Ponpon began dialing every one of the numbers she'd memorized.

She'd begin by speaking at length herself, before thrusting the phone into my hand, my cue to embark on a set string of pleasantries: "Hello . . . How are you . . . I'm fine . . ." This arrangement allowed Ponpon to dramatize the depths of my depression with a hair-raising description of my ruined health and cadaverous appearance, then move on to an excruciatingly detailed and heroic account of her own role in my salvation, from the shade of eye shadow she'd administered to what she'd prepared for each of my meals.

When headwaiter and gossipmonger Hasan heard my voice, he insisted on coming round. I had no doubt that he'd conspired with Ponpon to get his foot in the door. He is self-important and arrogant, but in fact he's the *only* waiter at my club, and he had kept the place going during my breakdown, for which I was grateful. We agreed on a time that day for his visit.

At my insistence, we also called my employer, Ali. I freelance for his computer security firm, working on a commission basis only. Our partnership has been highly profitable for us both. He knows what I am and what I do nights, but doesn't meddle; for my part, I overlook his yuppie ways and all-consuming quest for the almighty dollar. For days now, I hadn't been by the office, answered the phone, responded to messages, or returned his e-mails. It was only natural that he'd wonder what had happened, especially since so much of his business depends on me. I'd have to bite the bullet and phone him. I had no intention of losing my day job as a computer whiz, custom designing antihacker security programs.

When I was put through, he cursed at the sound of my voice, telling me in dollar terms how much my absence had cost us—that is, him. I was ordered to report to the office immediately to discuss several new projects.

Ali and I don't see much of each other outside work. Although our business relationship has lasted for years, and we've made each other rich, he's never even seen my home. In any case, Ponpon hadn't scheduled him in for a visit, so I promised to stop at the office as soon as I could.

"We're losing business every day you're in hiding," he grumbled. "Competition is fierce. They'll think we're not available anymore. Kemal Barutçu is snapping up all our clients. I hope you realize we'll be reduced to selling PC and standard software programs if things go on like this!"

I wasn't ready for his tirade, so in order to end it, I meekly mumbled, "Okay."

Perceptive Ponpon intervened on my behalf, snatching the receiver from my hand to interject, "He's still very weak. I'll have to ask you to keep it short."

"Who was that?"

"A relative," I said, grabbing the phone back. "My spiritual aunt."

Ponpon grimaced. She'd have preferred being described as a younger sister.

Visitors starting arriving even before Fatoş Abla had finished waxing my legs. The appointments Ponpon had so carefully spaced out over the late afternoon and evening were running like clockwork, but unfortunately our growing number of visitors appeared disinclined to leave as punctually as they'd arrived. My living room had turned into what appeared at first glance to be a coffee klatsch of housewives in rather risqué costumes, perhaps a Tupperware party or Avon lady demonstration. I was the only person in the room who wasn't engrossed in a screeching conversation. Occasionally, one of the girls would shoot me a glance of pity, but tinged with what was unmistakable envy.

I didn't bother to attempt to follow their conversations, just sat there amid an unintelligible buzz of baritone and falsetto voices. Nor was I interested in which girl had poached which boyfriend, or triumphant accounts of the miracles wrought by hormone injections and silicon implants.

That is, until my attention was caught by Dump Truck Beyza.

"I had such a shock this morning! An old flame of mine was murdered! And who killed him? Some high-society loan shark! You can't imagine how wonderful he was. Once he got it up, it never came down. And incredibly well hung, like he'd strapped on a Coke bottle. The sort of man everyone should experience at least once. Amen."

"His death has no doubt added several inches," Ponpon interrupted. "Feel free to elaborate as much as you like, sweetie. None of us will be able to verify what you say now that's he's dead."

"If I'm lying, may Allah smite me right on the spot," exclaimed Dump Truck Beyza, lodging a large hand between her considerable breasts.

Blackbrow Lulu jumped in, her mouth still full of cake.

"Don't say that! You've been smitten enough as it is."

"Common! You're all just common," Dump Truck Beyza spat, before turning to me with, "Excuse me. Not you, of course. But I can't think why you're still friends with this lot."

I was intrigued despite myself.

"So you knew Volkan? The guy in the paper today?"

"What do you think I'm saying? You're not even listening! You never listen to me!"

Ponpon responded to this unfortunate attack on my person by lifting a warning eyebrow. She wouldn't allow any bad behavior. Dear Ponpon was protecting me. Allowing her eyes to flutter shut dramatically, she pursed her lips and pointed to her head with the index finger of her left hand. Then she silently mouthed the word "medication."

What's more, she did all this looking directly at me. There's no way I could have missed it.

"What medication? What did you give me? When?" I asked.

"At breakfast," she said, slowly mouthing the words in a barely audible and slightly ominous voice.

"What medicine?"

"Xanax."

She smiled proudly, a child expecting a reward for a good deed.

"But isn't that a drug?" asked Melisa, gulping down a mouthful of coffee.

Turning in Melisa's direction, Ponpon slowly opened and shut her eyelids, thus replying in the affirmative to her question.

"I consulted a physician," she added in authoritative tones. "They don't sell it without a prescription."

"I'm sure you did the right thing," I said.

So the wave of fatigue hitting me was caused by Xanax, not the large breakfast.

"But darling, they say Xanax causes anxiety and suicidal tendencies."

It was just like Fatoş Abla to bring up side effects. She won't even use aspirin, relying instead on homeopathic remedies, herbal teas, and incense.

"Oh no," screeched Dump Truck Beyza, as though I had set off on a pathway to inevitable self-destruction.

"I told you, I asked the doctor," Ponpon said. "A pill or two won't hurt, he said."

Seizing the reins of general conversation, determined to steer us back to what really interested me—Volkan Sarıdoğan, Faruk Hanoğlu, and Haluk Pekerdem—I addressed myself to Beyza.

"Beyza sweetie, tell me all you know about Volkan. From the beginning."

I was depressed, in need of attention, care, and cheering up, so the girls conscientiously shut up and listened to Dump Truck's long-winded ode to the glories of Volkan, which I occasionally interrupted with a question. I'd intended to glean some information about Haluk Pekerdem, but was unable even to get to Faruk Hanoğlu. All Beyza would talk about was the well-hung stud.

Beyza met Volkan when he was fresh from military service and had just begun driving minibuses. It was one of the many occasions on which lusty Beyza, having failed to find a customer, began haunting the minibus routes in search of a man. As usual, she got on a minibus with a driver she fancied, sat next to him in the front seat, and flirtatiously crossed and uncrossed her legs until the last stop. If payment isn't expected, this method works nine times out of ten. As it did that night. Instead of going to the back of the line when the last passengers got out at the final stop, Volkan drove off to a secluded grove in Hacı Osman. Volkan's staying power astonished even Beyza, whose libido never quits. In fact, he wore her out. Volkan began visiting Beyza at home, a blissful arrangement that pleased them both and lasted for some time.

Volkan was "handsome as a movie star," in perfect shape as a result of his recent stint in the army, full of the stamina of the young and sex starved, and the proud owner of an impressive organ that would have guaranteed him superstar status in the adult-film world. Or so Beyza claimed, in descriptions so detailed I suspected she may even have been telling the truth.

"It was thick . . . and it was long . . . and it had a massive head the most luscious shade of pink . . . I mean, once you got your hands on it they had to be pried off. The edges of the crown were like delicate lacework, the snaking veins of the shaft like needlework. So rare; so fine! Wonder of wonders, wrought with the utmost care by the Lord above. And when he came, well, it positively gushed . . . Never in my life have I seen or feasted on anything like it."

Her audience had fallen completely silent and was on the edges of their seats, spellbound, sighing, hearts racing, palms sweaty.

Every good story has a bad guy, and in this case it was Volkan's brother by marriage, his sister's husband. The brother-in-law had a strange control over Volkan, who followed his advice to the letter and would do nothing without consulting him first. But the two were also known to have long and loud arguments. Volkan would say horrible things behind the brother-in-law's back but was reduced to an obedient child in his presence.

According to Beyza, the bad brother-in-law, who was also a minibus driver, had forced Volkan to go from being an amateur gigolo to a professional one.

Blackbrow Lulu was having none of it. "He must have had it in him," she protested. "He couldn't have done it otherwise. Do you really think just anyone can become a gigolo? You're all so gullible! Wake up!"

"I don't care if you believe me or not. The boy was an angel. It was that brother-in-law who spoiled him. And who put him off me. Of course the money had something to do with it. Volkan was up to his ears in debt. He owed for the minibus. I was helping him out but could only do so much."

"Didn't I tell you! See, he was taking your money!" Lulu roared triumphantly. "Instead of blaming him, why don't you take a good look at yourself? You're the one who got the boy used to accepting money."

"Look, Lulu," interrupted Melisa, "if you go on like that you'll get a good walloping. And Dump Truck's got a heavy hand. Take it from me, girlfriend."

"She got that right," growled Dump Truck.

I interjected. "Ignore them. What happened next?"

Not only was I their hostess, but these girls hung out every night at my club. My wish was their command. The girls shut up and Dump Truck continued.

Whether it was the brother-in-law's idea or not, it wasn't long before Volkan became the most sought after gigolo in Istanbul. Nor was it long before the visits to Beyza suddenly stopped. He still got behind the wheel of his minibus from time to time, but he usually left his vehicle in the care of a younger brother or a driver hired for the day. Volkan's time had become far too valuable for ordinary work.

"Such a pity," she concluded. "A lion of a man, and a dick unlikely to grace this earth ever again. What a waste. May Allah strike down whoever did it! May their hands be broken, their eyes blinded, their hearths extinguished . . . Have I left anything out?"

"That should do it, dear," Melisa assured her.

So, the part-time minibus driver allegedly killed by Haluk Pekerdem's brother-in-law, Faruk Hanoğlu, had also been a well-known gigolo . . .

Chapter 5

*T*he girls all left just before Hasan arrived. The chatter, Xanax, and waxing session had left me exhausted, but I still had him to deal with.

A gypsy-pink bag full of accounting books slung across one shoulder, Hasan came determined to fill me in on all that had transpired at the club during my absence, right down to every last broken glass, every restocked roll of toilet paper.

Pulling up his low-slung jeans, he settled into the chair nearest me, bemoaning the crushing responsibility and sleepless nights he'd suffered, as he worked his way through what was left of Ponpon's cake and a tray of spicy walnut canapés. Hasan's lack of a gut is yet another example of God's miracles.

I was overcome by fatigue at the sight of all those accounting books spread out before me. Ponpon took over, gracious hostess mode instantly replaced by a studious headmistress taking stock of pencils and merit badges. Slips of paper were occasionally presented for my approval, and I duly nodded, not bothering to look, and no doubt grinning like a total imbecile, thanks to the Xanax.

Hasan finished expounding on the conscientious discharge of his self-appointed duties in excruciating detail, filling his belly as he filled our ears. Now he moved on to the juicy morsels and choice bits of dirt that are his stock in trade.

The stream of gossip left behind by the recently departed girls was elaborated upon, corrected, and reinterpreted by Hasan: the real reason Afet and İpek had fallen out, and the true identity of the owner of the fur collar they'd scrapped over; the inferior quality of the silicone injections in Sırma's somewhat overripe lips; the crush our barman, Şükrü, had on the comely twink Kaan, who for his part drooled over our bodyguard, Cüneyt, for which reason Şükrü was sore at Çüneyt, who was ignorant of the feelings of either Şükrü or Kaan; and then there was the hapless Mehtap, still wearing her ridiculous red wig, believing it brought her luck.

My boss, Ali, dubbed "the money counter" by Hasan, had come to the club twice looking for me, sending his wishes for a speedy recovery when Hasan told him I was incapacitated by depression. (He hadn't bothered sending flowers at the news of my "condition," but I'd long since learned not to expect courtesies of that sort.)

Then there was news of my old archenemy, Sofya. In order to show off the winter tan she'd acquired during an extended holiday in Morocco, fabulous Sofya had thrown a dinner party, with those pointedly left off the guest list immediately relegated to the class of undesirables. Hasan, who naturally copped an invitation, said the entire affair was one of Sofya's typical events, designed solely for shameless boasting and showing off, but that didn't stop the guests from talking it up as a fete of legendary proportions. Those lucky girls claimed "the only thing missing was bird's milk," and described each item of fabulous furniture in Sofya's house, embellishing them to the extent that later gossips dared suggest that one or two pieces sounded a bit kitsch.

Hasan's final bombshell concerned that man of all seasons, the poet Refik Altın, who was also in advertising, a director, and a fixture on talk-show TV. The lover he concealed from everyone but droned on about ad nauseum had apparently simply disappeared. Refik had appeared at the club the previous night, drank heavily, wept into his cups, and attempted to pick a fight with anyone who dared approach him. Our staff had placated him somewhat, but once everyone left at nearly dawn and the lights were turned up, he was discovered under a far table, where he lay on the floor, snoring.

With the assistance of the bodyguard, Cüneyt, Hasan had managed to stick him into a taxi and take him home.

Not a single detail escapes Ponpon, and she jumped in to interrogate Hasan.

"How did you know where that contrary faggot lives?"

Despite his undeniably flaming ways, suspiciously precise speech, and the trademark jeans slipping down his hips to expose his butt crack, Hasan insists he isn't gay. Ponpon and the rest of us are eternally vigilant when it comes to Hasan, hoping for a slipup that will reveal all. That's why she'd interrupted.

"Well, if he was so drunk, he couldn't have woken up to give you his address . . ." she pounced.

The knowing look on her face said "gotcha."

Hasan faltered for a moment, eyes wide, shoulders hunched.

"It's not what you think," he stammered.

"And what is it that I think?"

"I've never been with Refik Altın."

"Really?" asked Ponpon disbelievingly.

"Yes, really! Even if I was into that kind of thing, surely I'd find someone better than . . ."

"Don't be so sure, sweetie."

The verbal sparring between Ponpon and Hasan was eternal and never ending. They adored each other, even as each did everything possible to get the upper hand. Their barbed brawls were a hoot to watch, but still quite dangerous. If Ponpon weren't my best friend, Hasan would long since have ridiculed her to all and sundry. It was only the prospect of a good dressing-down from me that made him hold his tongue.

"I used to be a huge fan of his poems," Hasan continued. "I'd buy his books the day they came out and read them right away, even memorize the ones I liked best. Of course, I didn't know him as a person. It was his poems I admired. Anyway, I was still young. A child, really."

"You're too much of a smart aleck to have ever been a child," Ponpon cut in.

"Hear me out if you want to. If not, don't. Anyway, I don't have to answer to you."

Hasan turned to me and continued his story.

"After a book signing we followed him home to learn where he lived. Then, one day, I gathered up all his books and went to visit him."

"Just who do you think you are?" asked Ponpon.

"Myself," Hasan answered coolly.

"So why are you using the plural? You said 'we followed him.' I suppose you went with your lady-in-waiting."

Ponpon was patiently pushing each of Hasan's buttons, one by one.

"Must be the 'royal we,' " she cackled scornfully.

Ponpon's laughter is a sight to behold. First, her entire body quivers, in all its bulk. Then, if she's still not finished, she repeatedly slaps her hands on her knees. Even when her laughter has finally died down, she continues shouting in the same ear-piercing tone. That's what she did now.

This was the first I'd heard about the apparent friendship between Refik Altın and Hasan. I was surprised. But it had all happened a long time ago, so I didn't take it seriously. And I'd long since resigned myself to the fact that Hasan had formed some sort of attachment to every dodgy character in town. What's more, everyone I knew had had some fort of feud, run-in, or disagreement with Refik.

Having dispensed with the subject of Refik Altın, we moved on to Istanbul in general. Hasan asked when I'd be stopping by the club.

"As soon as possible," Ponpon answered for me.

"Not tonight," I added.

"Well, what are your plans for tonight?" Hasan asked. "Why

not go to the cinema? There's a fabulous Cate Blanchett film out. It's just super. You'd love her. She plays a whore in this one. Just the most appealing thing you've ever seen."

"At the very mention of the word 'whore' he starts drooling. But still all the protests: 'I wouldn't; I couldn't!' "

"Really, it's a wonderful film. And Cate is something else! Go see it; you won't regret it. Just watching her will bring you around."

Ponpon was watching me with questioning eyes.

"I'm in no shape to go out," I said. "I want to sleep."

"At this hour?" asked Hasan. "It's not even six yet."

True, but it was getting dark.

"Come on, let's go out. You'll feel better," Ponpon urged. "Even if we don't go to the film, we'll have a nice walk and come back. Then you can come with me."

"To your *pavyon*?" asked Hasan, spotting an opening for revenge.

Ponpon can't bear to have the nightclubs she works at referred to as "pavilions," which in Turkish implies a clip joint with shady ladies sipping five-hundred-dollar bottles of watered-down champagne. For her, a gig at a pavilion is as low as it goes, and even whorehouse workers are a mark above. "At least they make dozens of men happy every day of the week," she remarks.

Ponpon wasn't about to let Hasan's comment go unanswered. Eyes narrowed, lips pursed, she hissed sharply as she drew breath. If her exhalation was as dramatic as that intake of breath, all hell was about to break loose.

I had to do something.

"All right," I blurted out. "I'll go to the cinema. Where's that film playing?"

I placed a hand on Ponpon's knee. Her lungs slowly deflated, but she fairly crackled with electricity.

Hasan picked up a newspaper and began reading out cinemas

and screen times. When he was done, he began flipping idly through the pages.

"That's him!"

"Who?"

"Refik's lover! The one who's gone missing!"

"Which one?" I asked.

"This one here," Hasan said, pointing to a picture of Volkan Sarıdoğan.

"But you said Refik never took him out or showed him to anyone. How do you know it's him?" demanded Ponpon.

"He showed me a photo. One he took at home."

"And you're certain this is the same man?" I asked.

"Of course I am," he said. "Volkan. His name's even written right here."

He quickly read the article, then raised his eyes to ours.

"So they killed the guy," he said. "Refik's going to take it hard."

He thought for a moment, his expression morphing from surprise to sadness, then to something rather alarming.

"But just think of the poems he'll write," Hasan cooed with an evil grin.

Chapter 6

Cate Blanchett really was fabulous. But becoming enamored of another willowy woman would mean betrayal of my all-time idol, Audrey Hepburn. Audrey would remain top of the list, while Cate would be given second place. I refuse to assign any rank at all to uncharismatic fashion model types.

As we left the cinema Ponpon said we'd have to dash back home to gather her things and head straight for the club. She was clearly determined that I accompany her. But I was preoccupied with thoughts of Volkan Sarıdoğan. Cate Blanchett's porcelain beauty had driven him from my mind during the length of the film, but now my mind returned to him. I wanted to sit alone, thinking, and perhaps even researching. I had somehow found myself sitting atop another unsolved murder. Back to my role of amateur detective. And all because of that dish of a man!

Feigning fatigue, I managed to push Ponpon out the door. Then I prepared myself a large mug of fennel tea and began thinking. In order to focus, I switched on the TV, looking for an idiotic game show. No luck. I quickly decided a music video channel would not do. They're more useful as a sedative or hypnotic agent.

My tea was nearly finished, but my mind was as confused as ever. The best medicine would be Handel. Scanning the shelves, I couldn't decide between the *Athalia* oratorio and the opera *Alcina*. *Alcina* would be best. The exquisite coloratura soprano of Arleen Auger, who died unexpectedly at the height of her career, trilled from my speakers. Like a bracing tonic.

Working-class lad Volkan had graduated from driving a mini-bus to a career as a gigolo. He'd bedded Dump Truck Beyza, God knows how many others, and then finally Refik Altın before being killed by loan shark Faruk Hanoğlu for reasons unknown but perfectly obvious to me.

The thought of Faruk Hanoğlu brought to mind an image of Haluk Pekerdem: that strong chin, the thick hair of the young Franco Nero, the crinkles at the corners of his eyes when he smiled, his incredibly even white teeth. Every bit as tasty as John Pruitt, every known photograph of whom I owned and treasured. It had been ages since I'd encountered such a perfect specimen of man-hood outside pictures and films, that is, in the flesh. He had awak-ened such deep desires.

It was still early. I decided to call him. After all, he had given me his card. I could always just thank him for the previous night. Just the thought of his voice gave me hot flashes. I imagined him hold-ing the receiver, speaking to me. Naked, of course. His reciprocal desire for me boldly apparent . . . I shivered.

He answered the phone himself. Even his self-assured hello oozed masculine mystique. My first disappointment was his failure to recognize my voice. Bastard! I reintroduced myself. He remem-bered now. I thanked him for the previous night, assured him how charmed I had been to meet him. I was careful not mention the wife, Canan. I didn't signify that I'd met her as well. I spoke of our night together as though it had been just the two of us.

"I saw the papers today," I began. "I'm so sorry. I didn't know you were Faruk Bey's brother-in-law."

He listened, demoralizing me by making no attempt to prolong the conversation.

"I just wondered," I said, "if there have been any further developments."

"We'll handle it," was the terse reply.

I had no idea what he intended to handle, or how, but contented myself with a simple "good." I heard him take a breath. He cleared his throat with a light cough.

"Hello," I said.

"I'm here." Silence.

"I thought the line had been cut."

He couldn't have made it any clearer that he didn't feel the same pleasure talking to me that I felt talking to him. I fought a sinking feeling. I had no intention of giving up so easily.

"It seems Volkan Sarıdoğan, the late Volkan Sarıdoğan, was a gigolo," I informed him, hoping to provoke a response. "Some of our girls knew him; even some of our gay friends."

If he didn't take the bait, there was really nothing more I could do.

"We know," he said.

"What I mean is, if there's anything I could do . . . I know everyone in those circles."

"That's kind of you. There's no evidence to incriminate Faruk. But they've detained him anyway. It's all sensation. There are those who like him. And those who don't. There's more to all this than meets the eye. He'll be out in a couple of days."

Now that's more like it. A bit terse, but he was speaking. I'd loosen his tongue yet.

"They can't pin it on Faruk just because the last three phone calls made by the deceased were to him, can they?"

"Apparently they can try," he said dryly.

"An acquaintance of mine claims to have been Volkan's lover." I hesitated at the word "acquaintance." Should I have said "friend"? No, Refik Altın couldn't be described as a friend of mine. I only knew him from the club. "If any information would . . ."

He cut me off.

"It's the police's job to find the killer. Whether it's an acquaintance of yours or not. It's my job to prove Faruk's innocence."

He'd interpreted my offer of help as a finger-pointing at another suspect. Funny, it had never occurred to me, but Refik Altın could well have been the killer.

"I see," I said.

He must have detected the hurt feelings in my voice.

"Still, thank you for your offer," he said. "It was most thoughtful of you to call."

There wasn't a hint of emotion behind his words. Spoken like a professional. No gratitude, no pleasure at hearing my voice.

Wishing him a good night, I prepared to hang up, then added, "Greetings to your wife" at the last second.

Haluk Pekerdem was a tough nut. If I played my cards right, he would be mine. But I'd have to work for it. And I couldn't blame him. The person he'd met had not been me. He'd met a badly dressed tranny in face paint. Me at my most clumsy and insecure. He was right not to have anything to do with *that* person. I accepted, when I put himself in his shoes, that I would have behaved exactly the same way. But I also had to admit that the person sitting at the table that night, smiling nervously, fabric hanging off her emaciated frame, was none other than me.

Dressed to the nines, I would visit him at the first opportunity! He was going to meet the *real* me.

Chapter 7

I was asleep before Ponpon returned, and up before she'd risen. Taking my morning cup of coffee, I sat in front of the computer. Hundreds of e-mails had accumulated during my depression and I'd keep busy sorting them until Ponpon woke up and we had breakfast together.

Off went all the spam to the recycle bin, unopened. Ali had forwarded every work-related e-mail to me. Some included a line or two asking how I was; to others he'd attached a joke of some kind. But most were simply forwarded. It would take at least a few days to go over them all. I sent them to a folder for later inspection.

Cihad2000, that is, Kemal Barutçu, had increased the frequency and intensity of the messages he sent me. The more fervent, the more likely they were to contain elements of Islamic radicalism. The latest was full of prayers, scripture, and condemnation. I replied with a brief e-mail explaining my silence. The last thing I wanted was to antagonize Kemal. He's one of the few computer geeks who faze me. At first I'd felt pity for the Stephen Hawking–like figure in the wheelchair, but the minute we'd moved on to the subject of sex—and that happened in no time—he was audacious to the extreme.

From the four corners of the globe hundreds of my fellow hackers, their true identities and faces unknown to me, had showered me with new codes, hacking suggestions, and the latest on gaining access to proprietary systems. I answered the shorter messages and filed away those I thought would be of interest, naturally deleting the identity of the senders.

Selçuk and Ayla Tayanç had sent me New Year's greetings. The three of us had grown up together in the same neighborhood. We'd played doctor. Up until we reached puberty, Selçuk would suck my lips till they swelled up; I'd do the same to Ayla. But then he fixed on Ayla exclusively and later married her. Our friendship had remained fast all these years, but no mention was ever made of my swollen lips. Actually, that was just as well. Selçuk was now pot-bellied and going bald. They had a pair of pimply sons, and wrote to me that it was with the older one's assistance and his new computer that they'd managed to send an e-mail. And they'd attached a family photograph. Selçuk was still a big shot at the police department. I often turned to him for help and was constantly indebted.

I was more pleased than usual to hear from Selçuk. I'd be indebted to him once again, this time over Volkan Sarıdoğan, whose demise obsessed me only because of my dream man, Haluk Pekerdem. I replied to the letter, attaching two photographs: one of me as a man and one as an all-out vamp. Beneath the pair of pictures I wrote "before" and "after." Just as I was about to hit the reply button, I remembered that the letter had come from the son. There was no need to confuse the dear boy, or undermine the morality of that little family. I had no way of knowing if he'd yet come face-to-face with the facts of life. Detaching the pictures, I sent just the message.

It was high time Ponpon got out of bed and fixed us breakfast. The handfuls of vitamins had whetted my appetite. It didn't matter how many crackers, cookies, and biscuits I ate, I never felt full. I put on a CD, planning to turn up the volume every five minutes. Dalida's rhythmic "Salma ya Salama" reverberated throughout the flat. The rain had stopped, and for the second morning in a row the sun shone brightly.

Before I'd had to ratchet up the sound another notch, Ponpon appeared, sleepy-eyed but with a cheery "good morning," singing out each syllable.

As Dalida finished the second chorus, Ponpon, wrapped tightly in a kimono, back straight and face free of makeup, began heading for the bathroom with tiny geisha steps, the floorboards groaning under her delicately placed feet.

While she took a shower, I began making phone calls. First I called Selçuk. It took a little while before they put me through, but Ponpon's morning rituals would last for some time to come.

"There's the fugitive!" boomed Selçuk. "Where have you been? Unless you're hot on some trail, you never think to call. Who knows what you've been up to, or where."

"I haven't been up to a thing. I've been here at home. I've just been going through a bad patch."

"So that's it! Just tell me what I can do for you. Whatever you need, just spell it out."

The sincerity in his voice, his eagerness to help me whenever I called, touched me deeply. But that doesn't mean tears came to my eyes.

"I was going through a bad patch in my personal life. It's all past now; I'm trying to get it together," I began. "I just wanted to sort out my thoughts and feelings, spend some time alone."

"But now you're okay?" he said hesitantly, unsure what else to say. "It happens sometimes. To all of us."

"How true," I concurred. "Anyway, the worst is behind me."

"Good . . . good," he said. "I'm glad."

"I got your New Year's message," I said, changing the subject. "Thank you."

"Not at all. Now that the boys are using the Internet, the wife and I are learning it, too."

"They must be growing up so fast. They're nearly full-grown men by now."

"You should come and see them. Çetin is thirteen and Metin

just turned ten. Really, come by for dinner one night. You'll have a chance to see the boys and we can talk about old times."

"Aren't you afraid to have me over?" I asked. "Don't you worry I may set a bad example for the boys? You never know, I may even fancy one of them."

"Don't even think about it," he laughed.

I had to laugh, too.

"There's something I'd like to ask you," I said.

"I should have known," he responded. "Here we go again . . ."

I filled Selçuk in on the Volkan Sarıdoğan murder, and gave him some background on Faruk Hanoğlu.

"I know it's not your job, but I'd appreciate any information you could get," I said. "I'm quite intrigued by the whole thing."

"One thing I do know is that nobody likes the guy. He's a real shady character," said Selçuk. "We also know about his loan-sharking. A troublemaker if ever there was one. I'm sure we've got a fat folder on him. Doesn't have many friends."

"They say there's no proof linking him to the murder."

"That's nonsense. If there wasn't any evidence, they'd find some."

I shivered. He was right. The police would surely have "found" some incriminating piece of evidence.

"Put your feelers out, if you would."

"If it'll help get you out of that depression, I'm happy to," Selçuk promised.

"And," I continued, "about that murdered fellow . . ."

"Will do. His family, his friends. I'll gather what I can and have it sent to you."

"Thank you; you're a real friend."

"An underappreciated real friend."

We said good-bye and hung up.

I had time for one more phone call before Ponpon took over the house. I called Beyza. Though sleepy, she still answered all of my questions.

"I'm looking for some more information about that Volkan of yours," I began.

"Actually, he's a real piece of shit."

"That's not what you said yesterday."

"Well, he was great in the sack. That much I'll give him. But as a human being, he was worse than useless. The things he did! Not just to me ... to everyone ... See what I mean ... But I ... How can I put this: He had a tainted heart. Always up to some evil. Things that helped no one but himself ... Actually, it wasn't him who thought it all up, it was that brother-in-law of his. He was the real piece of shit."

"Tell me a little about him. I'm intrigued," I urged her.

"What more can I say," Beyza snapped. "He's a minibus driver, too. But a real asshole. You know the type, not a toilet or sewer he hasn't jumped in. If you ask me, he's a cesspool of a person himself! So he takes a good look at Volkan: young, handsome, full of airs. He pulls his strings, pushes his buttons, and gets him right where he wants him. Not that it was difficult. Volkan was devoted to his brother-in-law, saw him as a real father figure and all that crap. Seems he was raised by this brother-in-law, learned all about life from him and so on ... You know, the classic story. Volkan kowtowed to his every whim. But the guy's a real piece of shit ... I did mention that, didn't I? ... A total sleazeball and greedy as all hell ... He starts working on Volkan, softening him up, brainwashing him ... 'That one's good for some cash, sleep with that one, too' ... He's the one who corrupted the boy. And I bet he's responsible for what happened to him! It's the brother-in-law they should have killed."

"How can I find him?"

"What for! Haven't you been listening to me? What good would it do?"

"I just might uncover something," I said. "There's something funny about the whole business, but I haven't put my finger on it yet."

"It's clear as day. He wanted too much money, or threatened someone or something. It would be just like him. Someone wasn't taking it and that was that . . ."

"I'd still like to talk to him."

"You know best, sweetie, but don't say I didn't tell you. He's not the talking type. I think he works the Bosphorus minibus routes."

"What's his name?"

"Completely slipped my mind. He's a big guy with a mustache . . . an unshaven, badly dressed piece of shit. Zeki or Zekai or something was the name."

"If he hasn't cleaned up, he shouldn't be much trouble to find," I said, half joking.

"Cut the wisecracking," snarled Beyza. "If you find him, let me know. I got a word or two of my own for him. The way he ruined poor Volkan . . . And be careful. He's a real piece of shit."

Ponpon emerged from the bathroom singing her lungs out.

Chapter 8

$\mathcal{F}$inding Ziya Göktaş, Volkan's brother-in-law, was a piece of cake. When I phoned the association of minibus drivers they were more helpful than I'd expected. They didn't know why I was calling, but clearly assumed from my questions that I was a reporter. The secretary did her best to be polite, addressing me as "sir" and answering my questions one by one, a real nightingale.

The association condemned the attacks on its drivers. This wasn't the first one. In fact, as a form of protest and to enlighten the general public, they intended to turn out in force at the funeral. It was hoped that taxi drivers, too, would show up and swell their numbers.

The entire community was in mourning. They blamed the state for not providing security. If they weren't safe, what difference did it make if they had insurance and health care? But they paid their taxes like everyone else. I was informed at length of the deep distress of the family, how brother Okan Sarıdoğan and brother-in-law Ziya Göktaş had the support and solidarity not only of the minibus drivers on the Sariyer line, but of all the drivers across Istanbul. So I was able to confirm what line the brother-in-law worked on, and learned that there was a brother: Okan. An interview with him could be helpful. The most useful tidbits often pop out of the least promising mouths.

I had just one problem to consider: In what guise should I pay a call? As a foxy lady journalist, or as a slightly camp correspondent? A short skirt surely would get me more information, but I would be a helpless sheep among a horny pack of wolves. I decided to go as a man.

I didn't tell Ponpon what I was up to. She was liable to revert to her role of guardian angel and refuse to leave my side. I dressed and left, taking with me as accessories a huge old camera and my minirecorder.

The old minibus stop in Taksim was gone, and I had no idea where they'd moved it to. I was sorry I hadn't thought to ask the association. It would be difficult to find in the hubbub of Beşiktaş. I hailed the next cab, and the driver's face lit up when I told him to take me to Sariyer. He even stopped slouching in anticipation of the fare. I seized the opportunity to tell him to switch off the harrowing music. I simply will not tolerate anguished songs drumming the message into my subconscious that life is full of pain and sorrow. Particularly when I'm just emerging from a deep depression.

I'd intended to use the long drive to the other end of the Bosphorus as an opportunity to do some serious thinking. But as we passed Maslak and traveled through forested land, I couldn't help reflecting instead on how few and far between green spaces are in Istanbul today, and how people like me, who live in the heart of the city and rarely travel farther than a kilometer from their homes, seldom have the opportunity to see the few trees that are left.

The final stop was full of minibuses. They were parked in a long line, as they always are, except for rush hour. Everyone had heard about Volkan, and they all had different theories concerning his end. Most subscribed to the belief that he had been robbed. A few ventured the possibility of a jealous husband or boyfriend. None mentioned the fact that Volkan had been a gigolo. In fact, they pretended they weren't even aware of it. After listening to a couple of the drivers I decided they spent too much time watching films on TV. One fact was obvious: a highflier like Faruk Hanoğlu wouldn't have been caught dead getting into a minibus.

They graciously supplied me with a glass of tea while they looked for Okan and Ziya. Neither could be found, but I was assured that if I waited, they'd come.

"Ziya is a total wreck," confided the older one. "He loved that boy like a son."

The virtues of Volkan were listed at length. Such a good heart, so multitalented and ready to help anyone in need; the story of his rise from a boyish fare collector to the owner of a minibus was repeated several times, either by a single voice or as a gruff chorus.

I sipped the awful tea. My stomach would be skinned from the inside if I drank it, but failure to do so would be a terrible discourtesy. I took tiny sips for the better part of half an hour. As various drivers headed for the road, others replaced them, each doing his bit to contribute to the legend springing up around Saint Volkan. But there was still no sign of the brother-in-law, Ziya, or the brother, Okan.

I was getting bored. If any of the girls were here they'd be astonished I could get sick of sitting amid so many hairy men. But bored I was. It must have been the waiting.

Finally, I thanked them and stood up. A man in his forties rose to accompany me. He clearly wished to have a private word. I thought I'd been fairly discreet, but someone had spotted what I was. Yes, that must be it. He threw a friendly arm around my shoulder and walked with me as far as the main road.

His name was Tuncer.

"Don't let on that you heard it from me, but Okan, Volkan, and Ziya—the three of them—are all trouble. Don't believe anything the others said. They think they're showing solidarity. It wasn't like that at all."

Interesting.

"What do you mean?" I prompted.

"I'm heading home, to Kurtuluş," he said. "If you like, I can drop you off somewhere."

"Thank you so much," I accepted.

It was too good to be true.

Between deep drags on a cigarette, Tuncer talked the entire length of the trip. The brand he smoked and his choice of words pinned him as an old left-winger.

"Okan's a substance abuser," he began. "Totally useless."

"An alcoholic?" I asked.

"At first he was, now he smokes hash. Actually, he takes whatever he can get his hands on. Then he runs out of money, of course. And he can't work. Not all spaced-out. He had a couple of accidents, nothing serious. Realized he couldn't go on. Couldn't keep driving. He started leasing his minibus by the day. Started sitting in the coffeehouse all day, waiting to collect his cut. Once he got his money, he'd go and buy booze, hash, grass."

"No one mentioned that."

"They'd all clam up if you asked about it. That's our way. All in the name of solidarity."

"So why are you telling me?"

"So that someone knows the truth, knows the truth so they can write about it," he said. "But like I said, I didn't tell you."

"I understand."

We drove for a while in silence. Traffic grew worse near Maslak; we slowed to a crawl.

"Another accident," Tuncer muttered. "At the sight of an empty road they floor it. And for what! We've all got the same gas pedals under our feet."

"How true."

It was a perfect time to change the subject and calm him down.

"I know about Okan now," I said. "What about Volkan and Ziya?"

"They say you shouldn't speak ill of the dead, but Volkan wasn't anything like what they told you. You'd think he was some kind of angel. Far from it. Those manicured sideburns, tall and fit, full of himself, hitting on anyone in a skirt. He was nothing but trouble."

He seemed hesitant to elaborate, unsure of exactly how much I already knew. I cut to the chase.

"He was a gigolo, they say."

"Good for you," he blurted out in relief. "So you know all about that. The word's out."

He'd begun by addressing me with the formal *siz* but had switched to the more familiar *sen* at some point. I wasn't entirely pleased about that.

"He was a good-looking guy, knew how to please old ladies and homosexuals . . . for the right price, of course."

The fact that he'd avoided a word more disparaging than "homosexual" was another indication of his left-wing background.

"Handy, was he?"

"How do I know? It's not like I took him to bed . . ." he guffawed, showing tar-blackened teeth.

"Once he started earning money on the side he stopped coming to work regularly. He handed his minibus over to his brother. Not a smart move that. Okan would spend all day getting high, then pick a fight with whoever was using the minibus for the day, claiming they hadn't handed over enough cash. And whatever he did get, he spent on booze and dope. Anyone with sense wouldn't work for him again, but some were desperate for a job."

"And their brother-in-law, Ziya?"

"He's another brand of troublemaker. The kind who gives us all a bad name. A shifty sort, no sense of right and wrong, doesn't know the meaning of words like 'sin' and 'justice' and 'shame.'"

"I see," I said, not really seeing at all what he meant.

"There's a lot I could tell you, but it'd be wrong to say too much. I'm not the sort to run my mouth. I was raised different."

We spent the rest of the trip talking about Istanbul's problems and life in general. He told me how we could save our country, how working conditions were going downhill, how his earnings were adding up to less, how ashamed he was to bring home so little money at the end of the day.

Just before I got out, I asked one more question about Volkan's death.

"Do you think the guy who's been arrested is the one who killed Volkan?"

"It could be anyone," he said knowingly. "Anyone. He was mixed up with a bad crowd. There's a price to pay for easy money. He'd managed to buy a minibus in just three years. Brand new. Including rights to the line he drove. They say you reap what you sow. I believe that's what he did."

Volkan Sarıdoğan was an even richer, more popular gigolo than I'd imagined.

Chapter 9

*W*aiting for me when I got home was a large manila envelope from Selçuk and an enormous bouquet sent by Money-counter Ali. I was truly astonished by the flowers. The gesture was as unexpected as it was secretly hoped for. I really had to thank them both.

Ponpon was sitting in front of the TV mesmerized by her favorite BBC cooking program, offering barely an indication that she'd noticed my arrival. On the screen, a lively black man gushed and enthused and jabbered as he diced potatoes. Sitting across from Ponpon, I opened the envelope from Selçuk. It contained copies of the report filed by the policemen who'd discovered the body, official records from the nearest precinct, the coroner's report, and details of the initial investigation—all of them classified, of course. How sweet of Selçuk to send them along. Of course, he was fully aware that it was my taxes that paid for them—that is, that paid for the transport, water, electricity, and whatnot of the police force. But still, confidential is confidential.

Volkan Sarıdoğan's body was found in the forest just past the Kilyos junction. Whoever discovered him could not have been on a routine foot patrol. A child or woodsman had most likely stumbled upon it and called the police.

He'd been stabbed to death. The stab wounds were all on the front of the body, seven of them, of varied depths, in the chest and stomach, but all from the same knife. So he must have come face-to-face with the killer. The coroner estimated that forty-eight hours had elapsed before the body was discovered. The assailant was right-handed.

Found on the body were an ID card, a wallet, and a cell phone. It appeared that the killer had not stolen any personal items. Well, if Faruk Hanoğlu was indeed the murderer, why would he? It isn't as though he'd need cash or a phone.

It had been impossible to identify the footprints of the assailant: The area near the body was muddy, due to recent rain, and a number of individuals had approached the body, including the police. Tire tracks were faintly visible near the scene of the crime, but it was not possible to trace them any further.

For whatever reason, no one had made off with Volkan's phone, despite the fact that it was switched on and the PIN code already entered; the last three calls had been made to Faruk Hanoğlu. Twice cell phone to cell phone, and once to a fixed-line phone.

So Faruk Hanoğlu really had been detained on what would seem to be the flimsiest of evidence. No prosecutor in his right mind would dream of accusing him on the evidence at hand, let alone having him jailed. It was just as Haluk, my Haluk, had said: He would be free in a day or two.

What was missing from the envelope was a print-out of all the calls made to and from Volkan's cell phone. There must be a copy somewhere, but Selçuk hadn't forwarded it to me. I compiled an imaginary list of my own, one full of society figures, each name enough to cause a citywide scandal.

Ponpon's program finished, she turned off the TV and faced me.

"How's it going?" she asked.

"How's what going?" I countered.

"How's whatever it is you're up to going?"

"I'm not up to anything," I protested. "Yet."

"I know you. The way you're sitting, the way you move, the glint in your eyes. The way you were just scrutinizing whatever's in that envelope . . . You're up to something. Miss Marple is back in business."

"But she's so old," I cried in mock dismay.

The Agatha Christie heroine, who manages to solve innumerable murder cases on the basis of what she overhears in the garden of her country home, where she seldom leaves her chair, is an elderly, white-haired spinster. I was nothing like her!

"What do I know? It's been years since I've read a detective novel. Hercule Poirot would have been a stretch of the imagination, so I hit on Miss Marple."

"You could have said Miss Peel. You know, Diana Rigg in *The Avengers*."

"That's true," she agreed. "The way you hop about and beat men up."

"I practice what is known as aikido," I informed her. "As well as a bit of Thai boxing."

Actually, I hadn't done any training for weeks. I was rusty, and would be unable to jump more than a foot. Not all that long ago I'd been able to soar nearly two meters, simultaneously delivering a sharp kick to the head with either my left or right foot.

Curling her feet under her, Ponpon settled into her armchair.

"So, tell me. What are you up to? What have you stumbled on? What have you unearthed?"

Ponpon was grinning at me.

"Nothing much" was all I said.

"I don't believe you! You never return empty-handed. What's in that envelope Selçuk sent you?"

Even engrossed in her cooking program, Ponpon hadn't missed a thing. And hadn't she already learned my computer password?

"If you call Selçuk to thank him, send my greetings. I suppose you won't object to that much," she added.

"I'm just about to call."

"Oh, and remind him that he and his wife were going to come

see me perform. They still haven't. Do convey my sense of disappointment, would you?"

A wicked grin had spread across her face. Her eyes were shining. I'd forgotten how beautiful Ponpon's eyes were. The color of rich honey, with chocolate speckles. Her pupils were huge, and made her eyes look all the warmer. They dominated her face. Her Roman nose had been whittled away by the scalpel to next to nothing, and she was forever reflexively pursing her tiny mouth. The only distinguishing feature left on that face was a pair of larger-than-life, luminous eyes.

"What are you grinning about?" I asked. "Someone's got a secret. Out with it."

At first she was coy, feigning reluctance. Then she let her little bombshell drop:

"Faruk Hanoğlu was released on lack of evidence."

"That quickly?"

"Well, how could they keep him without any evidence?"

Selçuk had implied they'd simply manufacture something. It sounded like someone had other ideas.

"It's proof once again of what a fine attorney Haluk is," Ponpon continued. "If I ever have legal problems, I'm going straight to him. It's true he's a bit pricey, but he deserves every penny. Good for him!"

"How did you find out he'd been released? Was it on television?"

"No, sweetie. When I called Canan to offer my sympathies, she told me. They were elated, of course. But it's still just too horrid: accused of murder, detained in a cell. May Allah not visit such a fate on even my worst enemies. Protect us, O mighty one!"

"But he still has some explaining to do. Why had a gigolo phoned him? If you're looking for a scandal, you've got it in spades. It's a bit early to pop open the champagne."

"That's true, honey, but you do agree that there's a world of difference between hiring a gigolo and killing one. I mean, any number of couples dabble in that sort of thing to spice up their sex lives. Some prefer a call girl, others get hold of a rent boy. There are even some who opt for a TV. What's the big deal?"

"I'm hardly one to judge, but try telling all that to his business partners," I reminded Ponpon, who was badly in need of a reality check. "The financial markets are full of constipated types who frown on that sort of thing. Don't you remember all the talk about that businessman who traveled in drag every time he went overseas?"

"So they talked. Then it was all forgotten," she argued. "You'd think those doing the gossiping were different! They've all got something to hide. Each and every one. The ones who haven't done anything yet are still fantasizing about it. You know that as well as me."

Wagging her head in a world-weary I've-seen-it-all-and-then-some sort of way, Ponpon got up.

"Now I'll go make us some *ekşili köfte*; we'll have a nice meal together."

Just the mention of the dish made my mouth water.

Chapter 10

*T*wo days of Ponpon's devoted care had worked wonders on me. I scanned myself in the mirror. The shadows under my eyes were gone. I could still count my ribs, but I looked thin rather than wasted.

I'm no stranger to the transformative magic of makeup. While in New York on a tourist visa, broke and jobless, I worked for a spell at an undertaker's. Illegally, of course. Young and fond of risks, I was struggling to establish a brand-new life, starting from zero. It didn't last long.

I was paid a pittance at the funeral home, but I learned all the tricks of the trade when it came to makeup. My boss, Alberto, a queer old Italian, was the best in the business, working wonders on even the most damaged corpses in order to make open casket viewings less distressing.

With his heavily accented English, and the odd exclamation and curse in Italian, he'd flounce his way through the task of making a body beautiful. And instruct me along the way. He was incredibly painstaking when it came to the male bodies, examining them in detail and at length; as for the women, he devoted considerably less time to them. No matter what the age, the object was to create an air of girlish innocence, and he was big on pale pink lipsticks and light peach powder. A dab of rouge on each cheek was deemed essential for the older ladies, as well as a bit of white powder on their foreheads. The young ones inevitably received brown eyeliner and a thick coating of mascara, carefully brushed from the root to the tip of the lash. That's the way families like it, he'd claim. The more innocent looking the corpse, the more cathartic the mourning process.

I also learned how to apply makeup to hands, which usually occupied pride of place, as it were, folded and clutching a string of rosary beads or a cross. Because the veins had collapsed, that is, because they'd been drained of blood, there were no unsightly bulges to deal with. Just a bit of powder was all that was needed, with some concealer if necessary. If the surface had been so damaged that even several coats of paint failed to create the illusion of dewy youth, warm paraffin was injected just below the skin. Alberto claimed the warm wax method was a family secret handed down from his late uncle, who was also a confirmed bachelor—that is, queer. Perhaps, by some twisted logic, my own sexual bent made him consider me a member of the family, for Alberto never hesitated to divulge all he knew.

When he died peacefully in his sleep one morning, I once again found myself alone, jobless and penniless, in deepest New York. I finally ditched the fantasy of starting a new life. I was an idealist back then, determined to earn whatever I got the old-fashioned way, through pluck and toil. I wouldn't have considered relying on my sexual charms. And when confronted by the odd sexual predator, I would protest in the affronted tones I'd learned from watching Hülya Koçyiğit films for so many years.

While reminiscing over those long ago days with dear old Alberto, I'd been busily making myself up. Although tastefully restrained, the result was stunning. It was now time to pay a call on Haluk Pekerdem. Just as the ugly duckling was transformed into the beautiful swan, so had Ponpon's snotty-nosed friend turned into a real showgirl.

The colors that suit me best are baby pink and baby blue. And black, of course, which suits everyone. I was far too thin to pull off anything black, though, so I settled on a pair of pink trousers with a matching coat over a white sweater. White gloves completed the effect.

When I emerged from the bathroom Ponpon let loose a low wolf whistle.

"*Maşallah!* You look wonderful . . ."

"Thanks to you."

We embraced, our heads held back far enough that we wouldn't accidentally brush cheeks and spoil our makeup.

"You could use a bit more color," Ponpon observed. "You look pale."

Ponpon makes no distinction between everyday makeup and stage makeup. Subtlety is not her forte: it's either absolutely nothing or buckets of whatever's on hand!

But she'd managed to shake my self-confidence, if only slightly. I looked in the mirror again. The lipstick I'd selected did look a bit dull. I could at least apply a bit of gloss.

As I got closer to Haluk Pekerdem's office in Harbiye, I realized how excited I was. I really must be head over heels. The thought of shaking hands, mine clasped ever so firmly in his, sent shivers down my spine.

The office was near the Hilton, on the side overlooking the sea. It was one of those prestige buildings from the forties and fifties, with high ceilings and impractically spacious rooms. Haluk Pekerdem's office was like a showcase for select art deco pieces.

My first major obstacle presented itself in the form of a secretary / receptionist well into upper middle age, the sort who insists on an exhaustive grilling before ushering guests to the magic door. Judging from the plaque on that door, Haluk has no partners or fellow attorneys using the premises. So the entire place, including every stick of furniture, was the exclusive property of Haluk Pekerdem.

"Have you got an appointment?" demanded the woman, after scrutinizing me for several long moments.

No, I didn't.

"We're quite busy today," she explained dismissively.

In the same way a nurse asks if "we" have a fever or have re-membered to take "our" medicine, the gorgon at the gate had so identified with her boss that "they" were apparently too busy to see me. As far as I could tell, the only item of business on *her* plate was to subject me to impertinent questions.

"You can wait if you like, but he may not be able to see you," she said. "Or you could speak to Sibel Hanım or Ertunç Bey."

My blank expression at the mention of the two names elicited the information that they were "Haluk Bey's assistants" and a pre-liminary meeting with one of them would be advisable.

"I really must see Mr. Pekerdem in confidence," I said firmly.

Damn Ponpon! It was because of her that I used dated expres-sions like "in confidence." I felt like an *a la turca* stage actress.

"Please wait here for a moment."

I was deposited into a room that was once no doubt used as a broom closet in this stately apartment, furnished with only a small conference table and two enormous armchairs covered in Moroc-can leather. There was a window, but no view.

Spinning on her heel as she left the room, the secretary asked if I'd care for refreshments.

"A glass of water, please, at room temperature."

Fashionable blends of tea or coffee don't hold a candle to the source of life, plain old water. Unless they drink expensive malt whiskeys or imported beer, health-conscious society tends to favor *aqua* these days.

I was turning over in my mind what I would say to Haluk, and how I would say it, when the door opened and a girl with glasses poked her head into the room.

"Excuse me," she said. "I thought it was empty."

But she kept her eyes locked on me. I smiled lightly, staring back. We were still sizing each other up when she decided she'd seen enough to satisfy her curiosity and shut the door.

The professional secretary / receptionist must have flown straight to her colleague and fellow gossip with the news that I had arrived. And she'd come for a quick peek. It was probably the Sibel Hanım mentioned as an assistant. She couldn't be called ugly, but she was unlovely, slightly sour, and far too curious.

I fought off boredom by going over in my mind the chronological order of Audrey Hepburn films, and also trying to remember her costars and costumes. My favorites were *Roman Holiday, Love in the Afternoon, How to Steal a Million, Charade,* and *Sabrina.* My least favorite ones were *Green Mansions* and *The Unforgiven,* directed by John Huston, whom I still admire. The former is set in a forest and features Audrey in tattered frocks. Nothing there for me. The latter is a western flick, with no changes of costume.

My Fair Lady had clothes galore, one outrageously over-the-top outfit after another . . . but nothing suitable for everyday wear. And I went cold on the film when I learned that they'd dubbed all of Audrey's singing parts. I still hadn't decided if I could rate it an overall success. My head hurt.

Just then the door opened and in came the gossip of a secretary to inform me that Haluk Bey was expecting me in his office.

Haluk greeted me on his feet and with the same insincere smile I imagine he presents to clients. His teeth were amazing, and he oozed charm in a light blue shirt and loosened striped red, white, and ultramarine tie. Not a trace of a belly. Were I to unbutton that shirt, well-toned muscle and golden chest hairs would await me. Of that much at least, I was certain.

The room had a splendid view over the gardens of the Hilton to the distant decorative bridges of the Bosphorus, smooth as a plate of china blue.

As he presented me with a chair, he murmured, "So pleased to see you again," without even looking at my face. He was a professional liar.

"As am I," I murmured breathily back.

He looked directly at me for the first time. He seemed to have detected a change in my appearance but couldn't put his finger on what it was. The corners of his mouth turned up in a half smile.

He must have noticed me blushing.

We sat across from each other, on ultrasuede art deco chairs with black lacquer sloping armrests, our knees so close they'd have touched if I'd dared to inch forward.

"What would you like to drink?" he asked. He was still looking me full in the face. I searched for a spark of interest in his eyes. They were most decidedly sparkle-free.

"I've just had something," I said. "Thank you."

"If you'd like something later, let me know," he said.

And that was that.

He was still addressing me with the formal *siz*. That beguiling specimen of manhood, honed and polished through years of work and play, full of self-assurance and effortlessly able to put any guest at ease, was looking straight at me, directly into my eyes. "So, what's this all about?" his eyes said.

I could have explained, at some length and with numerous asides, that it was "about" the fact that I fancied the pants off him.

"The murder that Faruk Bey's been accused of," I said instead.

He seemed impervious to my intense stare, burning with love and admiration.

"I'm often a bit captivated by cases like this," I explained. "They fascinate me. I like to do a little research on my own. Sometimes I stumble across things."

"A bit of an amateur sleuth, are you?" he said.

"That's one way of putting it," I replied, a bit peevishly. "I have managed to contribute to the solving of a number of murder mysteries."

He shifted in his seat, simultaneously shifting the expression on his face. I wasn't sure if he was now looking at me with grudging admiration or as though he'd just realized he had a crazy tranny on his hands.

"I've stumbled across some things in this case, too."

I didn't know what else to say. It would have been nice of him to help me out. But he just sat there, raking me over with those dreamy eyes, making me even more tongue-tied.

I wanted to reach over and caress his cheek, then lean forward and plant a kiss on those hungry lips. I restrained myself.

"So, what have you found?" he finally asked.

"Volkan Sarıdoğan, the late Volkan Sarıdoğan, wasn't particularly loved by those who knew him. He was a gigolo who managed to make a considerable amount of money in a short period of time."

"Yes," he drawled, not the least surprised.

The hand cupping his chin was exquisite. Was it possible to have come-hither cuticles?

"It appears I'm not telling you anything new."

"No, you're not . . . It's not exactly a closely guarded secret that the, ah, victim, was not popularly esteemed."

"He has a brother who's a drunk and a junkie. They say there's nothing he won't do for money. Nothing he won't do to feed his habit," I continued.

I waited for his reaction. Nothing.

"Go on," he said, after a moment.

"And there's the question of the cell phone. Were the police to trace all the dialed numbers and received calls on his cell phone, I imagine there'd be quite a series of scandals."

His laughter was genuine.

"I'm not so sure about that," he said.

"Don't be too sure either way," I said.

"The murder was most certainly not motivated by robbery," he said thoughtfully. "Whoever did it didn't touch his wallet, which contained some cash, nor his gold watch and chain or his cell phone."

Haluk was as up-to-date on the police records as I was.

"Don't you think the murderer made a stupid mistake, then?" I asked. "Why leave behind an important piece of evidence like a cell phone?"

Eyes narrowed, he studied my face for a moment. He was nibbling the thumb of his right hand. Delicious.

"It may have been deliberate," he offered. "Done specifically to implicate Faruk."

"But just as you said, planting a cell phone on the body wouldn't be enough to incriminate Faruk Bey. And if he didn't do it, who did? And why are they trying to make it look as though he's the murderer?"

"Bravo!" said Haluk. "Those are all perfectly reasonable questions, but I suggest you let the police answer them. I've done all I could, which was to get Faruk released and cleared of the charges as quickly as possible."

"But he hasn't been cleared," I pointed out.

"Well, he can't be charged either," he countered. "In a worst-case scenario he could be accused of having contacted a gigolo. That would be unpleasant but not damning. Rumors die down as quickly as they flare up. I only hope that his family won't be affected. His wife must be standing behind him. Otherwise, she'd have made a statement by now. At worst, he'll be branded immoral, a sexual pervert. A few people may turn their backs on him. That's all."

"That's all?" I asked incredulously.

Leaning forward, he placed a hand on my knee.

I was overwhelmed.

"When we consider that you must overcome this sort of thing, and far worse, every day of the week . . ."

I wanted to respond. But couldn't. All I really wanted was to

take him in my arms. I wanted that hand to remain on my knee forever. A warm glow spread through my body.

I placed a hand on his.

"You're so right," I whispered. "But it's not that difficult. One
just has to be strong."

An electrical current passed between us. My spine tingled. Our
faces were inches apart. I felt his warm breath on my face, my
throat, my skin. I breathed in his scent, my eyes traveling to his,
then to his lips. Just looking at him set me aflame.

"I have friends at the force," I suddenly said.

I had no idea why those words left my lips. It was important to
continue to talk, to maintain our pose. What we said didn't matter.

"I'll have access to more information, if necessary. Like the list
of phone numbers."

He removed his hand from my knee and leaned back.

"That could be interesting," he mused.

I'd provoked his interest.

"I wonder how far back they can trace his calls," he said.

"I don't know."

Looking deep into his eyes, I smiled.

"That would be a good starting point," he said.

He'd found something for me to research. I'd do anything for
him, I thought to myself. But I also had a few questions of my own.

"I heard that Faruk Bey isn't very popular."

"Who is popular in the markets? Successful men are envied."

On his neck, just above his collar, a few stray hairs glinted.
Clearly, even his wife, Canan, hadn't noticed after he'd shaven that
morning. If he were my man, I would never send him off to work
like that, I thought.

As he saw me off, he only shook my hand. Yes, he held it in a
tight caress, but I'd been hoping for so much more.

Chapter 11

If you like a man enough, you dote on whatever he does. Years ago, a vivacious great aunt of mine not greatly treasured by the family had said something that shocked us all: "After a certain point, every man I see turns my head."

She never married, and some of our family elders could be heard to remark, "born a virgin and going to die a virgin." But that's not what I overheard them saying behind closed doors. When I heard my mother and her friends refer to my aunt as a "nympho-maniac," I'd hauled down the unabridged family dictionary. I never looked at my aunt the same way again.

I don't take after my aunt: My sexual appetites are healthy, not excessive. But when it came to Haluk Pekerdem, I could see myself becoming a nymphomaniac, or anything else. Just the thought of him left me breathless and weak-kneed.

I floated out of his office. I don't remember how I walked to Taksim, how I got down the hill to my flat. I reenacted in my mind, over and over again, everything he'd said and done, every word and every gesture.

I didn't want to get my hopes up too high. I'd barely recovered from a breakup and couldn't face refusal at the moment.

Yes, it was true that he didn't fancy me as much as I fancied him. But that didn't mean he wasn't interested. He hadn't refused me; he'd fitted me into his busy day, put aside time just to chat with me. He'd touched me; I'd touched him. He hadn't retracted his hand after plac-ing it on my knee. Just that one act was surely a sign of something.

As I approached my apartment building I noticed Hüseyin at the taxi rank. His was the only taxi there. He was alone. I'd once taken him into my bed, worn down by his insistence and pleas. But then he thought he owned me. I'd been forced to correct him, to demonstrate to him with a good public thrashing that he'd gotten me all wrong.

He turned his head away when he saw me coming. He hadn't been my driver since the beating. Either it wasn't his turn every time I called for a cab, or he was avoiding me.

I still had to find Okan Sarıdoğan and Ziya. I knew taxi drivers and minibus drivers weren't on the best of terms, but they were both members of the same general community, members of the fraternity of the steering wheel. Perhaps the taxi drivers could be enlisted for help. And Hüseyin wasn't such a bad sort; he'd even proven to be quite handy on a few occasions, and he adored being involved in sleuthing.

I'm not one to stay put out with anyone, barring a few names I won't mention here. It was time to offer the peace pipe. I walked up to Hüseyin's cab; he pretended to be adjusting the rearview mirror, but I knew for a fact that he had seen me.

"Hello, Hüseyin," I said.

Lowering his eyes and turning his head, he looked at me. He was tense and hesitant.

"You're not cross with me still, are you?" I smiled.

He got out of his cab and stood there sulkily, hands stuffed in the pockets of his jeans, shoulders hunched, eyeing me suspiciously.

"Aren't I?" he asked.

A sulky child, he scratched at the ground with his left foot, his eyes never leaving mine.

"There's no reason to be, is there?"

"You . . ." he began, the informal *sen* slipping out before he switched to the formal form, "know best, I suppose."

That he'd remembered my insistence on good manners was a point in his favor.

"You hit me in the patisserie in front of everyone . . ."

My response was brisk and pleasant. "You asked for it, hitting on me all the time. Everywhere I looked, there you were. On my tail every second of the day."

"I can't face the other guys," he complained. "After they heard about it, they all laughed at me. Thanks to you, my reputation's shot to hell."

"Surely you exaggerate. And I didn't hit you. I knocked you flat with a couple of well-placed kicks to the head. That's all."

"That's all, huh, baby."

He pretended to have tacked on the "baby" by mistake. I knew all his tricks; he was quite the performer. Now he was pretending to be embarrassed, peering out at me from below his heavy eyebrows.

"I'm sorry," he said.

I gave him a friendly thump on the shoulder.

"All's forgiven," I beamed.

Then I extended my hand, taking care to remove my glove first, of course.

"Still friends?"

He took my hand without hesitation. His was rough and cold.

He made an "uh-huh" sound, which I interpreted as a response in the affirmative.

Smiling sweetly, I asked if he would be willing to help me out. Raising his head, he looked into my eyes.

No, that's not what I was after.

"I need some information about a couple of minibus drivers. I haven't been able to find out much. When I ask about them, everyone talks them up. I'm not entirely convinced. You've got sharp ears. You might overhear them saying things they wouldn't say to my face. Could you keep your ears pricked for me?"

"Not more of that detective business, I hope. I got the stuffing knocked out of me last time."

He'd once done an errand for me, just the innocent delivery of a package, as a result of which a bunch of thugs had worked him over. Now that's what I call a thrashing, not the couple of kicks I'd delivered.

"I'm afraid it is detective work," I said. "A driver was murdered. I indirectly knew both the guy who was killed and the one who's been accused of killing him. But there doesn't appear to be a motive, and the driver didn't exactly have clean hands."

"You don't mean that minibus driver from Sariyer, do you?"

"Volkan Sarıdoğan!"

"Yeah, that's him. Everyone's talking about him. If he'd been so famous when he was alive, he could have retired. Life's funny like that."

"What have you heard?" I pressed him.

The phone rang. There were no other cabs. Gesturing for me to wait, Hüseyin went into the taxi shelter to answer the phone.

When he returned he was smirking. Just two words from me, and he already was becoming insolent.

"I gotta run," he said. "But I'll stop by for a tea later, if you want. You can tell me all about it."

Here we go again.

"He's got a brother. A druggie they say. And a brother-in-law. Okan and Ziya. Ask around," I shouted after him as he drove off.

He gave me a military salute in his rearview mirror, flooring the accelerator of his Şahin taxi, even managing to lay a little rubber.

I suppose he thought I'd be impressed.

Chapter 12

By the time I opened the door to my flat I'd forgotten all about Hüseyin, my mind having flown back to Haluk. I was too horny to sit still. But it wouldn't do to sleep with just anyone, either. I know plenty of girls, and indeed real women, who are able to shut their eyes and pretend that whoever is screwing them is the man of their dreams. But I'm not one of them. I want to focus on whoever I'm in bed with. I expect both my mind and my body to be possessed by the same man, or, on rare occasions, very rare occasions, woman.

The house was filled once more with the tantalizing smells of Ponpon's cooking. I didn't like the thought of a roll in the hay with her around. If I were alone, I'd be able to do as I wished.

Before I had the chance to drop a subtle hint, Ponpon apparently read my mind and broached the subject herself.

"I'm going to the sauna. Would you like to come?"

I didn't know what to say. Ponpon and I have totally different approaches to saunas. She thinks it's a practical way to burn calories; I take a more sensual approach. Naturally, we go to different saunas: Hers are the sterile ones; mine are more like overheated dungeons.

"I just reek of onions," she said, untying her apron, "and I'm all sweaty. I thought it'd be nice to get rid of some toxins. And peek at a few prowling willies while I do it."

Anyone else would have used the verb "grab" or even "gobble," but it was just like Ponpon to satisfy herself with a peek. She wasn't

far from what they call "asexual." I'd never known her to get horny.
If she did get down and dirty with someone, it was always done in
the name of love. Then she'd bitterly regret it for days afterward.
After a series of blood tests and negative results, she'd finally relax
and shut up. A period of repentance lasted for what we creatures of
fleshly desires would consider an "eternity" before she'd "sin" once
more.

"I'm a little tired," I lied. "I thought I'd lie down." My second
sentence was closer to the truth, if lacking in detail.

"Of course you are, dear," she exclaimed. "I can stay here with
you if you'd like. It's not like I have to go to the sauna. Just say the
word and I'll stay."

"That's alright," I assured her. "I'm a big girl now. I'm not afraid
of the dark. Go on, have fun."

"I'd better hit the road before my sweat dries, then. All primed,
as it were," she sang out.

Once Ponpon was out of the house I switched on the PC and
began clicking though my collection of rare porn. Some of the
men looked a bit like Haluk. I searched for them, and found one.
His name was Taylor Burbank. He had a mustache in some pictures, a beard in a few others. So be it. Through squinted eyes he
still reminded me of Haluk Pekerdem. That would have to do for
now. I began undressing.

And the doorbell rang. Just as I got started. Ponpon must have
forgotten something. Not bothering to switch off the computer, I
raced to the door, wrapped in a pink jacket. I'd get whatever she
wanted and send her on her way.

When I opened the door it was Hüseyin who stood across from
me. I'd rather not have met him at the door nearly naked. I struggled to cover myself with the jacket. Unsuccessfully. I concealed
myself behind the door.

"Here I am," he announced.

He was staring at me.

"It was a nearby drop. I came right over. I was afraid of getting stuck at the rank if I went back there."

"You did well," I praised him.

Opening the door all the way, I ushered him in.

"Wait right over there," I said. "I'll go put something on."

"Don't bother," he said with a wink. "It's fine with me; I could get comfortable too."

We'd just made up, and I had work for him, so there was no point in overreacting. Ignoring his remark, I headed down the hallway, certain he was watching my ass and sighing as he did so. Spotting Ponpon's kimono, I threw it on and returned to the living room.

He'd wasted no time settling into my favorite armchair.

"Can I get you something to drink?" I asked.

"Whatever's easiest . . . Nescafé?"

"I'll be right back."

"And bring me a glass of water, okay?"

Not only the familiar *sen*, but the imperative, bossing me around in my own home! Still, I held my tongue. We had work to do, and patience is one of my many virtues.

Handing him his coffee, I put on some soothing music. The fourth, fifth, and sixth discs of Haydn's Opus 33 Quartets.

"That's nice," he said.

I smiled but didn't feel the need to furnish any further information. He could always go over and look at the cover of the CD if he was curious.

"So tell me what you know," I prompted.

"I hadn't heard of any of the three. That is, until they appeared in the newspaper. You know how we read all the papers to pass time at the rank. That's when I first heard of the guy. Actually, it's Nazmi the Catamite who knew them personally. He used to be a minibus driver, too. Working on the same route. Knows them from way back. Anyway, he repented, got married, and gave up minibus driving. Then he came to our stand."

"Who?" I asked.

"Brother Nazmi the Catamite," he replied. "That's a nickname he picked up from back then. I've never seen any signs that it's true, but we call him that sometimes just to get him going. You should see him whip out his knife. And the curses when he gets really mad!"

"What does he say about Volkan?" I asked. I didn't have time for taxi rank antics. It'd be best to finish with Hüseyin before Ponpon returned.

"Well," he said, taking a gulp of coffee, "Volkan was a fare collector back then, working with his brother-in-law."

"That's nothing new," I said. "I already found that out."

"The real bombshell's about to come, but it seems someone's a little impatient," Hüseyin teased.

"Out with it," I commanded. "There's no point in trying to build up suspense."

"Back when Volkan was a fresh-faced boy, Ziya, that is, his uncle, would use him."

In order to be certain I understood what he meant, Hüseyin opened his eyes wide and carefully enunciated each word, with special emphasis on the word "use." When he was finished, he looked at me expectantly, to gauge my reaction. My eyes, too, had flown wide open. We gaped at each other for a moment.

"The guy was a pederast. He used the boy until he went off to do his military service."

I was truly astounded.

"You look surprised," Hüseyin said, all pleased with himself.

"I'm sure I do; I am. That's the last thing I expected."

"Wait, there's more," he said. "Why do you think he married Volkan's big sister? So he could be near Volkan! When they got married, they had Volkan live with them. In the same house! Perfect. Not only were they working all day in the same minibus, but they spent nights under the same roof. Volkan must have been about thir-

teen or fourteen back then, but from what Brother Nazmi the Catamite says, he was a real knock-out. Everyone had eyes for him."

"Anything else?" I asked, still stunned.

"Isn't that enough? It's incredible news! Sell it to a TV channel
and they'd run it for a year."

"Yes, it's a real bombshell and all that, but what else did
Nazmi say?"

He thought for a moment, sipping his coffee.

"He says that if you ask him, it was Ziya who killed Volkan."

"What makes him so certain?"

"Jealousy," he says. "When Volkan came back from the army he
didn't give Ziya the time of day. It's true that our Nazmi wasn't
working as a minibus driver then, but he'd still get news of them
from time to time. Ziya was mad as hell. He even threatened the
boy, I mean Volkan. Pulled a knife on him and everything."

"A bloody love story," I remarked.

"I wouldn't say for sure that it was love," Hüseyin objected.

"What is it then? You told me yourself that he was jealous."

"So just because I act like a gentleman and don't pull a knife on
you, what I feel isn't love?"

Here we go again, having the conversation I least wanted. Yes,
Hüseyin was fond of me. I understood that. And it was only natural that he would desire me. What wasn't natural was Haluk Pekerdem *not* desiring me. But it was just like Hüseyin to confuse lust
with love. Perhaps he respected me, even liked me as a person, but
that didn't mean he loved me. There should be no such thing as un-
requited love. It's just so unfair. To him, and to me.

Chapter 13

aving sent Hüseyin on his way, I reviewed all I knew before Ponpon came back. It was getting more and more confusing. Volkan, the ardent lover, had died, leaving behind scores of men and women with broken hearts, teary eyes, and unsatisfied libidos. Apparently, everyone within spitting distance of the late gigolo had fallen head over heels and embarked on some sort of adventure with him.

Even if Faruk Hanoğlu was not responsible for the vicious slaying, and the media had, as usual, been overhasty in its pronouncement of guilt, there were still plenty of other suspects. Everyone I knew seemed to know something that would implicate someone.

That wonderful man, Haluk Pekerdem, had been cold to me and not the least bit helpful, but if he thought he had slipped through my clutches, he was taking me far too lightly. I would be visiting him on at least a few more occasions. I am nothing if not tenacious.

The list of people I wished to interview was growing: Volkan's sodomite of a brother-in-law, Ziya; his addict brother, Okan; Refik Altın, despite his seeming innocence; Faruk Hanoğlu, despite the difficulties I'd face in seeing him alone and in person; a separate meeting with Faruk's wife, whose name I didn't even know; and finally, there was the blue-blood lady herself, Canan Hanoğlu Pekerdem. I'd already started sharpening my claws and tongue when it came to the wife of dearest Haluk.

I didn't feel like haunting far-off minibus stands again. That meant I would postpone my interviews with Okan and Ziya for the moment. Ponpon could be tapped to arrange a meeting with Canan and her sister-in-law, Faruk's wife. Once she returned from the sauna, all relaxed and glowing, I'd put her to work on that. That left only one person: Refik Altın.

I dialed his number. A mournful voice answered. Explaining I'd heard of his loss from Hasan, I offered my condolences.

"Thank you, nursie," he said. "You can't imagine the depths of my despair . . . I was unable to attend the funeral of my lover. I shrank from contact with the family. Forbidden love and all its attendant complications. Deprived even of a simple burial service."

His possessive insistence on describing as his "lover," a person openly described in the newspapers as a gigolo, was a bit odd.

"I haven't been out and about much lately," I said. "Had you been together long?"

"Concepts like time are meaningless," he chided me. "It's the intensity of what is shared . . . You know that. I mean, look, you're only just recovering. And your affair ended so quickly, surely you remember that much . . ."

He was a master of rubbing salt in wounds. While he may have had a point, I still bristled.

"How can I help you?" I asked.

"I really don't need anything, nursie. I've been alone with my pain, letting it slowly flow to a place deep inside. In silence. I've been writing about it. Would you like to hear?"

That last question was a welcome one, but he began reciting his latest poem before I'd had a chance to respond no. So I imagined it was inspired by Haluk and listened to the end. I was actually quite moved.

"Beautiful," I praised him. "So beautifully expressed!"

I remembered what Hasan had told me. Refik really was pouring his grief into his work.

He wasn't going to tell me anything useful on the telephone. In fact, no one had told me anything of much use so far.

"Shall I stop around?" I asked.

"Don't trouble yourself," he said. "But if you do insist . . ."

It wouldn't be any trouble, but neither was I insisting. I wasn't even certain whether or not I wanted to see Refik. But I did want to see the photos of Volkan. The picture in the paper and the descriptions I'd heard wouldn't suffice.

I jotted down his address and we agreed on a time.

The phone began ringing the second I put it down. Whoever was on the other end would know that I was at home. It was Ali. Judging from his tone of voice and careful choice of words, whatever he expected of me was extremely important. He suggested we meet at the office as soon as possible. What he wanted to tell me was too detailed and confidential for the phone.

I'd been dodging Ali and our work for some time, and his polite and friendly tone could only mean that a major account was in the balance. He'd even sent me a huge bouquet of flowers. I decided to postpone my visit to Refik in order to see Ali first.

I called Refik to explain.

"Nursie, don't bother coming if it's an inconvenience," he said. "I only suggested it because you seemed so determined. I'm actually quite busy."

Taking into consideration his recently broken heart, I listened patiently to his barbed monologue. I promised to stop by as soon as I had concluded my business with Ali.

I taped a large note to Ponpon on the full-length mirror in the hallway. It was the first thing she'd see when she walked into the flat. Ponpon never misses a mirror.

I dressed and hopped into a taxi, arriving at the office twenty minutes later. Insipid Figen met me at the door.

"It's been so long," she said. "We've missed you."

Under rather different, more sincere circumstances there was nothing to object to in what she said. There was Ali, who must have heard my voice and suddenly appeared right next to me. No doubt afraid of being misinterpreted by the dour secretary, he skipped the usual bear hug and, taking me by the arm, propelled me straight to the room I occasionally use as an office.

As usual, Ali got straight to the point, one of his more admirable traits. After asking Figen to prepare two coffees, he shut the door and began outlining the task at hand.

An anonymous client or clients wanted me to crash their computer system, and to do it so thoroughly that it would never function again. Furthermore, I had to ensure that my work could not be traced. That was it, and it would be no problem. Previous clients had requested similar services in order to avoid the tax man or inspectors. Even if charged with fraudulent tampering or falsification, they would simply have their day in court and get off with a moderate fine. Or get whoever was on their tails off their backs.

Our work was to be confidential. No signed agreements. Just a handshake and the promised payment once our work was done. What was strange was their request that we do our job remotely. That is, not on their premises but long distance, using data cables or even telephones. And, of course, without leaving any tracks that could be traced later.

I asked for the name of the company we'd be working for.

"They sent an intermediary. I have no idea who they are," said Ali.

There was no reason not to believe him.

"They'll provide us with all the necessary telephone numbers and passwords. Easy as pie. Just go through their system like you were carding wool, leaving no records behind."

"We could be falling into a trap," I said. "What if they're having us crash someone else's system, not their own?"

"What difference does it make?" Ali objected. "They're the ones paying us; we'll do whatever they want. And if it really is someone else's system we crash, we may have just created a new client. Then we'd fix their system and earn even more."

"Look, Ali," I said, "if I do the job right, even I won't be able to get the system up and running again. It's easier to destroy than to create."

"So we'd ask for extra money."

"Look," I warned Ali, once again, "I'm not so sure about this. You know I'm not one to go on about principles, but wrecking someone's system because someone else is paying you for it seems a bit much to me."

"Princess, you've gone all soft on me," Ali said. "You never had a problem with this before. What's happened to you?"

"That was the old me."

"Oh, come on. Surely you remember all the systems we crashed just because the client didn't agree to meet our price. You do remember?"

I did. It was our favored response to companies that went too far in trying to drive down our fee. Once we'd crashed their systems, they'd come running, and would give us whatever we demanded.

"If we don't do it, Cihad2000 will. You know that! He's been undercutting us, snagging all our business. I've had to stop communicating over the Internet because of him, and I even have my doubts about using my cell phone. I've taken to arranging meetings in person."

As I sat there, silent, Ali continued for some time to try to persuade me to accept the project.

"All right," I finally relented. "I'll do it."

"They'll tell us the day and time."

"How systematic of them."

Once I'd agreed to do the job, Ali suddenly decided to agree with my reservations.

"Maybe you're right about this one. It does seem like something funny is going on, but as long as we don't know what it is, it won't affect us. We'll still have clean hands and clear consciences!"

"Give me the numbers and codes," I said.

"I don't know them. They're going to let us know over the phone."

"You mean I'm supposed to sit here day and night waiting for their call? Forget it!"

"Of course you don't have to sit here," he said soothingly. "I'll get in touch with the intermediary and he'll stay in touch with the client. We've only just agreed to do this in any case, haven't we?"

Ali went to his office to make the necessary phone call, leaving me alone. I sorted through my mail and scanned the latest magazines.

Figen brought in a cup of Turkish coffee, served with a piece of chocolate.

"I just got engaged," she announced. "The chocolate's from the party."

Hiding my surprise, I congratulated her. So Figen had landed a husband. Miracle of miracles! Ever since I met her she's been dreaming of finding a man, and considered each one she met, regardless of age and marital status, a potential suitor.

"Oh, by the way, I wonder if I could ask you something?"

"Go on, dear," I replied. That "dear" was in honor of her engagement.

"I wondered where you picked up your two-piece. I just love it."

I'd purchased the suit in question at NetWork but would never wear it again on the chance that Figen would now run out and buy the same thing. The very idea of appearing in public in the same costume as Figen sent a shudder down my spine. For one thing, she had a huge rear. Her acquisition of a fiancé did not mean she was in my league and could copy my dress sense.

"I bought it overseas," I lied.

"It's so cute," she gushed.

I thanked her once again.

"There's a photograph of my fiancé on my desk; I could show you if you're curious."

That's all I needed.

I continued flipping the pages of the magazine without really looking at them.

"I'm busy right now. Another time maybe," I said.

She was tactful enough to take a hint, and left the room without comment.

In less than the time it took me to flip through a second magazine, Ali returned.

"They want us to start today," he said.

"Perfect," I said. "We won't have to wait around. I'll get started immediately and you'll get your money."

"Perfect. I agree."

"Did you know that Ponpon calls you Money-counter?" I said.

"Who's Ponpon?"

Ali inevitably forgets every face and name who isn't in some way connected to earning money.

"She remembers you," I said. "You know, my big sister."

"Ah, that's right, that friend of yours," Ali lied, clearly as clueless as ever. "Anyway, about those numbers and passwords."

He handed me a sheet of pink paper.

"This evening," he instructed, "after seven p.m. will be suitable. They suggested between nine and ten as the ideal time."

"Talk about fussy!" I said.

"They pay; we listen," said Ali.

"I suppose you're right," I admitted.

"And please, whatever you do, don't leave any tracks. You may even want to go online at a café. Working from home or here at the office could be risky."

He was right. Just as I was sometimes able to trace Cihad2000, he and others like him could do the same when it came to me.

Then I had a stroke of genius: Why not make it look as though

Cihad2000 had done it? I could easily access his connections. Yes, I was taking a chance. If he found out, it would be considered a declaration of war. But I had learned all his tricks, and it would be no trouble to imitate his methods. And if I went online at an Internet café, it would be impossible to trace me.

I didn't tell Ali what I was thinking. We agreed on a code I'd use to let him know my work was done.

Chapter 14

An analog phone line would be preferable, even though it would be a slow connection. It's easier to detect someone—or be detected—on a digital line. The very fact that analog lines are so old and inefficient is a kind of built-in security system.

I took the office laptop away with me. Then I visited a few of the Internet cafés in Beşiktaş where students hang out. They all have digital lines. But I was certain there were still analog lines in use; Cihad2000 lived in Beşiktaş and he had both types. The last café I entered was nearly full, with groups of teenagers gathered in front of each screen.

The cubicles were tiny, and by massing in front of the screens the students concealed them completely. Their silence, punctuated by sharp intakes of breath, made me doubt whether they were in the café to do their homework.

I found an empty computer near the door. There would be a lot of traffic behind me, but it was worth a try. And it wasn't as though the content on my screen would attract attention. First I tried out the connection on the PC. Analog, just as I'd hoped. I turned on my laptop as well.

I opened a few browsers, so that if someone suddenly appeared behind me, I could switch to an innocent music, travel, or news Web site. The connection was slow, and the PC antique. I connected the PC to the laptop. Identity shield safely in place, I began browsing in security.

The first of the numbers Money-counter Ali had given me

worked at the first try. The site was not open to the public. I had been connected to a modem line that had been left open. It would make my job much easier.

Fine. I would cause the entire system to crash and not leave a trace of data behind, but I couldn't help having a peek at what I was about to obliterate. The connection was strangely primitive, full of redirections and substandard shield programs. It was obviously an outdated example of amateur software. The first image on the screen was a long list. A long list of numbers.

I scanned through the programs in order to get a better understanding of what they could be. The numbers were too long and irregular to be bank accounts. I began looking for alphabetical characters. I was in no hurry; I was just beginning.

One of the young café workers suddenly asked me if I'd like anything to drink. I looked nothing like the others at the café, and he wasn't about to leave me in peace and forgo the prospect of a tip.

"What have you got?" I asked.

Stuffing both hands into his jeans pockets, he shrugged slightly.

"Tea . . . Nescafé . . . cola . . . ayran . . ."

There was no need to cause a stir by asking if they had herbal tea. My outfit and open laptop connected to their PC already had marked me as slightly unconventional. Asking for a cup of fennel tea would have been downright eccentric.

Tea would be too cheap to justify a generous tip, so I opted for a cola. "Not too cold," I added.

I would have to leave my work and surf through other sites until the pimply youth returned with my refreshment. He reappeared in no time, his grubby fingers touching the yellow straw in my can of cola. I thanked him and asked how much.

"Pay on your way out," he said.

Alone and undisturbed once again, I got back to work. Lists of numbers were still flowing down the screen. If they were a code of some kind, it would be a tough nut to crack. We hadn't agreed to

anything like that. They'd asked us to crash their system, not decipher it. What's more, I had no way of even knowing if it was in fact
their system.

I activated a search program to locate any letters. The first characters seemed randomly ordered. Then I identified names followed
by cities and fragments of sentences. In the search program, I entered the first name that came to mind: Haluk Pekerdem. While
that name was never far from my thoughts, it didn't appear on the
screen. Deciding to be more rational, I canceled the search. If I was
looking at bank account numbers, the name Faruk Hanoğlu would
be more likely to appear. I entered his name and waited. I believe in
coincidence: There before me, clear as day, was the name Faruk
Hanoğlu.

Now I was truly intrigued. What was Faruk's name doing in
this system, and what kind of system was it anyway? I'd crash the
whole thing, as agreed, but I could well find something useful before I did so. There was no way for me to transfer all the data to my
laptop. It didn't have the hard disk space. What laptop does?

Something told me the information before me was valuable. It
would be foolish to destroy something that could be of use to me
later. But I had promised Ali. The terms of the agreement were
that I would crash the system that night. I had a few more hours. In
any case, in the name of professionalism, if nothing else, I would
have to become better acquainted with the system in order to ensure that I didn't leave behind any virtual fingerprints.

In order to get my thoughts in order, I imagined I was a game-
show contestant faced with four alternatives: a) simply look the
other way and delete all the data on my screen; b) somehow create
a copy for my personal use at a later date, then delete the data; c)
drop the whole project and face the consequences—even knowing
as I did that the client would then employ Cihad2000 to get the job
done; d) meet with Faruk Hanoğlu immediately, and let the shit hit
the fan.

Openly courting danger, that is; meeting now with Faruk Hanoğlu, who was a chief suspect in the case, would be ill-advised, to say the least. And compressing and copying the enormous system before me would be next to impossible in the time frame allotted. Not only would it take all night, but I'd have to locate a state-of-the-art computer with an expanded capacity. And I didn't have the option of merely trying to copy the bits that seemed important; I still had no idea what the file after file of numbers and names contained or what it all meant. And time was running out.

Cihad2000 was the only person who could help me. But getting him involved would be tricky, and I cringed at the thought of what he would then demand of me. I tried and failed to come up with alternative plans of action. There was no one to turn to for help but Cihad2000. I knew exactly how to enlist his help; seducing him would be easy enough. But I shuddered at the thought of coming up with the goods once our work was done.

Dispensing with security precautions, I entered a private chat room where I knew he always he lurks.

Good evening, sweetie,

I began.

There was no way he wouldn't recognize me. He immediately sent me an impressive float.

where are you? that's not your address!

Clever boy; he'd already checked where I'd logged in. Ignoring his question, I got straight to the point.

help!

I need your help now

are you free?

He answered back in a wink of the eye.

when have i ever refused you

but you'll have to pay for it

I wasn't about to go into more detail; it was too complicated for that.

Can I pop round?

NO WAY

I hadn't expected to be refused. A wheelchair-bound computer whiz, Cihad2000 was living in Beşiktaş with his parents. The capital letters indicated that he was either about to climax or that something strange was up. I repeated:

I need your help now

This time he took some time to respond. Perhaps he really was busy.

it's impossible right now

After a pause, a flood of letters appeared on my screen.

if it's what i think it is, stay away!

they're dangerous

stay away!

It wasn't like Cihad to pause before writing something. I knew he was monitoring me, but he couldn't know what I was doing or anything about the files I'd just opened. I'd taken every security precaution. Actually, I reminded myself, I was now chatting from a run-down café. Some security!

I don't understand

what are you talking about

I need extra storage space

find me some

to transfer some data

I can't transfer a whole system to a PC

There was no response for a couple of minutes. Then he sent me a float. Instead of the usual sermons and doomsday quotes, he'd inserted numerals into all the spaces between words and letters. It took me some time to decipher it.

it's that client!

drop it

or you'll burn

so many numbers

but not the lottery

stay away

I was confused. There was no way he could know whether or not we were working on the same project. And even if he was trying to protect me, in the end, we were rivals.

don't be an idiot

don't you recognize what's on your screen?

I finally got it. The numbers he'd sent, which I thought was just an ordinary float, were in fact the database of the system I had set out to destroy.

what do you think you're doing?

get out of my line

I was cross when I wrote that. Enough was enough. Despite having gone online at a café, he'd still managed to track me down. We were going to have to fight it out once for and all.

it's my contract

YOU SHOULD GET OUT, NOT ME

And he closed the connection.

I called him on his private cell phone number.

"You're starting to get on my nerves!" I hissed.

"What do you think you're doing? This is my contract. What gives you the right to steal my work? It's mine. I respect you . . . but get lost!"

"We landed this contract," I told him. "Don't try to pinch it. Stop tracking me. The market's big enough for both of us. You're always on my tail! I've had it. We both lose if we undercut each other."

"What do you mean *your* contract? I closed the deal a week ago and was waiting for an appointment with them. They give me a day and time, and who appears? You!"

"They gave us an appointment. We're supposed to finish this in two hours."

"Wait a sec," he said. "Who's your client?"

"It's confidential. Who's yours?"

"It's confidential."

Then an outrageous thought occurred to me: Two top-notch hackers employed to do the same job!

"What exactly did they ask you to do?" I asked. "They wanted me to crash their entire system, with all its data. What did they want you to do? Shield their system?"

"No, nothing like that," said Cihad2000. "All they wanted me to do was to create an intermediary link connecting their system to another system at a specified time. Theirs was too unwieldy."

"Look," I said, "I think they're using us both. Your computer is acting as a sort of intermediary portal, opening up their system to the outside. They've assigned you the task of bypassing security. Then I'm supposed to enter through the channel you've opened and obliterate the database. Don't you see? They're using us both, so we're both mixed up in this. Neither of us is fully responsible; both of us are kept in the dark. Speaking of which, this whole business is a lot shadier than I'd realized."

"You must be serious," he said. "You haven't said *ayol* even once."

I had to laugh at that.

"Technically, what you say is possible," he continued. "But why would they do it? Why should they pay us both?"

"I've got no idea. But take a look at the connection code they gave you . . ."

When I read out the code, it was his turn to be stunned.

"That's a virtual code I created just for my computer, so they could link to me from abroad."

"They told me to use a switching route from overseas, but when I found an analog line I decided not to bother."

"So that's how I found you," he teased. "You're not up to snuff these days. You've fallen in my eyes."

So be it. If I fell in his eyes, maybe he'd get off my back and leave me alone. But it wasn't just my skill as a hacker that drew him to me.

"So are you going to store that data for me?" I asked. "Have you got enough space?"

"I don't think so," he said. "It's such an old-fashioned database, too clumsy and unwieldy. And the codes are poorly devised. I can't make heads or tails of it."

"Don't you have any idea what it is?"

"I didn't really have a good look," he said. "I was at a video cam site. Two guys were doing the most unspeakable things to each other. I couldn't believe my eyes. Maybe we can try it sometime."

"Don't even think about it!" I said.

Cihad2000 is into things like S&M and rubber. That sort of stuff not only fails to turn me on, I don't even find it interesting.

I glanced at the clock. I'd been connected to the system for about an hour, Cihad2000 for even longer. If someone was monitoring us, and had even the slightest experience, he would have noticed by now. But there had been no indication that anyone had.

"I came across a name among the data. I don't know why, but it caught my eye," I said. "I'd like to do some further research before I crash the system. If you help me, you may find me a bit more . . . accommodating."

"But that's blackmail!" he sputtered.

"So what?" I said. "You scratch my back, I scratch yours."

There was a moment of silence.

"You're pushing me," he said. "I've got a bad feeling about this whole thing. The system I was linked to is an outside one. It's not theirs. And here we both are, doing their bidding . . . Not even knowing who 'they' are. I find all these extra security measures a bit alarming. If I were you, I'd finish the job, take my money, and shut up."

"Are you going to help me or not?"

"We're getting into hot water here . . . But how can I say no to you? Okay, but I can't copy the whole thing. Give me that one name."

I gave him Faruk's full name.

"And," I added, "Haluk Pekerdem."

I couldn't resist. And if Faruk Hanoğlu was listed, there was every chance Haluk would be too.

"At your service, your royal highness. Start when the flowers arrive! I'm signing out."

The flowers he mentioned appeared on my screen about twenty-five minutes later: a huge bouquet composed of brightly colored characters!

It was time to get to work. By ten I had sent Ali the agreed-upon text message: "I'm not hungry." I'd even left the pimply waiter a big tip.

Chapter 15

*P*onpon was waiting for me at home, in full war paint, ready for battle.

"I've been worried sick," she said the moment I stepped through the door. "You've got a phone. But it's switched off! I call, no answer. Then I phone Hasan, and he knows nothing. So I try the office . . . Money-counter won't tell me a thing. I don't know, he says, and hangs up. I was sure something had happened to you. You'll drive me crazy yet. It's not as though you're in perfect mental health yourself. The least you could do is leave me sane."

"Thanks," I said. "That was great for morale."

"Oh, I see," she said. "So now it's all my fault! We've been friends for decades, so I drop everything and leave my home to come here to yours. I've been cleaning and straightening for days— that is, when I haven't been slaving away in the kitchen. Why? To help you. And what do you do? Disappear, as irresponsible as can be. And until the middle of the night. Do you have any idea what time it is? I even considered phoning that police chief friend of yours. Enough. I'm going. I simply won't put up with this kind of abuse."

"Come on, Ponpon," I said. "It was an important job . . ."

Ponpon melts if she's hugged. And that's what she did. Actually, her leaving was a good idea, but I couldn't deny that thanks to her I'd been living in comfort and feasting like a queen.

"See, I'm fine," I went on. "And it's all thanks to you. Go if you want to, of course. I know I've been a real bore. I've worn you out."

"Don't think you can soften me up like that! And I was so busy answering your phone calls, I burned dinner. We've got nothing to eat!"

That was the worst possible disaster scenario for Ponpon.

"We'll eat out," I said. "My treat!"

"It's too late . . . I'll barely make my show as it is. I've got to leave now."

"We'll meet up later," I said.

"You mean you're not coming with me?"

"It's high time I stopped by my own club. To see if the place is still standing."

What I'd just said was perfectly reasonable, but it didn't stop Ponpon from scrutinizing me from head to toe before glancing at her watch in a panic and darting out the door with:

"I suppose you know best."

I raced to the bathroom to get ready to go out. I had two choices: to knock them out as my usual glamorous self or resort to tragedy, winning their sympathy as a piteous creature who'd only just crawled out of her deathbed.

I decided on the former.

I've got no time for unpleasant surprises, so I phoned Hasan to let him know I was coming. He feigned pleasure, but I could see right through him. I was certain he'd been enjoying playing the tyrant while I was away. It was time for me to topple him from his throne, claiming my place as queen bee and relegating him to the role of drone if need be.

When I hung up, I scanned the list of messages Ponpon had written in a flowing hand perfected at a series of French schools. The name Hüseyin jumped out at me several times as I vainly looked for the name Haluk Pekerdem. How was I supposed to concentrate on anything until I'd landed that man?

I knew I'd see Hüseyin on my way to the club in any case. Now that we'd made up he'd be waiting at the rank at the usual time. If he had anything to say to me, he could do it on the way to the club.

I put on my favorite sleek black dress, collarless and sleeveless like the one Audrey Hepburn wore in *Breakfast at Tiffany's*. The effect was completed with three strands of large fake pearls and a pair of long satin gloves. All that was missing was the cigarette holder and French twist. I was at least as thin as Audrey, but far sexier.

When I called for a taxi, Hüseyin arrived, as expected. He began speaking before I'd even settled in.

"I've been ringing you all day, but you were out. And I left a message, but you didn't call back. Brother Nazmi the Catamite had some more amazing news. It's about that minibus driver you were asking about, the brother of the dead guy . . . He's disappeared! Hasn't been seen for days. The whole taxi stand is looking for him."

"You might have tried 'good evening' first," I reprimanded Hüseyin.

"Yeah, right, good evening and all that. I suppose I got a little wound up, and I thought you'd be excited too."

"So how did this Nazmi of yours find out he'd disappeared?"

"Some guys from the stand stopped by to offer condolences. The minibus guys over there said Volkan had socked away a lot of cash. They think the brother ran off with it when he was killed."

"It's entirely possible," I reflected. "Likely, in fact."

Huseyin paused. "I swear there's something funny about you tonight. You didn't use to sit there like a statue when I brought news like this."

"What am I supposed to do?"

"If that's how you feel . . ."

"Let's get going. I haven't been to the club for days. I miss it."

"Where have you been all day?" Hüseyin asked, as soon as we were on the road, driving up the hill.

"Since when do I answer to you?" I replied, raising my voice. "I was wherever I was."

I wasn't having any impertinence just because we'd slept together twice.

"Get a grip and don't bother getting your hopes up," I continued. "Whatever happened, happened. Don't go reading anything into it."

He slammed on the brakes, stopping in the middle of the road. Throwing an arm over the seat, he spun around to face me.

"You're like a cat playing with a mouse," he said. "I know you'll thrash me if you get mad. You've done it before. But I've got feelings, too. I'm not a toy. You can't order me to come and go whenever you feel like it."

"Then don't," I snapped. "And keep driving."

"Then get yourself another taxi!" he shouted.

"Don't be silly, Hüseyin! We're halfway there."

"I'll drop you off back at the rank," he said.

"So are you going to sulk like a child again?"

He started driving.

"Well, you treat me like a child. Why shouldn't I act like one?"

"Stop being so stupid!" I said. "Let's get going. I'm tired, you're cross . . . Let's not drag this out."

"I waited for you at the stand all day long. I didn't take any other fares."

"Did I tell you to wait for me?"

"No," he admitted.

"So?"

Cüneyt the bodyguard met me at the door to the club, holding it open for me. He even kissed my hand. I must have looked as surprised as I felt. Where on earth had Cüneyt learned that?

"They always do that on *The Hülya Avşar Show,*" he explained. "And what has she got that you haven't got?"

"Quite right. And I've got something she can never have," I said.

I had only a split second to feel ashamed of my little joke, for the moment I stepped into the club flashes popped and confetti dropped and Hasan was squeezing me so hard I thought I'd suffocate.

When Hasan found out I'd be dropping by the club, he, along with the other boys—Cüneyt, Şükran the barman, DJ Osman, and the regular girls—had organized a surprise party. I was touched, despite myself. Amid cries of "welcome home," I was dragged onto the dance floor.

My favorite song of all time, "It's Raining Men," as performed by the Weather Girls, began playing. I was given even more space than usual on the floor, and had barely finished my second twirl when it filled with well-wishers hugging and kissing me in turn. I was about to burst into tears of joy, gratitude, and pride.

No doubt my high spirits were a bit too much for Hasan, who danced his way to my side to say, "Refik called you twice. You were supposed to stop by. He's been waiting for you all night long."

Congratulations. He'd manage to spoil my good mood. I'd completely forgotten about Refik Altın. It was just like him to track me down at the club. Refik had been talking down his nose to me for months, humiliating me at every opportunity. But he still didn't hesitate to come to the club—my club.

"Oh, I forgot all about him," I said. "That's not like me at all. Remind me to give him a call and apologize."

"He's the last person who deserves an apology from you."

"If anyone has any apologizing to do, it's him," added Hairy Demet. So, no doubt due to Hasan's big mouth, everyone at the club knew I hadn't kept my rendezvous with Refik Altın.

They'd immediately misinterpreted the concerned look on my face.

"Don't worry about it," continued Demet. "If he doesn't come here anymore, so be it. We don't need the likes of him!"

Hairy Demet was right, I thought, but Refik Altın and his sort did lend a certain intellectual air to the premises.

I was distracted by the front door. It had opened, and three people were walking in. Three men. I glanced hopefully at each in
turn. Was that Haluk Pekerdem bringing up the rear? . . . No. In
the dimly lit club, whoever it was had looked remarkably like my
Haluk, and I'd held my breath, waiting for him to turn toward me.
What was I thinking? What would someone like him be doing in
our club? He'd be terrified just to walk through that door.

The excitement I'd felt at seeing a pale imitation of Haluk
turned to frustration. I was hooked. I had to get my hands on him
one way or another, or I'd lose it.

My pulse was still racing. "It's Raining Men" was still playing,
but I stood stock-still. Breasts straining against filmy fabric, as always, Aylin came up and took my arm.

"Sister, are you all right? You've gone all pale." Screeching,
"Clear the way!" Aylin led me off the dance floor and made me sit
down.

Hasan and Şükrü pushed their way through the crowd, coming
to my side with worried looks.

"I'm fine," I said.

"You're awfully pale," said Hasan. "Why don't you sit down for
a minute? Şükrü, go and get a lemon soda."

"Soda won't help," Nalan intervened. "Get something sweet.
Her blood sugar's dropped."

A serious junkie, Nalan was considered an authority on such
subjects.

"Get some cola then, and throw in some sugar! Run!" said
Hasan, still bossing Şükrü around.

"Cola won't do it either. It's carbonated," Nalan informed them.
"Plain sugar water is best."

"It'll make me sick. I don't want any," I said. "I'm fine. Look!"

As I stood up, I toppled over. Either my blood pressure had
dropped or a lack of sleep was taking its toll.

Chapter 16

Opening my eyes to the sight of Haluk Pekerdem would have been wonderful, but it was Hasan who was leaning over me. Yes, it was Hasan who was bringing me around by slapping me repeatedly. And I do mean slapping. One of the girls was massaging perfume onto my wrists, probably because there was none of the customary cologne on hand. The intoxicating scent of Guerlain Samsara filled the air.

"His eyes are open!"

No doubt hoping they'd remain closed forever!

"I'm fine," I said. "Just give me a little air."

Chief fusser Hasan began barking orders. The crowd moved back. Taking an arm each, Hasan and Cüneyt assisted me to the door. I must have been grinning foolishly, perhaps even sheepishly.

It was only the second time I'd passed out in my life. The first time had happened years ago. A headstrong little boy, I'd thrown a hysterical fit when my mother had refused to buy me a pair of gold lamé boots. When I came to, the boots were resting next to my bed, with the stipulation that they were to be worn only at home, and never in front of guests. Blacking out had helped me get my way. But that hadn't happened this time. There was no Haluk Pekerdem waiting for me to open my eyes, his strong arms ready to scoop me up and carry me off.

Instead, I was flanked by Cüneyt, who's considered cute only because of muscles regularly inflated at the gym, and Hasan, whose orientation and tastes remain a mystery, but who works for pennies at a transvestite bar, traipses around with his butt crack showing, and refuses to put out for man, woman, or anything in-between. This must be what they mean when they talk of cruel fate.

"Shall I drop you off at home?" Hasan asked.

"No!" I said. "I've just come to. And I'm fine. I just need a bit of air."

"Boss, you gave us such a scare," Cüneyt chimed in, his eyes like saucers. "And you've only just risen from your sickbed."

"Do you want me to tell Ponpon?"

"No, Hasan," I said. "It was hard enough to get rid of her. Let me rest in peace."

"But you've been resting for weeks," said Cüneyt.

"Keep out of this!" I scolded him, before turning on Hasan. "It looks like everyone knows everything. I'll have a word with you about that later."

"Oh, come on, is Cüneyt a stranger?"

He imagined he'd get off the hook by seeming to spring to Cüneyt's defense. He was wrong.

"I've had quite enough air, and quite enough of you," I snapped. "Let's go back in."

A special table had been prepared for me, the one Hasan dubs the VIP corner. At a strategic point just between the dance floor and the room, it's the best place to see and be seen. I sat down. Şükrü brought me my virgin Mary. It was perfect, the best I've had except for mixes imported from America. Not only could he make a perfect drink, Şükrü was also one of the last of the twink-chasers. Just Şükrü and Ziya, the brother-in-law of that most accommodating of gigolos, Volkan.

The girls took turns sitting with me, outdoing each other in expressions of concern and sympathy. But even as I nodded mechanically and smiled graciously, I continued thinking of Ziya Göktaş. What was he up to these days? And what about his wife, Volkan's sister? Did she know?

The moment I felt stronger, barring any more fainting spells, I'd go see Ziya. Yes, first thing tomorrow morning. Then I'd pay a visit to Cihad2000 to get the data he'd promised to download for me. He'd hit on me, as usual, and I'd either have to ignore him or give him a good dressing down. Not that the latter would do any good: He loves nothing better than being humiliated and abused.

My body still felt a bit wooden, but my mind was working a mile a minute. I fastened my eyes on Shrewish Pamir, who was dancing up a storm and almost certainly looking to start a brawl. As far as I knew she enjoyed playing the dominatrix with her tricks. With her tall muscular frame, toned by years of basketball in her youth, long legs, tiny leather skirt, and vinyl stiletto boots reaching hip high, she'd be perfect for the little job I had in mind. I called her over.

"Yes, *abla*," she droned as she made her way over to me. Pamir is one of those who imagine that speaking through one's nose produces a more ladylike effect.

"Have a seat," I said. "I need to have a word with you."

"Anything wrong? What's happened?"

"Nothing's wrong. I've got a little proposal to make you."

She listened intently as I gave a brief sketch of Cihad2000: a computer genius in a wheelchair who looks a bit like Stephen Hawking and is an insatiable masochist.

"Just have a go," I said. "If it's too much for you, I understand. I'll pay your fee no matter what. I owe him a favor."

"What do you mean, sister? I wouldn't dream of taking money from you . . . When I think of all you've done for us . . . Wasn't it you who took me to the emergency room when my eyebrow was split open and made them promise not to leave a scar? You saved my face. I've never forgotten it. And I tell everyone about it."

"Really?" I said, truly touched.

I could feel myself beaming, just as I had been earlier that night.

"Of course," she went on. "No one ever helps anyone anymore. I can never repay you. Think of all the times you got me out of jail; I'm not even counting that. Just tell me who you want me to do—I don't care if it's Woody Allen or Yılmaz Erdoğan. And not just once, for a whole week, if you want."

So Pamir had no idea who Stephen Hawking was. As specimens of manhood, I'm not an Allen or an Erdoğan fan myself, but she hadn't yet seen Kemal, alias Cihad2000.

"You may want to meet him first," I warned her, "before you decide anything."

"No problem, if I have to I'll just shut my eyes and do my duty . . ."

Rising from the table, she exploded in a nasal guffaw, still convinced she was a tempting siren.

My creative solution to the problem of Cihad2000 had improved my mood immensely. If only someone would speak to Haluk Pekerdem on my behalf, win him over for me! Just once! Once would be enough. Like winning an Oscar, Grammy, or Nobel prize. If I could just seduce him once, he'd be back for more. I knew it. One taste, and he was mine.

Watching the girls display their most erotic, even obscene, dance moves for prospective customers, I sat at my table dreaming of Haluk until dawn.

Chapter 17

With the address Selçuk had given me in hand, finding Ziya Göktaş's home was dead easy. His apartment building was on one of those narrow streets in Ihlamur where the weekly market is held. He lived on the top floor of a nondescript building distinguishable from the others only by the smells of cooking that wafted out onto the street.

The stairwell looked as though it hadn't been painted since the building was constructed. The steps were shiny with years of constant wiping and smelled faintly of soap.

The doormat of his flat was completely concealed by shoes, as was much of the floor on either side of the hallway. Shoes of all shapes and sizes, the men's unpolished with heels worn down.

The door was opened by a young girl wearing the self-important expression of a school monitor. In this case, she'd been assigned the task of receiving guests coming to offer their condolences. Determined to live up to her grown-up duty, she was suitably somber, with just the hint of a proud smile playing around her lips. Moving to one side, she gestured for me to come in.

"Come in, uncle," she said.

I wasn't about to let that one word spoil my mood. "Uncle" indeed!

Heading toward the sound of soft weeping, I was cut off by a neighbor determined to play the role of hostess. She was way past middle age, her bracelets and gold earrings a calculated display of wealth and status.

"Welcome, my son," she said. "I was like an aunt to him. His mother and my mother suckled together . . ."

She was expecting me to make a similar announcement. I quickly made something up.

"My condolences," I said. "I'm so sorry."

"So many loved him. They've been coming to pay their respects all day long. Bless them all. Come in . . ."

I was waved into the living room. It was full of men. The women must be sitting in a second parlor, with the guests separated by gender. The man with bleary eyes sitting right across from the TV had to be Ziya Göktaş. He looked like the typical baddie in an old Turkish film: dark and mustachioed. Right out of the school of Erol Taş, Bilal İnci, and Hayati Hamzaoğlu. He looked up at me. His expert eye immediately determined what I was, and assigned me points. Suddenly, he rose to his feet and embraced me.

He reeked of tobacco.

I was taken aback by the unexpected attention. He must have confused me with someone else.

"Have a seat, chum," he said.

The word "chum" spoke volumes. He wasn't at all upset. Or if he was, he'd recovered in no time. Beneath black brows, his eyes shone with the shifty cunning of the film villain plotting some dastardly plan.

As is the tradition, everyone in the room droned at length about the flawless character of the newly departed and his endless good deeds. I would have to say a word or two. I did.

The brother-in-law stared at me, the kind of look that imprisons its target. He was on to me; in fact, he fancied me. But he had no idea who I was, why I had come, or how he could make a move on me without anyone else noticing.

I, too, wished to be alone with him. But for entirely different reasons.

None of the sitters seemed to have any intention of leaving

their chairs. Whenever there was silence, someone would emit a long, heartfelt "ahhhh," and begin a lengthy monologue on the implications of death and the relative meaninglessness of life. Ziya and I appeared to be the only ones there who actually looked at each other. Everyone else was either staring at the floor or contemplating the distant corners of the universe.

Like any troublemaker, Ziya was quick on his feet.

"Come, my lion, let me show you Volkan's old room," he said. I assumed I was the "lion" he referred to, since he didn't know my name.

Holding up an arm in a gesture meant to urge the others not to interrupt their floor gazing, he threw the other one around my shoulders and led me off. I was able to shake it off with a light shrug, but he then moved behind me. I could feel his eyes on my bottom as we walked down the hallway and into a tiny bedroom. There was no indication that the room had ever belonged to Volkan. In it was only a single bed, a chair piled high with blankets, and a rickety-looking wardrobe.

As he'd opened the door and lightly pushed me in, Ziya had copped a feel of my arm and my shoulder.

"You're him!" he exclaimed, once he'd closed the door. "I knew it the minute you walked in. Well, I've got to admit it. Our boy had good taste."

There was nowhere to sit but the bed. I didn't want to sit right next to him and be subjected to more groping, so I headed toward the window, intending to sit at the foot of the bed, as far away from him as possible. I pretended to look outside at the dark courtyard garden, which contained two fruit trees and a pile of junked furniture.

"Volkan and I were real close," he said. "He showed me some of your poems."

So that was it! The idiot thought I was Refik Altın, the latest lover Volkan had sponged off of. I decided not to correct him for as long as the mix-up suited my purposes.

"I needed to see you," I said, "to clear some things up."

"Come sit next to me," he coaxed. "Let me give you a hug."

"Volkan told me all about you," I said, as I pushed him off. It wasn't as though Volkan was going to come and contradict anything I said. Ziya changed color.

"*Aman!*" he exclaimed. "Keep those pretty lips sealed. You hear me?"

I studied him for a moment. I tend to purse my lips while I think. He misunderstood.

"I could eat those beautiful lips," he leered. What a creep.

"You pulled a knife on him," I continued.

"That's a lie!"

"Aren't you ashamed of yourself? You claim to be in love with him, then you pull a knife on him when he leaves you."

That same villainous look was still plastered on his face as he lewdly looked me up and down. Pulling a cigarette out of his shirt pocket, he lit it.

"There's nothing to be ashamed of," I said. "Burning love! It'd be great if all love affairs were like that . . . such passion . . . lasting for years."

Taking a long drag on his cigarette, he looked thoughtful.

"Is that what he said?"

I figured flattery would be the best way to get him to talk. "Of course," I replied. "He told me so much about you."

After another puff of his cigarette, he paused for a moment. I was watching him. He seemed lost in thought, like he was contemplating the mysteries of the universe.

"That's right, I loved him," he said finally. "I'd never met anyone like him, and I haven't since. Such airs, so beautiful. You wouldn't know. You should have seen him when he was young. Like an angel. Before his beard grew . . . Before hair grew on his pink and white body. Skin like cream, and he smelled so fresh. And what a fast learner. You know what I mean? Even at that age . . ."

I have never understood pedophilia. It may be because I prefer more mature men, but I just don't get it. In fact, it's deeply disturbing.

"You should be ashamed of yourself. A young boy like that . . ."

"He wasn't that young," Ziya argued. "When his stepdad came, they gave him to me. He'd finished middle school. He was old enough to come. And he enjoyed it, too. I'm no child molester. You know what I mean?"

So there were apparently alternative definitions of pedophilia.

He must have sensed my discomfort, even disgust.

"In a lot of countries in Europe the age of consent is sixteen," he pointed out. Had this brute of a man actually bothered to research this?

"What difference does it make?" I countered. "A child is a child!"

"It's not like that at all. Why won't you understand me? I mean, what about here in Turkey? Girls of thirteen and fourteen get married off all the time. My dad got married in the village when he was only sixteen or seventeen. He hadn't even done his military service yet. He went off to the army after I was born. It's not what you think!"

"I see," I said, just to put the conversation to an end.

He was lost in the "old days," and absentmindedly reached under the bed, pulling out a bottle of cheap cognac. He'd obviously been making frequent visits to the bottle all morning long. Taking a swallow, he offered me the bottle.

"It'll warm you up . . ."

If I intended to get him talking—and I did—I would have to join in. Most of the mouthful I took under his watchful eye went right back into the bottle.

"Feel better now?" he asked.

I nodded, grimacing as though my throat was burning from the cognac.

"He loved me too . . ." he said. He was staring off into the distance again. "I had to keep him to myself, so I went and married his sister. She's a good person, but she doesn't know how to be a real woman. All these years, and she still hasn't learned how to really get me going. She won't even suck on it . . . But Volkan, he was something else. I'd go straight from his sister's bed to his. I'd make up excuses, tell her the boy was crying, that I couldn't sleep. I knocked her up three times just so she'd be too busy to notice. She was too busy nursing and looking after our kids to catch me, even once. Summers I'd send her off to her mother's, along with the kids . . . And it would be just the two of us. Then we'd get to sleep in the big bed. All night long . . ."

I'd known about their relationship, but hadn't expected such passion. At the mention of Volkan, his eyes shone and he practically licked his chops.

"Enthralling" was all I said.

"I can tell you're a poet," he commented, with not a hint of irony.

"But how did it all start?" I prompted. "Weren't you afraid? Or wasn't he?"

"I've always had a thing for young guys. When I first saw Volkan I just melted. Like a tall glass of cool water, he was. I took him on as my assistant. I wanted him so bad, I couldn't look at him. I stopped hanging out with the other fellows at the coffeehouse, and would sit with him in the minibus waiting for my turn to come. Oh, he was interested, too. Interested in just about everything. His dad was dead, his mother living with another man . . . You get the picture? He was all mine . . . Finally, one day, I couldn't stand it anymore. I drove off with him toward Kilyos, pulled over onto one of those dirt roads. I told him how I felt . . . the way he made me feel . . . then I offered him money, said I'd increase his weekly wage."

So that's how Volkan began his career as a gigolo. Gay for pay right from the start. Ziya took another swig from the bottle.

"And did he agree?"

"Did he ever . . . Knew how to drive a bargain even back then . . . And he deserved every penny. I'd do it again. When I think of the pleasure he gave me . . . I'd hand over a hundred times more and no regrets!"

He started crying. I had a lovesick villain on my hands, and it wasn't a pretty sight. There's something about a badly dressed ruffian in tears that gets to me. I can't take it.

I waited for the unhappy spectacle to end. He wept silently, tears streaming, face screwed up in anguish.

"Come, let me give you a hug," he said.

A shoulder drenched in spit and snot would have been bad enough, but there was the possibility that I'd have to deal with even worse. If he crossed a line, I could always incapacitate him with a few aikido moves, but that was hardly appropriate behavior in a house of mourning. As a man, I found him revolting; but as the abandoned partner in a tragic and marginal love story, I was sorry for him nonetheless. Fighting competing feelings of pity and disgust, and a not inconsequential but grudging sense of respect, I gently sat down next to him on the bed. He took me in his hairy arms and continued crying—on my shoulder, just as I'd feared.

"I gave him everything I had . . . Did everything I could for him . . . I closed my ears to what they said behind my back. They called me a child molester, a boy bugger, a pervert. You name it, they said it. But I just ignored them. He was worth it! He was never treated like a minibus fare collector. He was like a little prince. The sultan of my soul . . . And when he grew up, I kept on loving him as much as ever . . . even more . . . and when he came of age, thinking he might have needs, I took him by the hand to a brothel . . . nothing happened . . . but the whores were amazed by his tool . . . You know, he was something else down there . . . a feast for the eye and the hand."

Actually, I didn't know, I'd never seen it. But Dump Truck

Beyza's account had left us all drooling. I nodded, and even managed a rather convincing sigh.

"So why did you two separate?"

"I didn't . . . I wouldn't, couldn't . . . He left me. There was
something strange about him when he came back from his military
service. He was distant. Something had come between us, something cold. I wondered what had happened to him, tried to get him
to talk. I mean, he was a stunner, and just that whopping big thing
of his was enough to get him more than enough attention . . . But
no, nothing had happened, or at least he didn't tell me anything . . .
I offered to take him on holiday . . . He wanted to go to Bodrum.
I'd never been. Okay, I said. I rented out the minibus to another
driver . . . And we went . . . He changed completely. The way he
sat, stood up, dressed . . . When we walked together, he'd keep a
few steps ahead or hang back, pretend to be looking at the shop
windows. Like he was ashamed of me. Like he didn't want to be
seen with me."

He swilled down another mouthful of cognac, the searing liquid no doubt the perfect accompaniment to his burning emotions.
He paused for a moment, eyes shut, jaw clenched. Then, as he went
on with his story, he seemed lost, hesitant, his voice rising and falling. All the time, as a surrogate Volkan, I was squeezed in a most
unpleasant way.

"The ones who know tell me to put it behind me, to forget all
about him. How can I forget him? He's not the kind you forget. Do
you think it's easy? Could you forget him?"

"No," I murmured, with some feeling. "I'm sure I won't."

"He's unforgettable. Just unforgettable . . . We'll find you a boy,
I said, if that's what you want . . . or if you'd rather have a preop
tranny, we'll get you one of those . . . I was willing to get him whatever he wanted. We shared women and boys, but we'd always end
up in each other's arms. It was real love! If that's not love, what is?

"When we came to Istanbul he started talking about living in separate flats. I agreed. We fixed him up with a place . . . All the furniture and trimmings . . . Like a dowry. I went up to my ears in debt to get him the best of everything. Then one day he just changed the lock. He wouldn't let me in. Can you believe it?"

"You're kidding," I exclaimed.

"I couldn't believe it. It wrecked me something terrible. I waited outside for him, just to have a word or two . . . he wouldn't give me the time of day! So I sent his sister, but he kicked her out."

"What about Okan?"

"That was later. Okan was back home with their mother. That's where the pimp grew up. Volkan hadn't seen his face for years. But then, for some reason, he found him and brought him to Istanbul. He said something about not letting him be raised by a stepfather. That's where the trouble started. It was all downhill from there."

This version of the story was different from what Dump Truck and Catamite Nazmi had suggested earlier.

"It seems Okan is . . . fond of a drink . . ."

"A drink! The boy's a junkie! Stoned out of his mind half the time . . . Supposedly got hooked back in the village. Claimed his stepdad would put opium in his milk to keep him from bawling. What a load of crap! Well, I'm not buying it. Never did."

Ziya was off on a bender. And his hands began moving across my body. I ignored them.

"So why'd you pull a knife on him? You haven't explained that one," I pumped him.

"It's like I told you. He wouldn't let me into his house, our home, the flat I bought and decked out for the two of us to live in. You can imagine how I felt about that. Like I told you . . ."

"I don't recall your mentioning a knife," I said. "I suppose I missed that bit."

He was now openly and unashamedly caressing me.

"You don't miss a thing, do you?" he leered. "With big bright eyes like that, not a thing . . ."

Seconds earlier he'd been blubbering over the love of his life, Volkan, declaring he'd never forget him. Now he was slobbering all over me.

I gave him a hard push as I rose to my feet.

"What do you think you're doing?" I demanded. "Shame on you, *ayol!*"

"I could eat that *ayol* of yours!"

"I'm going," I said, raising my voice a little.

"Where are you going? Stay a while for a bit of nookie."

He grabbed me with one arm and clasped his free hand over my mouth to keep me quiet.

"Just a kiss," he said.

His breath smelled of stale tobacco and cheap cognac. I gave him a little push.

"But I like you," he said. "You're a reminder of my Volkan!"

I had no wish to be anyone's memento. Nor would I be.

"Don't be ridiculous!" I was tempted to admit that I'd never even laid eyes on Volkan, and that I'd come here only to satisfy my curiosity about his family, but I thought better of it. He was emotionally unbalanced as it was, and I didn't have the heart. I held my tongue.

"Try it one more time and I'm leaving," I warned him. "Or I'll yell. Don't say I didn't tell you. Everyone will know your little secret."

"Don't get so angry, dear. So much rage and grace squeezed into one little package . . ."

The cognac was definitely going to his head.

"You're drunk."

"It's you who's turned my head. It'd take more than cognac to get me drunk."

"Think of Volkan!" I scolded in a last-ditch effort.

"But I'm trying to forget him!"

"The police suspect you. You do know that," I changed the subject. "They know you threatened Volkan, pulled a knife on him. Someone at the minibus stand must have told them."

"You're kidding? Which of those troublemakers spilled the beans . . . I'm clean. I swear, I'm clean. The police know that."

"How's that?" I asked. "Did you tell the police what happened?"

"There's no need for that. I pull a knife on someone about once a week. There's not a guy in the whole apartment building I haven't pulled a knife on. That's different, though! I'm not out for blood. Anyone who knows me knows that. If they're looking for a real scoundrel, why don't they go talk to that infidel Okan! He's the parasite who was feeding off my Volkan."

Again, this is where his story differed from what I'd heard earlier. So Okan and Ziya didn't get along. And judging from his squalid flat and shabby clothes, it wasn't Ziya who'd gotten his hands on Volkan's earnings.

"He worked for a while as a gigolo," I said. "He told me."

"For a while?" he snorted. "He was doing it when he was with you, too. You must have been blind with love. Where do you think he got his money? He never wore the same thing twice. He used aftershave. Stuff he paid a fortune for! He bought a brand-new minibus. Brought it to our route, just to spite me. But he knew he wouldn't be up for it forever . . . knew he wouldn't be young forever . . . no matter how big his tool, no matter how good in bed . . . he wouldn't be getting paid for it forever. That's why he always said he had to put something aside for later."

I was supposed to look stunned and hurt at this revelation. I duly did. He seized the opportunity to console me with a bear hug.

"Don't worry. I'm here to comfort you anytime you want," he said. "I may not be as hung as Volkan, but I'm packing a pretty good one myself."

When he pulled my hand down to his crouch I let him have it. He was shaken, but smiled.

"Wow! Looks like I've got a real wildcat on my hands!"

I'd heard all I needed to. I left him there, rubbing his cheek.

There was one more thing left to do this morning while I was in the neighborhood.

Chapter 18

I headed off to Beşiktaş in the first taxi that passed, to the Akdoğan Sokak address of Kemal Barutçu, otherwise known as Cihad2000. The apartment building was every bit as shabby and every bit as redolent of cooking as I'd remembered. I couldn't help wondering what he spent his money on. He had to be pulling in a tidy sum. But he was still stuck in this run-down building with his mother and overworked, largely absent father. And that meant he was constantly under their supervision and control.

His mother answered the door, the same worn expression on her face.

"Welcome, my son," she said. "Kemal's expecting you. He's a bit uptight today. Come on in . . ."

Showing due respect, I leaned over and kissed her hand. It reeked of onions.

"Go on in. Make yourself comfortable. I'll make you two some *sahlep*. I've made a fresh batch of *poğaca*, too. Once they cool you can have some with your tea."

If Cihad2000 let his mother have her way, he'd be the size of an elephant. It wasn't like he got any exercise. Actually, as far as I knew he never left his chair in front of the computer.

"I've got a wonderful surprise for you," I cooed as I walked into his room, all ready to tell him about leather-clad Pamir.

"We're in trouble," he said.

It seemed we weren't reading from the same page.

"And I mean big trouble," he continued gravely. "I've been researching since last night. The place we hacked was Türk Telekom. The phone records. If we get caught, we're really done for. If the police find out—and they're bound to sooner or later—we'll have everyone from the National Security Agency to the State Security Council on our backs. We're in deep shit!"

His mother was right; he was tense. He looked like he hadn't slept a wink all night. And what he said was truly startling and extremely serious.

"Calm down," I said automatically. "Start from the beginning, nice and slow . . ."

Far from calming down, he looked like he was on the verge of a nervous breakdown. Mouth twisted, lips quivering, face beet red, he began:

"Like I said, we hacked Telekom last night. The records we sifted through belong to the national telecommunications company. Don't you get it? Türk Telekom. It's a crime against the state. I don't know what the punishment is, but it's a lot more than a slap on the wrist, that much I can tell you. If we get caught, we're done for. They'll finish us off. We've been used. I swear to Allah, if I get away with it this time I'll give up hacking completely. All those figures and numbers were nothing other than telephone numbers and records. When I realized, I almost peed my pants. It's terrifying. We're in trouble. They'll all be after us. And we're bound to get caught. Red-handed. I'll rot to death in prison in my wheelchair. You can imagine how they'll treat me there. I can't face that. I'm afraid. May Allah save us."

I couldn't allow him to go on like this. He had to come to his senses. The *sahlep* would take some time to make; his mother wasn't likely to appear at the door anytime soon. I gave him a hard smack across the face.

"Get over it; calm down!"

The slap seemed to work. He was calmer, if only a bit . . . But he kept jabbering in the same hysterical tone.

"Did you know about it?"

"How was I supposed to know?" I said. "We landed the job. That's all Ali told me. There was a go-between. The money was good, so he didn't ask questions. Anyway, since when does anyone ask a lot of questions about this kind of work?"

"Exactly. We asked no questions and now we've landed in the shit. Up to our necks, no less. They paid me in advance, every last cent. What idiots, I thought to myself, as I counted it. Good God, forgive me my trespasses. I repent. Do you think He hears me?"

I tried, and failed, to suppress a chuckle. Here we were in the middle of a crisis, and I still couldn't help laughing at the religious fervor of poor Kemal.

"Do you really think it's so easy to get hold of Telekom's records? To access the main cache?" I asked, my mirth cut short by a chilling awareness that, as Kemal put it, we were in deep shit. "Haven't they got all kinds of firewalls and shields in place?"

"It's child's play," he said. "The system's extremely vulnerable. Anyone determined to access can."

"So why didn't they do it themselves?"

"What they actually had us do—had me do—was to make a tiny fraction of the records accessible, amid all that data. Then you accessed what I'd opened up and did what you wanted."

"I basically destroyed the records they wanted deleted . . ." I said.

"It's all over! I jump every time the doorbell rings. I expect the police to come and take me away any second."

"Don't be silly," I said. "We're experts. We both took every precaution to cover our tails. At least, I did. I didn't leave any tracks. And you're a pro, too . . . I know you are."

"That may be, but I was working at home. If they pull out all the stops, they could still trace me."

"What are you getting so worked up about?" I continued. "We'll destroy any traces you may have left behind. They'll never find you."

"I've already done that."

"So what's the problem?" I asked. "Why panic? You've taken care of things."

"I don't know," he said. "I'm still scared. What if something happens to me and . . ."

He never finished his sentence. The door opened and in came our cups of *sahlep*, borne by his mother on a garish plastic tray. She must have heard the last bit of our conversation, and she looked worried.

"What happened, son?" she asked. "Why are you so scared?"

"Don't interfere, mother!"

"But son . . ."

"Keep out of it! You wouldn't understand."

His mother looked at me for a sign of sympathy. Embarrassed at having been a witness to the sight of a mother scolded by her son, I examined the ceiling, avoiding her eyes and smiling sheepishly.

"Look, your friend's here. I'm sure he can help. You'll sort things out . . ."

"That's enough, mother! Just go and mind your own business!"

With a resigned glance at me, she left the room.

"Shut the door and stop listening in!"

Kemal was speaking from experience. Holding a silencing finger to his lips, he put a CD into the player.

"She often eavesdrops on me out of sheer boredom. Now that she's actually curious about something her ears will be pricked up like Lassie's."

The last thing I wanted was to get mixed up in a family feud.

"Just drop it," I suggested.

"No," he said. "It could be dangerous for her, too, if she knows what's going on. I need to protect her. As a son, that's the least I can do. And if she was ever called on to testify, she'd sing like a nightingale. Then we'd all be in trouble."

"Stop exaggerating," I said. "Don't be such a wimp! What kind of a man are you, anyway?"

Even I was astonished by my words. Kemal was still for a moment, then shot back with:

"A lot of good my manhood will do me in prison!"

"Look," I said, raising my voice before remembering the mother and lowering it again, "we did a clean job. That's a given. It's impossible for anyone to trace us. Anyway, who could they get to do it? It's not like they have any experts on the payroll."

"You're right about that, but there's no point in getting too complacent. A new whiz hits the scene every day. Some of them are still kids. It's unbelievable . . . Sharp as tacks. I caught one of them trying to penetrate my system. Can you imagine?"

That was true. There was a whole new generation of hackers waiting in the wings. I had confidence in my abilities. And in Kemal's. But we could well meet our match one day. You'd think those little bastards would be happy to play street football and chase after girls; but no, they sit in front of their computers all day and become self-taught crackerjacks.

Kemal was too panicked to think or talk about anything else. At the moment, at least for today, fear would dominate his life, if that's what you could call his rather limited existence. I decided not to mention my arrangements with Pamir. If it were kismet, it would have to happen another time.

The *sahlep* was delicious. I added a thick dusting of cinnamon to my cup. Once I finished it, I'd leave Kemal to panic on his own.

Chapter 19

Some feelings are contagious, and panic is most definitely one of them. The soothing logic I'd used when confronted by an unraveling Kemal had quickly evaporated once I was on my own. I was scared.

I'd intended to jump into a taxi and go home, but instead ended up walking down to Beşiktaş to sit in a seaside café and think things over.

Luckily, the skies had cleared. It was a crisp, sunny day, the kind that helps clear heads and allay worries. The waters of the Bosphorus shimmered serenely, silver and deepest blue.

To date, I've broken the law any number of times. I take a different view of many things considered crimes by ordinary people. In fact, some of them strike me as being the most natural things in the world. And, to date, I have regretted none of my actions. That may sound a bit bold, but I can honestly say that I have never done a single thing that has weighed on my conscience. Actually, perhaps there are one or two things I'm not particularly proud of, and would choose to do differently. Still, I can truthfully say that they were mere details in the grand scheme of things.

Even though I knew Cihad2000 was a half-crazed genius and insatiable masochist, he'd managed to infect me with cold fear tinged by panic. Worst of all, the seeds he'd planted were growing by the minute. It was time to turn inward, to calm myself with soothing thoughts.

I tried imagining Haluk Pekerdem. That sex god of a man could be just the distraction required. It wouldn't be long before the juices were flowing, and I was warmed by a pleasant heat that was far from cerebral. The sun beating down on my table would enhance my steamy fantasies. I began . . . and failed. My mind flitted to his brother-in-law, Faruk, which of course led me to those damned Telekom phone records.

Round and round, those earlier thoughts came crowding in: What on earth would we do if the police, intelligence officers, Interpol, and all the others caught up to us? Either we'd be quietly locked away in an undisclosed location or our names would be released to the press. We'd be disgraced and scapegoated, and they'd be baying for our blood. My personal life, which I'd carefully kept just that all these years, would be dredged up. Society's most feverish suspicions about my dubious character would be confirmed by half-remembered near strangers from years back appearing before the cameras to feed them a steady diet of fresh blood (mine) and bile (theirs).

There was another, even more sinister possibility: a silent end. No one would hear a thing, not a trace would be left behind . . . One night a car with darkened windows would take me from my home and I'd never be heard of again. How many people would notice my absence and dare to make official inquiries or demand a full investigation? As I pondered this last question, my spirits plummeted, my head throbbed, and a bitter taste flooded my mouth.

Coming to my senses, I dispensed with that horrible thought. There was no way the authorities could hush up something like this. No, they'd be duly impressed that a pair of local boys could manage such a thing. We'd be lauded as evidence that our country boasted secret talent, with the potential for much more . . . The nation would rise up as one to applaud us. We'd be splashed across the press and forced to appear on TV news programs. In other words, we'd be subjected to a fate worse than prison. And then? Well, when it all blew over I'd have full cosmetic surgery.

I found myself imagining which aesthetic procedures I'd opt for. I considered which features I'd change, what I'd augment, the bits that needed nipping and the areas that could do with a simple tuck: My prominent cheekbones could be enhanced, and a curvaceous smile designed for the corners of my mouth . . . and why not have a couple of dimples tacked on? So traumatized had I been by Kemal that I completely gave myself over to these whimsies. That's how Raquel Welch had been created: a series of thirty-six operations, transforming her completely from head to toe. And, to give credit where due, the scalpels and silicone injections had constructed a femme fatale who for decades enlivened the dreams and fantasies of men right across the globe.

I was losing it. Alright, I was a little scared, quite panicked, and a bit tense. But to sit lost in a reverie about plastic surgery and the merits of being transformed into a second Raquel Welch, with rocket breasts, lips perpetually blowing kisses, buttocks that with each sway sent ogling admirers reeling, eyebrows slightly raised into an alluring semiscowl—no, that was going too far.

A group of male students a table away at the sidewalk café were staring as they obviously discussed me. Judging from their white-and-blue shirts and loosened dark ties they were still in high school. Their five o'clock shadows told me they weren't all that young, though. They were undoubtedly the oldest bunch in school and had probably had to repeat several grades. One of them was good-looking, a tall, lean boy. He was tasty in a way none of the others were. Almost involuntarily, in a habitual response developed over years, I winked at him. He instantly responded right back. Like any true gentleman, and any man who knows the ropes and truly intends to get laid, he kept this exchange hidden from his friends. After all, he obviously knew he was the gem of the bunch.

Despite this pleasant distraction, my mind returned to Cihad2000, and I remembered that, due to his hysteria, I hadn't found out why the name Faruk Hanoğlu had appeared among the telephone records he'd downloaded for me. Well, even if I had asked for information, it wasn't as though he'd have had the presence of mind to furnish it. Once he calmed down, I'd have to dangle the prospect of a session with Pamir in front of him; that way, he'd be sure to cooperate.

The boys over at the next table were still busily eyeing me, no doubt making lewd comments as they guffawed and carried on. Rambunctious laughter wasn't the only thing radiating from their table; there was also the primal scent of male sexuality, an almost palpable perfume of lust and desire. Those who recognize it can't help being affected. There's something about boys that age, something raw, rapacious, and dizzying: libidos spinning out of control.

Unleashed libidos or not, I had more important things to do, chief among them phone calls to Ali, to find out if he had any news, and to Ponpon, to get her to arrange a meeting with the Hanoğlu family. I went into the café to use the telephone.

The phone was in the back, in a quiet corner just outside the toilets. First, I dialed the number for the office. Figen, the miserable secretary, picked up, her voice that of someone about to fade into oblivion.

"I need to speak to Ali Bey at once," I said.

"Yes, of course," she droned. "But I'll have to put you on hold. His line's busy. He must be on the phone."

A show of her efficiency was not what I required from Figen at that moment.

"Figen, I'm calling from a pay phone. I can't wait. Interrupt him; it's urgent."

I was astonished by the note of panic in my own voice.

"Well if he gets mad, it's not my fault. If he yells at me you better tell him it was all your idea."

"I will," I snapped. "Now hurry up and do what you're told!"

"Fine, give me a second to go and tell him you're on the line. I'll have to put you on hold," she said, as though I needed a blow-by-blow account of switchboard procedure.

The line automatically switched to Ali's CD player and Leonard Cohen singing "I smile when I'm angry" reached my ears. I attempted to do just that.

As I waited with a meaningless, tense, and completely artificial smile on my face, I glanced up to see the dark boy approaching me. He was taller and thinner than I'd thought. Although he looked slightly bashful, he was striding toward me with an air of purpose. I had no doubt that as he bore down on me he was rehearsing what he'd say.

I realized too late that the fake smile was still on my lips. I'd been caught.

"Hello," he said.

He had shiny, well-shaped lips.

My boss spoke to me at the same moment the boy did, Leonard Cohen suddenly replaced by Ali's tense voice.

"What is it?"

The boy's eyes were on me, his ears pricked to catch everything I said. I was nearly at a loss for words.

"I think we have a serious problem," I managed, simultaneously producing a little smile for the boy. Old Leonard was right, of course, but I wondered if the boy realized that anger can also produce a smile. I didn't want him to get the wrong idea.

"A problem? What do you mean? We got the job done, didn't we? They've even deposited our money."

It was just like Ali to use "we" and "our" even though it was "me" who had done all the work and who would face the consequences.

I could smell the fresh sweat of the boy an arm's length away. He'd hung his head in a show of bashfulness, but the eyes peeping out at me from below his eyebrows were bold and proud. And the half smile was as cocky as could be.

Covering the receiver with a hand, "It's confidential," I told him. "I won't be long," I added, as though he was in line waiting for the phone.

"Hello? I can't hear you. What's wrong? Like I told you, they've even paid up. Let's not spoil things now."

"Didn't I tell you to find out who the client was? I'm coming to the office. We'll talk there. Yes, the job went off without a hitch. But that's just the problem."

I could tell the boy wasn't listening to what I was saying, only looking me up and down hungrily. It wasn't what I was saying, it's what I was that intrigued him. His right hand was fumbling around in the pocket of his charcoal trousers. When he noticed my eyes had shifted, involuntarily drawn to the action, he increased his toying.

Muttering a few more words, I hung up the phone. Ali still had no idea what I was talking about, but he soon would.

"I'm sorry to keep you waiting, dear," I said.

The "dear" had slipped out of my mouth somehow.

"It's not important. No problem . . ."

He grinned.

He was standing right in front of me. I was pinned in the corner, and forced to take a step toward him as I tried to get out. He didn't budge.

"Can we talk?"

If I refused him on the spot, there would be a scene, and I'd end up harassed by the whole lot of them.

"Not right now, I'm afraid," I said. "You heard me on the phone. I've got to go to work."

"We like you. We think you're really something."

Why the "we"? Was he going to propose a group?

"That's very kind, but I'm afraid I haven't got the time for . . ."

"We're all crazy about you. Couldn't you help us out?"

Yes, it was an orgy he had in mind.

"Well, I never!" I bridled, not sounding entirely convincing or at all outraged.

He felt secure enough to take another step toward me. Inches apart, I could now smell his mint chewing gum. Having undressed me, his eyes, feverish and full of urgency, moved on to doing unspeakable things to my person.

"It won't take long."

His open desire was seductive, his bravado repulsive; I was wedged between the two. But his fresh masculinity, youthful brazenness, and fumbling hand were getting the better of me. He emanated a raw animal lust rarely seen in older men, who normally play by the rules and care for conventions.

"A friend of mine lives nearby. His place is free. It's safe. We could go right now."

He was taller than me. I was impressed by the way he stood, the way he carried himself. He had a narrow face but broad shoulders. I had no doubt that his stomach was flat and his bottom tight and well-rounded. Even standing there in a shapeless school uniform his wiry body promised so much. He swallowed, his well-developed Adam's apple rising and falling. His fingers were long and tapered. How could I resist?

"I'm not interested in the others," I said. "Just you."

He relaxed, relieved that I'd caved in so soon. He was now more confident than ever.

"But it'd be rude to my friends," he said.

I have no tolerance for being treated like the neighborhood whore. But the boy was a dish, and he'd gotten my blood flowing. Fortune had smiled on me, and I didn't want to spend the rest of the day horny and full of regret. I decided to flatter him.

"What do you mean 'rude'? You're the only one I like. And you're the only one I want to be with."

"They're good guys. And one of them's hung like you wouldn't believe. Like in those dirty movies. Come on, it won't take long.

They're dying to be with you. They're only kids! Don't leave them high and dry . . . Please, do what you can . . ."

"Stop insisting. It's not going to happen!"

"What's the big deal? If there's someone you don't like you don't have to do anything. No one's going to push you. Just suck on it, or let them rub against you. Some of them have no experience. They just about lost it when they saw you."

"Oh, and I suppose you are experienced?"

He smiled wickedly.

"You don't know me yet," he said. "I've been together lots of times."

"Where and how?"

"At the cinema . . . at the *hamam* . . . with some friends from the beer house. I also met a couple of people on the Internet . . ."

I believed him. He clearly knew what he was doing. In fact, he was even a bit jaded.

"Which cinemas and *hamam*?" I asked, just to confirm.

He told me. He knew all the ones in Beyoğlu and Aksaray. Considering where he apparently spent much of his free time, it was no wonder he was still in high school.

He interpreted my silence as a refusal. He had no intention of letting me get away so easily.

"We could go to the *hamam* if you're afraid to go to a strange flat . . ."

I wasn't afraid of anything. At any sign of the slightest misbehavior, the theft of my wallet, request for money, or discourtesy . . . I'd beat them all up. I'd leave the five of them in a bruised heap and simply proceed with my business.

It was funny, but I couldn't even remember the other boys; I suppose I'd been too busy looking at the dark one. As a public service, in the name of furthering the education of callow youth, helping them to gain experience and become better acquainted with their own bodies, I wasn't particularly averse to "getting men off," as the girls put it. And depending on the degree of pleasure this selfless service gave me, I would most likely invite the dark one to visit me one day.

"Go on, introduce us," I said.

A warm glow induced by the pride of seeing a potentially tricky mission accomplished with flying colors spread across the boy's face. The day was growing cooler, positively bracing. When the other boys saw us approaching they stopped talking and shifted positions in a valiant effort to appear taller. All eyes were on me. I took my time as I walked over to meet them, looking into their eyes, those eyes widening with desire, as I approached their table, savoring the attention and carrying myself as regally as Queen Elizabeth herself.

We were formally introduced.

I politely refused their offers of cola, tea, coffee, and toast.

The house was, in fact, nearby. And I ended up staying there far longer than I'd anticipated.

Chapter 20

$\mathcal{U}$nexpected developments were forever forcing me to alter my best-laid plans. By the time I got back to Ali, that is, to his office, it was getting dark. I felt completely smoothed out, from the tips of my toes to the roots of my hair. Yes, I was a bit spent, but that sensation of sweet limpness was just what I needed. Tension gone, I had a completely new take on myself, on life, and even on the dark night pressing in on the inhabitants of blessed Istanbul.

My mind was blissfully clear as I flew into the office on winged feet. Soulless Figen was getting ready to leave. Unused to seeing me at this hour, she didn't know what to say. In any case, she was off to meet with her fiancé and in a big hurry. Her makeup had been freshened, with predictably dire results. It would be well worth my while to take the poor girl aside one day and give her some tips.

After requesting that, before she left for the day, Figen bring in some coffee for me and Ali, I burst into his office like a bat out of hell.

"Where on earth have you been? First you get me all wound up on the phone, then you disappear until evening!"

"Well, I'm here now," I said. "I think we need to have a serious talk. Why not have a seat and wait for our coffee. Then we'll get started."

"You're making me even more curious. I hope you're not getting me worked up for nothing, *abi* . . ."

I was, of course, the "big brother" to whom he referred. And he was older than me. Deciding to take him to task later, I let it pass for the moment.

"Just wait till you hear."

"Come on then!" he said. "Tell me!"

Eager to run off to lover boy, Figen was unusually swift in serving the coffee.

"I'll be leaving now if there's nothing else you need."

"That'll be all, dear," I said, with meaningful emphasis on the word "dear."

As Figen rushed out the door, Ali had already taken his first swallow of coffee.

"Oh, and I really have to tell you. I don't know what it is, but whatever you've done, you look great. Just bursting with life. Ever since you walked through the door, I've been unable to keep my eyes off you."

"That's my little secret," I purred. "A secret formula."

"Well, whatever it is, *abi*, let me in on the secret. I'm green with envy."

"You wouldn't dare try it." I smiled knowingly. And that was the truth. For as long as I'd known Ali, and we'd been working together for years, I hadn't sensed, heard, or seen the faintest evidence of any interest in such things.

He knew me well enough to appreciate what my smile implied. And didn't insist I divulge any details. Ali simply returned my knowing smile and the subject was closed.

"Well then, tell me what's going on. What were you talking about on the phone?"

I gave him a quick rundown. Taking small sips from his mug, his eyes were serious and he didn't interrupt even once.

"I know the job came from an intermediary, but we've got to find out who the real client was," I concluded. "It's critical. Considering that they've used not only us but also Cihad2000, they can't be all that clean. And they seem to have taken every precaution."

Now it was my turn to sip coffee.

"I did what you said and began investigating. Not wanting to raise any suspicions, I asked just a few casual questions. So much for extracting a name or two; I wasn't able to get the smallest clue."

"And who is this intermediary?"

"A lawyer," he said. "The lawyer of a friend of mine."

Haluk Pekerdem wasn't necessarily the lawyer he was talking about, of course. And it certainly wasn't normal for the mere mention of the word "lawyer" to make me think of him. Had I become the victim of a one-sided crush, turned into the type of person I mercilessly tease about their so-called platonic relationships?

"So you don't really know him or her?"

"I do, actually. We have friends in common. That's how we met."

His halting speech patterns could only mean he was holding something back.

"And?"

"Unless you drop that significant stare, I've got nothing else to add," he warned.

I'd be the first to admit that mockery could be read in my eyes. Tilting back my head as though to finish the last swallow of coffee, I hid my face behind my mug.

"We went out a few times, that's all," he said.

"So it's a woman . . ."

"Uh-huh . . ."

"And when she has work for you, she still calls," I continued. "How nice . . ."

"We're still on social terms. We have friends in common. There just wasn't any chemistry. Still, whenever we run into each other, and we do from time to time, we exchange greetings, chat."

I've never understood that. It's something I could never do. Particularly once we've been to bed. If my intention is friendship, there's no sex; if what I'm after is sex, and it doesn't work out, I make no effort to remain friends.

"You still haven't told me who it is," I prodded. "Is it top secret?"

"No, more like it's private."

"Look," I said, "among the names we stumbled across is that of the shady loan shark Faruk Hanoğlu, who was accused of murder just two days ago. I don't know where all of this is leading us. But no one, at least no one sensible, suddenly decides to have Telekom's records scanned. And even if, for whatever reason, someone did, they wouldn't cough up a small fortune to hire two hackers to do it. Start thinking clearly, send for your common sense, wherever it's gone, and get over your misguided idea of what is and isn't 'private'!"

The look he gave me was thoughtful, or perhaps he was just focused on retrieving his common sense. And back it came, reclaiming its rightful place.

"Sibel Yıldırım," he exhaled deeply. "She works for a large law firm. She's a good girl. Not the sort to get mixed up in something like this."

"This has got nothing to do with 'good' or 'bad.' Nothing whatsoever."

"It could only be a client of hers. She hasn't got that kind of money."

"I didn't say she was directly responsible. We've got to find out on whose behalf she was acting."

"I'll give her another call," Ali said, talking to himself. "It may be a good idea to bring round a bottle of wine. In a relaxed environment, face-to-face, just the two of us . . . it's no good talking on the phone . . ."

"Well, she's your friend, and you doubtless know the most *effective* way of dealing with her . . ."

Ali may have appeared to be ignoring me, but he caught my little dig. Our eyes met. I smiled wickedly, the all-knowing big brother or sister.

"Alright then!" he burst out. "I'll suck it up again and sacrifice for the team!"

"Oh, I see! A real sacrifice, was it? And all for a little profit!"

"She's not much to look at, but she's sharp as a tack. Well brought up, cultured . . ."

"Sounds like the perfect business prospect. Is that how they reeled you in?"

"You could say so, I guess."

He'd managed to overcome the genuine sense of embarrassment real gentlemen feel when talking about their conquests. We'd strayed into new territory, and he seemed relieved that we'd broached the sensitive subject for the first time ever.

"Try to create an opportunity to thank her. Without delay. I think you should call her now."

"You mean right this minute?"

"Yes, of course." I said. "And I'd like to come, too, unless you think I'd be a distraction."

We arranged to meet at the rooftop bar of the former Sheraton, a place I hadn't visited or even thought of for many years, ever since it had changed hands and become the Ceylan Otel. When I remembered the stunning view, I could have kicked myself for not having paid a visit earlier.

Less than an hour remained before our rendezvous. Evening traffic is always horrendous, and we'd have to leave almost immediately. I wouldn't be able to stop at home for a shower and change of clothes, so I phoned Ponpon, just to ensure that she wouldn't have a panic attack at my absence. She must have been busy with God knows what, for she didn't pick up. In soothing tones, I left a message informing her I would be late, and that there was no need to worry.

Ali and I got into his two-seat sports car: a dark red Aston Martin DB5 like the one he'd fallen in love with as a child watching a James Bond film. At around the same time Ali was transfixed by fast cars, I would have been having a huge crush on Sean Connery, or enviously admiring a Bond girl. I remembered the gadget-laden vehicles, but I couldn't recollect an Aston Martin like the one in which I was now sitting. I suppose that's what sets boys apart from girls. Ali had been ordering spare parts and working on his car for years, but it still wasn't to his liking. Doubled over in our seats, and likely to end up in each other's laps at any moment, we proceeded through heavy traffic toward Taksim. As always, Ali exuded Calvin Klein One.

"Forgive me for saying so," he said, screwing up his face, "but you smell a bit funny."

I wasn't pleased by the unexpected comment.

"Bad?" I asked, instinctively opening the window.

"Not bad, really, just . . . different," he said. "Sharp and sour. Not an odor I'd associate with you. It's familiar, but strange. Anyway, you don't have to open the window in this weather. I've got some aftershave in my bag, if you like."

When I finally realized what was behind the smell, and remembered how much fun I'd had, my body was once again flooded with sweet warmth. That mysterious odor is, of course, familiar to all men. Swollen with a contradictory mixture of pride and shame, I kept my mouth shut for the rest of the ride. Ali whistled along to a CD. He only whistles when he's tense.

By the time we made it to Taksim, it was time for our meeting.

Stepping out of the elevator into the roof bar, we took a couple of chairs in front of the floor-to-ceiling windows. It was late enough for me to order a Virgin Mary; Ali requested a neat whiskey, specifying that it not be J&B. Like anyone claiming to know his whiskey, he has only contempt for that particular brand. The panoramic view was just as breathtaking as I'd remembered: to one side, the green valley of Maçka and the Bosphorus Bridge brought to life by a glittering red and white stream of flowing traffic; to the other side, beyond the rooftops of Taksim Square and the Golden Horn, the domes and minarets of the old city. We seemed to be hovering over Taksim, the heart of the city, as it pulsed with a rhythmic surge of cars and people.

The sound of approaching footsteps reached my ears even before the drinks had arrived. To be more precise, coming up behind me was a woman totally inept at walking in high heels, as evidenced by the clacking racket she made. A woman not possessed of grace or elegance. Someone who now had a black mark against her.

Ali, who was facing the door, rose to his feet to greet the stomper. My feminine side paid no mind to the men's clothing I was wearing, and I remained seated and graciously ladylike. Had I been riled by the approach of a rival? I gracefully swiveled my head slightly to one side.

The woman approaching our table wore what she took to be fashionably pink sunglasses, but I still recognized her. Yes, it was the lawyer from dear Haluk's office, the nosy creature who'd peeked in at me when I was in the waiting room. The phony smile on my lips froze. I had no idea what to do.

A thousand images ran through my mind. A chain reaction of interconnected conspiracy theories, each more dire than the last! I hadn't played chess for years, but my skill at forward strategic planning was undiminished.

She had never seen me in a "civilian" getup. The person she'd met was a girl, dressed to the nines and formidable. Sitting here before her now was an unshaven man in a V-neck sweater and black jeans, the occasional flourished hand a dead giveaway only to the astute eye of an experienced observer. It was unlikely, but still possible, that she would recognize me. But so what if she did? There was no reason to panic. She was the one with a problem, and in much deeper than me. The only thing was, she might not have realized it yet.

We were introduced and she took a seat. As she pretended to

chat nonchalantly with Ali, she kept an eye trained on my every move and gesture, trying to place me. It was, of course, quite an undertaking: Even if she thought she recognized me, she couldn't openly ask me if I was "she." I was determined not to make her task any easier. Every once in a while, I'd join in the conversation with a subtle riposte or jibe, then fix her with a compassionate stare, looking directly into her eyes and effortlessly winding her up. For some reason I was finding it impossible to warm to our Sibel. Nor did I have any intention of doing so. Isn't it enough that she spends every day in close proximity to the divine Haluk?

Chapter 21

$\mathcal{A}$s I made my way home, shivering, I pieced together a clearer picture of what we were up against. Lawyer Sibel had been tight-lipped, careful not to give the game away. Her very presence spoke volumes, however. No longer able to endure the little piece of theater going on, I'd gotten down to brass tacks.

"It's only natural that you wish to conceal the identity of your client. I appreciate that," I'd said. "But considering that the name of Faruk Hanoğlu, and even that of"—here I was extemporizing—"Haluk Pekerdem, was listed in the Telekom records we accessed and destroyed, it may well be in your best interests to be a bit more . . . forthcoming."

I had threatened her openly. Her professional lawyer's mask firmly in place, she'd foolishly attempted to stare me down. Seconds later she'd glanced away and said, "I can't say I fully comprehend your exact meaning here. Still, I'll give your words the consideration they're due."

That was enough for me. The dots had been connected. Faruk Hanoğlu had sought to destroy any phone records that could implicate him in the murder. And he'd used his brother-in-law to do it. The total extent of the crooked and devious manipulations involving the phone records was anyone's guess.

The question running through my mind that night as I walked past the Atatürk Cultural Center in Taksim Square was "why?" All that money and effort had been spent in the name of protection, or, more accurately, concealment. Why? What exactly were they trying to hide? What was behind a seemingly routine murder that had brought together two completely different groups of people?

My cozy home was empty. There was no sign of Ponpon. I resented her for having disappeared right when I needed her most. Of course she couldn't have known, but even so . . . One doesn't need a good reason to take offense. Just the impulse.

Remembering my aromatic state, I raced to the shower. Standing under the stinging hot water, I asked myself why I keep getting mixed up in things that are none of my business. Actually, this time things had landed right in my lap. Still, I needn't have rushed in as an amateur sleuth. Had I left well enough alone, the case would most likely have been closed. Why had I gone digging? What was I trying to prove to myself—and others? Knowing full well that the answer to that last question would be far from agreeable, I dropped it. I stepped out of the shower. My stomach was grumbling with hunger. When I saw that Ponpon had stocked the fridge, I felt better. I helped myself, loading a large plate, buffet style. *Alcina* had been left in the CD player, and I pushed "play." Handel's soothing strings filled the room. Self-reflection had done nothing to dent my appetite; I gobbled up everything on the plate.

There was no getting out of it. The time had come to pay a little call on Faruk Hanoğlu. I wouldn't be able to arrive unannounced. Men like him are always sheltered from surprise visitors; even if not flanked twenty-four hours a day by bodyguards, he'd be living in a high-security walled estate. I'd have to find a less conventional way to impose myself on him.

I called Ponpon, who answered drowsily.

"*Merhaba.* I must have dozed in front of the television."

"Have I been abandoned?" I half joked, half grumbled.

"What kind of talk is that?! Consider it unsaid!"

"Just kidding." I laughed. Then I got straight to the point: "Arrange a meeting with Faruk Bey. If possible, for tonight."

There was silence on the other end.

"Hello? Ponpon? Are you there?"

"Yes, *ayol*. I was thinking."

Ponpon never thinks in silence. She must have been trying to come out of her sleepy stupor. It wasn't long before she had the presence of mind to fire a question back at me.

"Why?"

"I suspect he's got me involved in something dodgy. We need to talk, face-to-face."

"You mean about that boy with the big thingy?"

"It could be relevant. I'm not sure. I did something I'm not entirely comfortable with. I need to get the bottom of it. Only then will I be able to relax."

"Hmmm . . ."

I didn't know how to interpret Ponpon's response. Silence. I waited.

"I'll give him a call and get back to you."

"Whatever you do, don't mention that funny business! I don't want to raise his suspicions."

"I figured out that much, *ayol*! Good-bye!"

I decided to give Cihad2000 a call while I waited for Ponpon. By now he could have calmed down, had a good look at the records he'd downloaded, and discovered something useful. He didn't answer his private phone. Convinced he was busy, I didn't persist. I also didn't want to drive the sad-eyed mother to answer her son's phone, forcing me to speak to her. Instead, I tried reaching him on the Internet, but there was no sign of him in any of the usual chat rooms. Sorting through my extensive porn collection for two pictures I knew would appeal to his tastes, I attached them to a message and sent it. They'd pop up the second he went online.

I had a million and one things to do, but no intention of doing any of them. No, I'd savor the tension of waiting, the discomfort of being unable to do anything. The picture hanging on the wall directly across was slightly crooked. It showed me posing with Ru-

Paul at the London Gay Pride Parade. My eyes were closed, but my outfit was fabulous. Even RuPaul had admired it. I'd just returned to my seat when the phone rang. Certain it was Ponpon, I lunged for the receiver.

On the other end, drawing out every syllable of his *"Merhaba"* as always, was Hasan. "I called to ask how you were. Are you okay?"

"Yes, I am," I said. "Thank you. Much better now."

"I'm so glad to hear that. So, will you be round tonight?"

I hadn't yet decided whether or not to drop by the club. It depended on the news from Ponpon. Actually, Faruk Hanoğlu was not likely to devote an entire night to me, even if we did meet.

"Yes, I'll be there."

"We'll talk then," he said, and hung up.

Chatterbox Hasan had hung up in record time. Something was up. I rang him back immediately.

"Yes?" he asked. "Did you forget something?"

"No, but you always have something to say. Anything wrong? Don't go getting all funny on me. You know I've only just come right. I can't handle another shock."

I managed a light laugh, but I was dead serious.

Hasan was silent. Something had come over everyone tonight. No one was prepared to give me a quick answer or response.

"It's nothing . . ." he finally said. Then, he reversed himself with "Well, there is something, but we'll talk when you get here. It'll take time."

I wanted to tell him that I had plenty of time, or even ask him to come over, but I was expecting an important call from Ponpon. I left it at "fine."

I could have mulled over all I hadn't told Hasan. I could even have produced a tiny prick of conscience for having left him in the dark. But I didn't do either.

Chapter 22

Faruk Hanoğlu lives in Yeniköy, right on the shores of the Bosphorus. At the front gate, apparently expecting me, was an elderly creature in the early stages of fossilization. As soon as I told him my name, I was waved through into an enormous, beautifully manicured garden that stretched from the main road all the way to the sea. Although it was night, I was certain not a single dried leaf had been allowed to fall to the ground, not a single wayward branch allowed to live. It was a secret paradise hidden behind high walls. The house stood in a small wood at the end of a long, well-lit path lined with ancient trees. A few steps led up to the glass door of the main building, in which a rather younger, better-dressed figure waited to greet me. In his forties, he wasn't in traditional butler gear, wasn't even in a suit. Over a beige shirt, he wore a brown V-neck sweater.

"Welcome," he said. "Faruk Bey will see you in a moment. Come in."

I was led to a ground floor room built virtually over the sea.

"Could I get you any refreshments while you wait?"

It was the most cordial offer I'd had for some time. His tone was refined and reflected a perfectly modulated courtesy, the correct balance of respectful distance and gracious warmth. Whatever he was, he did it beautifully.

He ushered me into a room at least half the size of my entire flat but clearly not furnished as a living room, or even a sitting room. It served only as a waiting room for guests like me. Facing each other were a pair of antique sofas. Two spindly chairs with wooden arms and threadbare Gobelin cushions stood guard. Heavy, matching gilt framed a series of wall mirrors and an ominous still life of a watermelon and a bunch of grapes.

As for the view from the window, only a string of adjectives like "fabulous," "marvelous," and "extraordinary" could begin to describe it. The dark of night lent the scene an element of mystery and otherworldliness; in the murky waters of the strait glowed the lights of the opposite shore and passing ships. I felt that if I leaped through the window I would become a part of the fairy-tale world outside.

As I sipped water from a fine antique glass, I tried to decide what to say to Faruk Hanoğlu. I'd just begun losing myself in the watery view when the door opened and the master of the house entered dressed in a Muzaffer Tema costume: a silk dressing gown and crimson ascot. I had no idea that anyone actually dressed like that anymore. A film had come to life. On his face was a smile of the sort favored by his sister, an affectation of snobbish nobility.

"*Merhaba*," he said, shaking my hand. "Welcome. I hope you haven't waited long. Ponpon's call took me by surprise. But when she said it was urgent I couldn't bring myself to refuse her. We're so fond of Ponpon, you see."

I thanked him.

"Do forgive me," he said, "but I haven't got much time. As you know, we don't normally work nights."

Right from the start the guy was trying to make me feel guilty. He was still standing and his smile couldn't conceal the tension around his lips. I had been granted an audience under duress, and I was meant to realize as much.

"How funny, we just get going at night," I chirped. "You know, the nightclub business."

"Look," he said, "let me be frank. Normally I don't offer special treatment in cases like this. But Ponpon called. And was most insistent. She told me you required a fairly insignificant sum, and that you needed it immediately, tonight . . . Something about a difficult creditor or a routine payment of some kind. Of course, none of that interests us."

"Yes . . ." was all I managed in reply.

"I think you'll appreciate that large amounts of cash are not kept in the house. In fact, we don't deal in cash at all. Our business is making money from money. We put everything to work, all we have. But you're in luck. We've retrieved a certain amount just tonight."

"Well, aren't I the lucky one?" I grinned.

If he detected a note of sarcasm, he didn't let on.

"How much do you require?"

When I didn't answer, he continued, "As I told you, we never have much cash at hand."

We'd never get anywhere if we went on in this vein. He was anxious to slap a cash loan into my hand at a not entirely exorbitant rate of interest and to see the back of me. And the sooner the better. The thought of taking his money and never paying him back gave me a certain wicked pleasure. After all, in his eyes I was the manager of a fifth-rate tranny club, a lowlife in difficult straits for reasons undoubtedly connected to the underworld, a credit risk who happened to be a friend of Ponpon's. But I hadn't come here to rip him off.

It was time to lay my cards on the table.

"Look," I said, "the loan was just a ruse to get my foot in the door. There's something else we need to talk about."

As I talked, he became less smug, his shoulders falling along with his face. He even deigned to sit down across from me, growing more and more tense as he listened.

As I was finishing, I added, "Don't forget. I'm on your side. I never really thought you'd killed Volkan. With your help, I can find out who did, and why. But I wasn't happy about that business with the phone records. Just what did you think you were doing?"

He stared at me blankly.

"What can you prove?" he finally said. "You haven't got a shred of evidence."

"I have all I need."

He laughed nervously.

"You mean nothing!"

His voice had reached a new pitch.

"I have enough evidence both for myself and—if it's appropriate—the police."

Once again, I was winging it. But I sincerely believed that with Cihad2000's help we would turn up something.

He carefully scrutinized my face before looking deeply into my eyes. His left eye seemed slightly out of synch. If he wasn't careful, he'd end up cross-eyed. It could be a blood sugar problem, I mused.

"You'll have to excuse me," he said. "I've got nothing to say to you. I told the police all they need to know. They're doing their jobs. None of this concerns you."

"Perhaps. But the police know nothing about the phone records."

"That's your problem. It has nothing to do with me. I didn't even know about it. You're making unfounded accusations and nonexistent connections."

"But I can prove it . . ."

"Sure you can," he said. "We'll never get anywhere like this."

Standing up, he walked over to the door.

"Now, if you'll excuse me, I've got work to do."

I was being thrown out. Slowly rising to my feet, I stole one last glance at the amazing view, hoping to keep the image alive forever.

"You know best," I said. "I have no choice but to protect myself. If I find myself in trouble, don't blame me for getting others involved—and that includes the police."

Icy eyes were on my back as I left the room. I wished I had long hair, or at least a shoulder-length wig. I'd have proudly raised my chin, narrowed my eyes . . . and delivered a crushing toss of the head. Just a single toss. Like so. Humph!

The same two silent servants relayed me back out of the house and to the front gate.

Faruk Hanoğlu could only have treated me this way because he had something to hide, or perhaps because of his intolerable insolence. But whatever the reason, I'd been unceremoniously thrown out! It was an official declaration of war. If that's what he wanted, that's what he'd get!

A dark red BMW slowed in front of me, blocking my path to the opposite pavement. Thinking the vehicle may have decelerated just for me, I leaned down and looked inside. Sitting in the driver's seat of the car entering the front gate, which had silently swung open to allow access to the garden I'd left seconds earlier, was none other than Haluk Pekerdem, in all his glory.

He hadn't even noticed me. Haluk Pekerdem! Me! Unnoticed! I was furious! Hurt! I took it hard . . . I needed to be loved and desired, especially by someone like him. I ran to the opposite pavement.

Waiting for a taxi in the chill air of the Bosphorus, I hissed out a cloud of steam and the words "This means war."

Chapter 23

I'd had more than enough humiliation, degradation, and mortification for one night, and was now filled with a burning desire for revenge. I mean, really, who did they think they were? Fire smoldering in my belly, I applied *the* most exquisite makeup.

"A real doll. What a doll . . . *Maşallah!*" I said to the reflection in the mirror, taking care to spray it with a healthy dose of spit to ward off the evil eye.

I was on a roll. Unless my fury faded away, I'd be hell on wheels at the club tonight, taking it out on the boys, making them hop and jump. I considered the way they treated me when they were cross and their transparent efforts to hide their resentment.

If DJ Osman played ludicrous tracks, claiming they were the latest hits, I'd shit in his mouth. He'd had it coming for a long time. The second I turned my back he'd play Sertab Erener, stretching my nerves like an overly taut bowstring. And when I'd intervene, he'd grin an apology out of the corner of his mouth. How many times had I told him that I simply would not have either that voice or its vessel in my club. If he tried it tonight, he'd be eating the shattered pieces of that shrill siren's CD before he knew what hit him.

And as for Cüneyt, that groveling excuse for a doorman . . . the slightest slipup in manner, word, or conduct would be noted ruthlessly on the spot. In any case, the boy was too simpleminded and pure of heart to take a hint, and his earnest response would only serve to sharpen my wrath further. So be it. Once I was through the door there would be any number of targets to choose from.

It would be tough to stick it to that incorrigible boy lover Şükrü. He'd put up with whatever I dished out. After all, the club was his idea of paradise, and he wouldn't allow it to be spoiled by anything I, his nominal boss, said. He'd simply tilt his head to one side, gaze into the distance, and put his trust in God.

And then there was Hasan! I had a real mouthful for him, an unending litany of abuse. I suddenly remembered that Hasan had wanted to talk to me. Even though we couldn't be considered close, he'd always come through for me, no questions asked. It's funny, though. He'd never expected me to reciprocate, almost as though he was determined to keep his distance.

I realized that I'd never made a special effort to get to know him better, or to lend him a hand. All I'd done was criticize and condemn. He, too, surely needed a kind word and a show of respect from time to time. I thought about his family, the one he never mentions but that I know live somewhere in Istanbul . . . the men, women, or boys he'd no doubt fallen for but never spoken of . . . the fact that to date he had not once complained or grumbled about his life to me or anyone I knew . . . Who knew what he suffered in private, the difficulties he faced in coming to terms with himself and his place in the world?

As I pondered the riddle of Hasan, the wind went out of my sails, blustery malice replaced by an almost maternal inner stillness. It was an unfortunate development: The grudge I harbored against Haluk also vanished. Those amazing eyes and wondrous face appeared in my mind's eye, and all was forgiven. He'd been reelevated to divine status. I imagined myself folded in his arms. And instantly turned to jelly. As I caught myself caressing my own arms, which were wrapped around my own body, I cursed aloud. Had I fallen in love, just like that? Where would it lead? Let's say my wildest fantasies came true, just once. Would he be prepared to divorce that rich, condescending, and stylish wife of his? Or would I become his mistress? An unfortunate and unreciprocated love. A tiresome and tiring adventure, the ill-fated course of which was clear from the start! That's all I needed right now!

Resentment welled up once more, buoyed by a bubbling pool of self-pity. *Bonjour, tristesse* . . . Good morning, *hüzün*! *Merhaba* and welcome back, depression!

"Hey!" I scolded myself aloud. I had no intention of returning to those dark days, of becoming a sorry creature with the mental faculties and *joie de vivre* of a sponge. Erkan Koray's "Sevince" always raises my spirits. I set the song to continuous play. Singing along, I completed my preparations. As always when determined to be cheerful, I'd laid it on a bit thick: sylphlike Audrey Hepburn buried under garish early Madonna gear. Now, if I only had a pistachio green fake fox fur detachable collar. And I did, of course. I had to laugh at myself in the full-length mirror. The impression I made tonight would be a lasting one indeed!

Cüneyt was not manning his customary spot at the door when I arrived. His absence must be due to the chilly weather or an unusually slow night at the club. I pressed the tiny doorbell and waited. After peering out through the grate, Cüneyt quickly opened the door. I handed him my cape, which was as thick as a blanket. After looking me up and down, and obviously unsure what to say, he fixed his eyes onto my face. I tossed him a hard look and entered.

It was nearly empty inside. Just two or three customers to a full ensemble of girls. Bored, they'd flocked to the dance floor. When Çişe saw me she hastily bundled her free-floating breasts back into her blouse. She's perfectly aware I won't permit such displays. Zero tolerance.

Şükrü winked as he gave me my virgin Mary. I asked how he was. He responded with a smile. After handling Hasan I'd return to his side prepared to listen sympathetically to his troubles. *Ay!* I'd been transformed into the very picture of a morally upright, considerate proprietress.

Hasan trotted to my side with short, quick steps. He'd been thrashed.

"What happened to you?" I asked. "What's all this?"

"Let's go upstairs and I'll tell you about it."

I left my drink on the bar and Hasan and I climbed up to our infamous storage room/office. He shut the door behind us the second we entered.

I cocked an eyebrow in an attempt to look sufficiently inquisitive.

"I was beaten," he said. "It wasn't an accident."

"Oh? Why? Who did it?"

"In my neighborhood. I was beaten up in my own neighbor-hood. You know the grocer on the corner of my street . . . He's got a son. Turan . . . Just back from military service. A good-looking guy."

I was preparing to spring to his defense when he silenced me.

"He may not be your type, but he's a real drink of water. In a Tom Cruise sort of way . . ."

"Did you hit on him?" I asked.

What really annoyed me was that after running around for all this time with his jeans hanging off his hips, butt crack exposed for all to see, flirting and carrying on with everyone in his path, stead-fastly rejecting various admirers of all ages and both sexes, he'd de-cided to hit on some grocer's boy. Just to initiate him, and uncertain of his tastes, I'd even gone so far as to offer to arrange a tryst with one of our girls or our gay-loving clients. He'd refused them all.

"That's not it," he said. "I liked him, is all. I started doing my shopping during his shift, having it home delivered. You know me, I'm the friendly sort. I warm to people straight off . . . I joke around . . . I liked him. We'd chat now and then. That's it."

"So that's why you got beat up?"

"No!" he said. "He has friends in the neighborhood. Real scum.

They hang out in front of the grocer's, talking and poking fun at everyone passing."

"Did they beat you up?"

"Yes, they did it. I'd just turned the corner one evening on the way home when they cornered me over by the rubbish bins. They jumped me."

"But why? Just because you were flirting with the grocer's boy?"

"It's a bit complicated," he said. "It was only later that I found out why they did it. It seems Turan has a thing for the girl on the floor below me, Şengül. He'd been hitting on her for a while. I joke around with Şengül sometimes. We lend each other books. Borrow things from each other when we run out. Once in a while, on Sundays, we go to the cinema. We're friends. We live in the same building and all that . . . Anyway, it seems Turan got jealous. He's got a thing for the girl, thinks he owns her. Sometimes I'd joke around with him about Şengül. He thought I was making fun of him for being jealous. So he decides that not only am I after his girl, I'm rubbing his nose in it. Then he sends his friends after me . . ."

"How'd you find all this out?"

"When Şengül saw them beating me up she came running out to help. She's the one who told me about Turan. He'd been sending her love letters, you see . . ."

"So they let you go when she turned up?"

"No, that's not what happened. They just ignored her and kept hitting and kicking me. That is, until Şengül, at the top of her lungs, so she was sure they'd hear her over the racket we were making, screamed out that I was a faggot, that there'd never been anything between us and never would be . . . When she finished, you could have heard a pin drop. They all froze, gaping at me. Then one of them shouted 'faggot' and they started beating me up again."

I'd heard enough. I was feeling sick to my stomach. I wanted to rush over and flatten the grocery first, then the entire district.

"How'd you get away?"

"When they'd had enough they left. I'd passed out . . . Şengül dragged me home and dressed my wounds . . ."

"I'm so sorry," I said. "My condolences. Have you told the girls?"

"Of course not. They'd run off and raid my neighborhood . . . It wasn't easy finding that flat!"

"Fine," I said flatly.

I hadn't yet decided what to do.

"What would you like me to do?" I asked.

"You've got friends in the squad. Arrange a good thumping. A night in jail, even . . ."

"There's no need to get the police involved," I said. "I can handle the whole lot on my own. How many are there?"

"Four or five, tops."

"If necessary, I'll go around with Shrewish Pamir or a couple of the other girls . . ."

"That's no good," he said. "This thing'll turn into a blood feud. And what about my standing in the neighborhood? As you know, I'm not gay. It'd just give them another reason to call me a faggot."

"So what can you do, file for slander?"

"Not only would the police make it official," he insisted. "They'd realize I have friends in high places . . ."

"And were you to be rescued by transvestites, just think what it'd do to your reputation, right?"

His face, already distorted by swelling, became deformed with astonishment.

"How can you say that? I've never been ashamed of you or the girls. Never."

Yes, behind the windowless walls of the club, at home or in our own specially designated spaces, there was no problem, no cause for embarrassment; still, I knew, deep down, that I was right to take offense. Even worse, so did he.

Chapter 24

When I woke up the next morning, at an hour ordinary people refer to as "the afternoon," I felt like a sharp blade had pierced my forehead, entering just below my right eyebrow. I pulled back the thick curtains; bright winter sunshine filled the room. A wonderfully crisp day, the kind that brings joy and energy! I sighed contentedly. Pity about the headache. Such things simply should not be on a day like this.

On the way to the bathroom I ignored the flashing light of my answering machine. Whoever had called at such an early hour deserved to wait. First I'd enjoy a long shower and the sumptuous breakfast offerings laid in by Ponpon. Followed by a couple of Advil, if required. The brilliant blue sky urged me to find an outdoor spot to warm my bones and to spend the rest of the day lazing about.

Wrapping myself in a robe, I began fixing breakfast. Flitting across the floor on tiptoe amused me, as well as minimized contact with the freezing tiles. As the bread toasted, I switched on one of those determinedly dispassionate but in fact utterly partisan twenty-four-hour news channels. One simply must remain abreast of current affairs!

Only watched bread toasts just right, so I turned up the volume and returned to the kitchen. I listened to the latest on the financial markets: international stock market closings; dollar, euro, and yen parity; and fluctuations in oil and gold prices. The information did nothing for my pounding headache, but still I listened. I am not the sort to surrender to pain.

When each slice had begun to turn a golden brown, I flipped them over: I like my bread toasted on both sides. The market reports, so avidly followed by the good people of our nation, ended, and the regular news began.

I couldn't believe my ears. The female presenter failed to repress the thrill in her voice as she announced: "Leading financial consultant Faruk Hanoğlu has been killed in an unfortunate accident."

I rushed back out to the living room. The news account was accompanied by stock footage of Faruk Bey, tensely holding forth on the consequences of foreign direct investment. Looking more unpleasant than ever in a tailored suit that did nothing for her complexion, the presenter droned on in a small window in the bottom right-hand corner of the screen: Faruk Bey was fifty-three years old, had been educated abroad, and had served as a financial consultant for many years. He had recently been arrested for murder but was subsequently cleared of all charges.

No additional information about the "unfortunate accident" was provided.

The smell of burning bread had me racing back to the kitchen. It had happened again. I'd turned my back for a moment and the last two slices of bread had turned to charcoal. Shortly after my visit, during which I'd been outrageously mistreated, Faruk Hanoğlu had died. And how? An "unfortunate accident." Whatever that meant!

The stabbing pain just above my right eye suddenly spread to my entire forehead. I'd scared myself: Surely I couldn't have called down a curse on the late Faruk . . . Or could I have? No, I was being silly.

I didn't know whether to blame the headache on the news of Faruk's death, on an empty stomach, or on having spent such a long night in the stuffy smokiness of the club. I definitely needed an Advil. After downing half a glass of cold milk to coat my stomach, I took two. I would remain seated until I felt better.

I tore to shreds a now stale slice of cake made by Ponpon, reduced the shreds to crumbs, and unenthusiastically chewed as
much as I could as I sat there in the kitchen. The tiles were freezing,
I was getting cold feet, and things were getting more complicated. I
couldn't find rhyme or reason for the seemingly random series of
events in which I was now hopelessly entangled.

First I needed more details about the "unfortunate accident." I
nearly called Selçuk, my police connection, but thought better of
it. Pestering him every time I had a question, particularly when it
had nothing to do with his job at the force, didn't seem fair. I decided against it. Then I remembered Olcay. These days he was
working for that insipid twenty-four-hour news channel. Once
upon a time we had enjoyed intimate relations for an entire weekend. His career had since taken off.

I dialed his number at the network and was connected almost
immediately. So, he was not yet important enough to warrant five
layers of screening.

I told him who I was.

"What's up, girl? Where you been?" he began. It is a manner of
speaking I detest. I even considered hanging up on the spot.

"Oh, I'm around. And fine," was my terse response. "What
have you been up to? How are you?"

"I'm around too, my rose . . . So you're alright then?"

He hadn't changed a bit. Even that single weekend had been
overlong.

"There's something I need to ask you," I said. "I missed the
cause of death in the piece you just ran on Faruk Hanoğlu. I knew
him, you see, and I can't believe this happened!"

"My condolences," he said, a note of respect creeping into his
voice for a moment. "Just a sec, babe. I'll find out for you." Put on
hold, I was forced to listen to whatever the channel was broadcast-
ing. The experience was not unlike one of those brainwashing
scenes in cold war films.

"I hope you haven't been waiting too long. There are no more details. The police reported an 'accidental death.' That's it. I guess no one's investigating further . . ."

"I see . . ." I said.

"I hope you don't mind my saying so, but the guy was a real piece of shit. I don't wish to speak ill of the dead, but people really do die as they live. Divine retribution and all that. Still, my condolences, since you knew him personally. Afraid I've got to go. We're real busy here."

"Okay. Thanks, anyway. Bye."

Boorish Olcay had been as tactless as ever. Not only had he failed to provide any worthwhile information, he'd aggravated both me *and* my headache. One more performance like that, and he'd be deleted from my address book. That would serve him right!

Once again, Selçuk was my last, best hope. I called him up and explained. He listened patiently until I was finished, promising to do what he could. I'd get him a nice gift and visit him at home.

Chapter 25

aiting inspires me to total inaction. When forced to wait, I tend to do nothing, and if I do act in any way, it always comes to naught. But I had to find a way to keep busy until Selçuk got back to me.

I called Ponpon. There was no answer. Either she was still asleep or she wasn't taking calls. I insistently left two messages, one after another. Perhaps the blinking light of my answering machine meant she'd done the same. I went and listened.

Addressing me, in order, were Ali, Pamir, Hüseyin, Pamir, and Kemal Barutçu (alias Cihad2000), intermingled with the annoying electronic signals of those who had hung up without leaving a message. Pamir said she had spent two days at home waiting for me to get back to her. In the first message, she wondered if I was alright. In the second one she said she was sick of sitting at home and asked me to give her immediate instructions for whatever it was I wanted her to do. In light of Cihad2000's quite understandable panic attack, I had thought it best to postpone a session with Pamir. Naturally, I'd then forgotten to inform her.

Cihad2000's message was short and snappy: "Call me." The authoritative tone in his assured voice indicated that he'd overcome his feelings of paranoia.

The phone rang. It was Selçuk.

Sounding worried and dispensing with the formalities, he got straight to the point. "You're in deep shit this time."

"What do you mean?"

"You paid a little house call on that loan shark Faruk last night . . ."

So, our police actually were hard at work on the case.

"So what?" I said. I then coughed a few times, to account for my strangled voice. The sudden lump in my throat could be put down to all that stale cake, I reassured mysef. Surely there was no cause for alarm?

"I'd suggest you lay low for a while. That is, you'd better not pursue this any further . . . Just a bit of friendly advice."

"So what if I did go to Faruk Hanoğlu's house?" I protested, my voice cracking this time. "He has dozens of visitors every day."

"Look," said Selçuk, "the circumstances of his death are some-what complicated. That's all I've been able to find out. Best not go digging for now. Keep your nose clean for a while. Let things die down a bit."

"Well, now you've made me even more curious. At least tell me how he died."

"You know what our guys are like. We talk about everything, especially in a routine case like this one. But this time it's different. They're all as tight-lipped as can be. Something's going on, and I haven't been able to get to the bottom of it."

"How'd you find out I'd visited Faruk? Who told you?"

"Stop pestering me! They were watching footage from the se-curity camera in the garden. Just as I walked into the room you ap-peared on-screen. That's how!"

"Are you suggesting that just because the camera picked me up I should consider myself to be a suspect? Even though we don't even know how the guy died?"

"Listen up, friend," he said. "Just after I entered the room they switched off the tape. Or, maybe the camera had been disengaged at that point. All I know is that two high-ranking commissioners and three policemen wouldn't be involved if this were a routine death. I mean, the guy wasn't even a minister or anything! They're onto something. It's not normal! Now do you get it?"

"I'm trying, but failing to manage it, I'm afraid . . ." I said.

"You're quite the manager. So manage this, too. If anything turns up I'll call you. Alright?"

I managed a halfhearted "alright" before hanging up.

The murder of a third-rate gigolo was now connected to a high-profile homicide, and I was being sucked in deeper and deeper. Faruk Hanoğlu, the number-one suspect, had been killed in an "accident" the cause of which the police were hiding. As someone who had visited the late Faruk just before his untimely death, I found myself a suspect. I had no idea why I was under suspicion, but Selçuk had strongly implied that I was in trouble.

As I pondered various courses of action, I found myself resorting to the vulgar format so beloved of TV game shows. I really must shake off this obsession with presenting alternatives in multiple-choice form. I thought I was over it, but here I go again:

(a) I could drop everything and let the dice fall where they may. Whatever happens, happens. If the situation is as serious as Selçuk suggests, the police might even pay me a visit sometime soon.

(b) I could stubbornly persist in my sleuthing and risk finding myself in even bigger trouble. "Trouble comes in threes," or so they say. Was I prepared for a real disaster?

(c) Considering I was likely to be accused of murder in any case, what was the harm in bringing down a few people with me? Nothing had made any sense so far. Perhaps I could rub out a few of my enemies without anyone noticing. If nothing else, the world would be a better place, and I'd have considerably more elbow room.

(d) I could take a long holiday, all on my own. A place far away; a place no one would ever think of. Months later, when everything had blown over, I'd resurface. That is, a slightly more relaxed, tanned, healthier, and happier version of me would fly back to Istanbul and resume my life.

I weighed up my choices, juggling their order and carefully considering each alternative. It did no good.

I became sidetracked by choice C, and spent quite some time mentally composing a list of the people I'd like to eliminate. Once I got started, names started mushrooming out of control. Acquaintances and complete strangers, people I knew only from TV, newspapers, and magazines, some famous, some not, dozens of names without faces, and faces without names. The list grew and grew, and when I realized that I had no intention of removing a single victim from the lengthening list, that I was incapable of finding a single redeeming quality in any of my condemned souls, I frightened myself. There were so many!

The holiday fantasy was more pleasant. A hot, sunny spot far from the streets of Istanbul . . . No need for layers of clothing, just shorts and a T-shirt. Somewhere I could live on tropical fruit, frolic in the surf, stretch out on the sand, book in hand, sighing at the half-naked men parading past . . .

Visions of a dream holiday relaxed me. I'm only human, after all! I felt myself winding down and loosening up. It was almost as good as being there on the beach. The tension in my muscles, the middle of my forehead, and my temples was easing. I only realized I'd been grinding my teeth when I stopped clenching my jaw. The perfect holiday: sea, sun, shopping, and men. Men marching in front of me, dressed in a kaleidoscope of brightly colored bathing suits, swim trunks, and Speedos—even a few G-strings displaying bronzed apple cheeks . . . Haluk Pekerdem, suddenly materializing in knee-length board shorts. Hey, what was he doing here in my fantasy? I began thinking about Haluk and the spell was over, my holiday finished. "One's real life is so often the life that one does not lead," someone once said.

I began murmuring an old dance favorite: "Back to life, back to reality . . ."

Chapter 26

*T*he realities of life demanded that I call Cihad2000. I complied.

"What's going on?" he roared excitedly. "You start digging around for information about some guy and now he's dead. Boy have you got some explaining to do."

First I'd been named a suspect and now I was apparently being openly accused of murder. That was going too far.

"How am I supposed to know?" I snapped.

"We both know you've been poking around. I'm sure you're not telling me everything. You're hiding something. Even worse, you're getting me mixed up in your dirty work."

"Believe me, I don't even know how he died. I found out about it on TV, same as you."

"You'd better listen in on some phone calls then. All hell broke loose. Everyone who's had dealings with that loan shark is in a panic. The lines are crackling. You'd break out in cold sores if you heard some of the names being mentioned."

"You don't mean you eavesdrop on phone conversations, too?"

I really hadn't expected that.

"If I need to, yes," he said. "How do you think I manage to rustle up so much business?"

If Money-counter Ali ever heard about this he'd never pick up a phone again. So that was how Cihad2000 managed to steal so much of our work.

"Cat got your tongue?"

"I was thinking," I said.

"Therefore you are!"

If it weren't for his silly sense of humor, Cihad2000 would be unbearable. He always catches me by surprise. I even laugh.

"Stop laughing!" he shouted. "The situation's serious. Never mind that I'm laughing, too. Now that he's dead, those phone records we destroyed will become even more important. The police and everyone else will be hunting for clues. And where's the first place they'll look? The phone records. And what will they find? Surprise! Gone. Deleted. How did that happen? And guess who's responsible?"

"Us," I responded automatically.

"Bravo!"

I hadn't thought about that. I'd already felt as though I was being drawn into a complicated maelstrom of events outside my control. I didn't even want to consider the implications of this new information.

"Well then, were you able to find anything among the bits you managed to copy?"

"Who do you think I was listening in on? Did you think I was picking phone numbers at random? That would have been a waste of time. And like I told you, his list of clients is a real who's who of movers and shakers. You won't believe it: politicians, businessmen, singers, high-society types, the usual underworld figures . . ."

I really was surprised at the names he reeled off. And astonished that Kemal seemed to recognize so many minor celebrities.

"And I've got more than just tapes of their phone calls," he continued. "There are lots of money transfers arranged over the Internet and by phone. Transfers to domestic and international accounts, numbered and official, taxed and untaxed, in the Cayman Islands, Bahrain, Switzerland, Luxembourg . . . You name it!"

"Well then," I repeated, "what does this tell us? I mean, what good is it?"

"What good is it?" he nearly shouted. "Just think of the implications! A loan shark . . . Shady money transfers . . . Imagine what
you could do with information like that! Of course . . . as you know,
the records are all dated. The new ones are gone. Deleted. That is,
a huge chunk of the most recent information is missing. Good on
us, we wiped them out together."

"Don't be silly, *ayol*! It's not as if Telekom would have archived
records of every single phone call. Or do you think we're talking
White House here?"

"I see you're using *ayol* again! Anyway, I suppose you have a
point."

We'd gone off on a tangent, but we were now back to the central question.

"You say you've deciphered the records you copied. What I
need to know is this: What's going on? How did he die?"

"Let's take things one at a time," he said. "I don't think I can answer all your questions in one go."

"Just tell me everything you know," I urged him. "In exchange
for any useful information, I've got a big surprise. A hot little
number with your name on her. Just the kind of preop sweetie you
love, a real lolly on a stick. And she's ever so stern!"

I detected an immediate change in the breathing patterns on
the other end of the line. For someone unable to escape the watchful eye of a fawning mother, someone unable even to stand up un-
assisted, the prospect I dangled before him was intoxicating indeed.
Gone was the bellowing, replaced by a whisper.

"Who?" he breathed thickly. "Tell me who it is . . ."

"You tell me first," I said. "Tell me all you've found out. That
way you'll truly deserve my little surprise."

"Who is it? Tell me and I'll . . ."

"You wouldn't know her," I said, just to increase his curiosity.
"But when you lay eyes on her, she'll knock your socks off. I
swear!"

I'd expected silence on the other end as he weighed my offer, but I hadn't expected it to be so brief.

"Faruk Hanoğlu fell into the Bosphorus just in front of his house, and drowned."

"You must be joking," I said. "A grown man like him didn't know how to swim? He grew up in a *yalı*, right on the water . . ."

"That's what makes his death a tragicomedy. And a mystery. Apparently, his feet got tangled in some rope, and he couldn't get his head above water. Despite the strong current, they found him bobbing in the water right in front of his house, a length of rope wound around his ankle. In fact, they say his body was smashing into the dock with each wave. The seagulls had done a real job on the bits of him above water."

"That's enough," I cut him off.

I could visualize the scene all too easily, and felt nauseated. A hairy calf, bloated and bleached in the saltwater, and torn to shreds by voracious screaming seagulls, like the attackers did in Hitchcock's *The Birds*. After seeing that film as a child I'd had nightmares for weeks.

"Don't you think this all sounds suspicious? I don't know about you, but I smell a rat."

If even Kemal smelled a rat, my sensitive, highly experienced nose should have been overpowered by the stench of bloody murder, two truly vicious ones, no less! But it wasn't. I needed a moment to recover from the image of gulls pecking away at a pale leg.

"Can I call you back in a bit?"

"But you haven't told me who it is! You can't hang up now!"

"I'll call you right back. I've got to get to the toilet."

"I'll crash your system! I'll show you!"

I had reason to fear Kemal. He meant what he said. And he'd be perfectly capable of making good on his threats.

"Pamir!" I shouted. "More details soon."

I slammed down the receiver without waiting for a response.

Dashing off to the bathroom, I threw up. The cold water I splashed on my face did me a world of good, though the retching had left my eyes watery and bloodshot.

The intricate workings of the brain remain a great mystery, and mine is no exception. During the few seconds I spent looking into the mirror, flashing through my mind were: Alfred Hitchcock, *The Birds,* Tippi Hedren looking like a frigid drag queen, her hunky leading man, Rod Taylor, Hitchcock's efforts to transform Hedren into the new Grace Kelly in *Marnie,* her costar in that film, Sean Connery . . . and then, Haluk Pekerdem.

Yes, I now had the social and moral obligation of paying my respects to one Haluk Pekerdem—and of doing so in person. None other than the Haluk Pekerdem who only last night had completely ignored me as he pulled into the driveway of that ill-starred waterfront mansion! When it comes to collecting one's thoughts and getting back on one's feet, a heady brew of rancor and exhilaration is just the ticket.

I was ready to return to my phone conversation with Cihad2000, to arrange the promised tryst with Pamir, and to present myself, in all my glory, to Haluk Pekerdem. An opportunity had arisen, and it would be duly seized. Kismet wouldn't necessarily come knocking again any time soon.

Cihad2000 had told me that Faruk's wife herself was fielding all phone calls made to the mansion. However, most of the talking was done by Yalçın, a man with the voice of a butler. As well as by the lawyer of the deceased, brother-in-law Haluk Pekerdem. Despite myself, I couldn't help sighing at the very mention of the name Haluk Pekerdem.

"I gather the house has been flooded with visitors. Everyone who's anyone is there. A well-placed bomb would effectively wipe out the Turkish political, business, cultural, and hooker communities. We'd be left empty-handed and destitute," Cihad2000 continued. "While the phone calls are full of the usual sympathy and commiserations, there's also a lot of talk of money. Dollars, marks, yen . . . Turkish lira are even mentioned, if rarely."

"*Ayol*, what do you mean 'marks'? It'd be euros!"

"Look at you, getting hung up on currencies! As if that's what's important! I'll stop now if you're not interested!" he scolded.

Kemal softened as I elaborated on Pamir's special talents. He then repeated, at great length and in full detail, everything he had heard, been told, and discerned. We may be the fiercest of rivals, and at each other's throats more often than not, but I definitely have a soft spot for geeky Cihad2000. A pervert and a paraplegic he might be, but he was also a goldmine of useful information.

"When are you two coming?"

"She'll come on her own," I said. "Not with me. I'll just give her your address. Make sure your mother's not around."

"Don't be ridiculous!" he declared proudly. "I'm not doing it at home. I'm going to reserve a nice room at a classy hotel. What's money for?"

I hadn't thought of that.

"Any recommendations? You know more about that kind of stuff than me . . . But I want the best service. And not too many questions."

"Would you like a room with a view?" I asked, stifling a giggle.

"I doubt we'd have time to admire the view."

Chapter 27

My chief suspect for Faruk's suspicious death was, of course, Volkan's burnout brother, Okan. Even as I was pondering Okan's murderous motives, others had drawn the same conclusion: Television pundits were even now noisily accusing the brother. Up flashed the juicy caption "Drug Abuser Avenges Slaying of Elder Brother?" and the usual gang of windbags duly pontificated. The accident reported just a few hours earlier was now a sensational murder case. Police were searching everywhere for the main suspect. A snapshot of the brother appeared on the screen: dark, shifty, and ugly, with hangdog eyes, he looked nothing like Volkan.

Typically opportunistic, one of the channels seized upon Okan's sudden notoriety to reair a program on drug addiction featuring grim doctors in white coats droning on and on. While abusers of marijuana were bad enough, anything could be expected of users of heroin. Random violence of a maniacal nature was apparently scientifically linked to doses of X opioid and Y hallucinogen. Sometimes I seriously considered giving the TV set to Fatoş Abla or the janitor, or even throwing it out of the window. I'd easily come up with something attractive to fill the empty space. As a matter of fact, that black, plastic box had always clashed with the room's overall color scheme.

I hadn't thought talking to Okan would be of much importance, nor had I managed to find him. Now I had to. I'd be racing against the police to get to him first. If he was arrested—as he no doubt would be, eventually—he would speak only on the record, nothing else. But I was only too aware of the methods employed in extracting official confessions and testimony. I'd have to be quick.

I hurriedly threw on some clothes that wouldn't draw too much attention: a black sweater and a pair of relatively high-waisted jeans. Ever since waists started heading south, I haven't bought a single pair of jeans measuring more than a hand's length from crotch seam to belt loop. And my hands are not like those of the other girls: while strong, they are slender and elegant.

As I walked out the door, it occurred to me that I had no idea where I was going, and no idea where to find Okan. A street-by-street search would be less than effective. In fact, in this day and age, it isn't even the preferred method for apartment hunting, let alone a hunt for a murder suspect. Undeterred, I locked the door and walked off.

Having silenced the nerve-racking music in the taxi, I gave the driver Refik Altın's address. Less than fifteen minutes later I was entering his new apartment building in Esentepe. While there was nothing particularly grand about the place, it reflected him perfectly: well past its prime but stubbornly pretentious. As I rode an elevator redolent of Ajax to the top floor, I examined myself in the mirror. An impertinent hair had grown out just above my nose. I struggled to pinch it between two fingernails, but it was too short to pluck out. The hair won, and I was left with a red spot right between my eyebrows. Let's hope for the best, I remarked to my third eye as I stepped out of the lift.

Refik was expecting me.

"Look, sister, you got me all wound up on the phone. I'm taking tranquilizers as it is, just to pull myself together. You can imagine the state of my nerves. It's an understatement to say I'm not feeling particularly lucid these days. I haven't got the slightest idea what I'm saying, or even what I'm being told. Do forgive me . . ."

It's never too late to know thyself, I thought.

I was determined to keep the ritual expressions of sympathy to a minimum; he was equally determined to blubber and bawl over every last detail, embroidering and embellishing ad nauseam. Of the most recent news, he had not a clue.

"*Ay*, please, you can't be serious. As though I have the strength to pick up a newspaper or switch on the TV. I'm in mourning, sister, scorched and in pain, utterly incapable of finding amusement in the simplest pleasures of life . . ."

I'd always been astonished that someone whose speech oozed treacle of such a vulgar nature could manage to produce such compelling poetry.

"If I weren't worried about the neighbors, I'd be listening to hardcore *arabesk* at full volume. Gut-wrenching music belting out as I throw myself to the floor, thrashing and weeping, grieving to my heart's content . . . But a sea of salty tears won't bring him back, will it? Quiet! I know . . . But still!"

This final outburst, accompanied by facial contortions meant to simulate anguish, was all the confirmation I needed. Yes, once again he was performing. *Puro teatro!* The green light on his stereo was still burning; he must have switched it off just before I arrived. I was up against an *a la turca* Blanche DuBois at her most ludicrous, provincial, and overwrought.

"Look here," I said, pointing my right index finger at his left eye. "I do believe you're grieving and in pain. He was your lover, after all. However, please try to understand what I'm about to say. I speak not out of a lack of respect for your suffering and your love but because you're about to spin completely out of control. So cut the drama for a moment, or I'll smash you and your flat to bits."

The lightning in my eyes convinced him I was serious. He knows all too well what I'm capable of when I lose my temper. Once upon a time, back when I was practically apprenticed to stupen-dous Sofya, I'd been provoked into breaking into Refik's flat, tearing the place apart, and demonstrating for the benefit of Refik and my so-called lover boy at the time a series of recently mastered

Thai boxing moves. And with bonus background information on each kick and slam thoughtfully provided free of charge. After that it was a long time indeed before I was able to refer to any man as my lover.

I was short and snappy as I summarized the latest for him. He was a bit thrown by my criticism, a bit miffed that his portrayal of an inconsolable widow had gone unappreciated. Eyes fixed on my wagging index finger, he meekly nodded from time to time to confirm that he was listening.

"Oh good," he said, when I told him about Faruk. "He got what he deserved. Thought he'd get away with it. It's called divine retribution, sweetie. I sometimes believe in it. There you go."

When it was time to bring up Okan, I stopped. I'd been talking so fast and so loudly my throat was dry.

"Don't look at me like that," he said. "I didn't do anything."

"Have I said anything about you having done something?"

"No, you haven't . . . yet. But you've been banging on for so long, I can't help but wonder if I'm next. I ask but one thing: If you must beat me up, please don't touch my face. As you well know, it took two operations to straighten my nose that last time."

Reminded of what had happened, I couldn't help laughing. He had no idea why, of course.

"What is it, sister? What happened now?" he ventured timidly.

"Nothing," I said. "It's just that I remembered how you wet yourself when I smashed your windows that time."

"That's not the least bit funny. I've chosen to forget all about it. I attributed your behavior to a fit of jealousy, temporary insanity. Otherwise, I'd never have spoken to you again."

I didn't bother to remind him that he'd slandered me all across town, that he hadn't spoken to me until the club opened, and that when he'd arrived there, hoping to bag a boy, none had shown any interest in him, which was the reason he was now pretending to have forgotten the whole thing.

"You weren't entirely innocent," I said.

"That was different. You still haven't let go. You're so vindictive!" He was as determined as ever to get the upper hand.

"The boy you bedded happened to be my lover," I said.

"He was like Kleenex, nothing more. One of those one-night, one-use types. I didn't take it seriously. But now I see that you did; you're still obsessing. Aren't you a funny old thing."

We weren't getting anywhere. I couldn't even remember the boy's face. All I recollected was throwing everything that came to hand at the windows, stuffing a huge towel into the toilet, knocking over the lit candles so they burned holes in the carpets and upholstery, and, of course, my little Thai boxing exhibition. Oh, and the sight of Refik scampering around the room wearing nothing but a pair of pink panties.

"Whatever," I said. "That's not what I've come to talk about. I'd forgotten the whole thing. To tell you the truth, I can't remember the boy."

"What do you mean, can't remember?" he said, out of sheer spite. "His name was Ufuk. He was medium height. A bit on the thin side. Big eyes, like chestnuts. Had a mole on the right side of his chest that looked like a third nipple."

The flourish with which he indicated, on his own chest, the location of the third nipple just begged a good thrashing.

"Shut up, *ayol!*" I shouted, glaring at him. "End of subject. Forget Ufuk. It doesn't matter. Okan, your Volkan's little brother, has been proclaimed a killer. They're going to pin it on a drug abuser and close the case, nice and tidy."

"No, that can't be! Okan wouldn't have. He couldn't have . . ."

"How can you be so sure?"

"He's here, sleeping in the bedroom. He hasn't been outside for two days. Neither have I."

"What are you saying?" I said. "Okan is here with you?"

"That's right," he answered calmly. "I called him, to hand over some of Volkan's things. He was good enough to come right over. We had a few drinks, wept on each other's shoulders . . . Then he . . . comforted me."

An inappropriate and groundless note of pride had crept into his voice. As though he'd pulled off a difficult stunt. Lips twisted into a wicked smile, he continued.

"And I comforted him right back . . . then . . . he spent the night . . . with me . . ."

"So neither of you has gone outside for two days?"

"Well, not since yesterday. As I told you, Okan has been here with me. He couldn't have killed that money-lender. Anyway, why would he do something like that? After all, Faruk Bey helped him out, gave him tons of money."

"Run that by me, again," I said. "Nice and slow. I'm a bit confused."

Ponpon's Xanax couldn't still be affecting me. I seemed to have suffered lasting damage.

"Let's call the police and tell them! They'd better leave him alone . . ."

"Yeah, right," I said. "The police have been waiting for a call from you. They're just dying to cross their top suspect off the list, I suppose. Get real!"

"So what are we going to do?" he said, biting his lower lip anxiously. "He can't hide here for the rest of his life, can he? That would be impossible."

The combination of campy vamp and imbecilic child star was too much for me. Wincing, I looked him up and down.

"Stop staring, sister! Say something!"

"Go and wake him up. We need to have a little talk," I said. "Then you can go write a bit of poetry."

As I watched Refik going off to rouse Okan, I couldn't help wondering what kind of underwear he was wearing.

Chapter 28

*R*efik's low murmur reached me from the bedroom, where he was trying to wake up his new favorite, the boyfriend he had, in a sense, inherited from his late lover. One question—other than Refik's underwear—burned in my mind: What else and who else had been recorded by the security camera at the Hanoğlu mansion? If I had made an appearance, and I had no reason to doubt Selçuk's account, there must be footage of Okan as well. Otherwise, why would he be a suspect? But if it was true that Okan had been at Refik's side for the past two days, he couldn't have been captured on camera. Someone was being economical with the truth. But who?

It would take some time for Okan to wake up, come to life, and be ready to meet me. I walked over to the window to enjoy the luxury of being on the fourteenth floor. The Bosphorus lay before me, stretching from Ihlamur Valley all the way to Sarayburnu. It was overcast. The night I'd smashed the windows I hadn't even noticed the view. I'd been in no condition to do so. Gravity would have ensured that the pointed shards of glass were lethal weapons by the time they reached the ground. I hadn't heard anything in the days following, so I assumed no serious accidents had been reported.

Why was I able to remember every detail of the havoc I wreaked that day but absolutely nothing about the boy, Ufuk? So he had a mole like a third nipple. I racked my brain but came up empty.

"Good morning . . ." said a sleepy but tense voice.

Okan Sarıdoğan was standing in front of me. He was taller and stockier than I'd expected, and not nearly as dark and shifty as his photo had indicated. But he was obviously nothing like his older brother, the brother so highly recommended by one and all as a "once in a lifetime, must-try" experience. It wasn't just that he wasn't handsome; he couldn't even be considered "charismatic," the term in popular use these days to describe ugly men. He had thick, unruly hair and a sulky expression, just like in the somewhat blurry photo. Even so, the doleful look in his eyes aroused one's protective instinct.

"Good morning," I responded.

"Refik said some things, but I didn't really understand what he was talking about. I must have overslept. I'm still a bit woozy."

He glanced over, as Refik spoke.

"I'll make you some coffee. That'll help."

So, the period of mourning was officially over. The new romance was in full bloom.

"Would you like some?"

"Yes." I smiled. "Black. No milk, no sugar."

When Refik disappeared to prepare the coffee, I sat opposite Okan and we studied each other. Conflict or concord, which was it to be? I, myself, opted for the latter.

I related the breaking news, and told him he was wanted by the police. I also added that no one would think to look for him here, at Refik's place—at least for the moment.

"But how could they accuse me? I didn't even go to that house yesterday. There must be a mistake."

The coffee arrived. Refik served *him* first. Welcome or not, I was a guest. Because they were sharing a bed, Okan was in fact an honorary member of the household, not a guest. I should have been served first. He must have considered Okan to be the man of his life, and the two of us to be no more than concubines or slave girls. Ha! I said to myself. What good are all those pronouncements on homosexual rights and feminism if this is the way you act at home? So much for all your politically correct articles, your egalitarian ideas. Of course, all of this was irrelevant to the task at hand. I'd allowed my mind to become hung up on detail and exercised by other things.

Okan pulled a small foil-wrapped disk of dope out of the pocket of his designer sweatpants and began rolling a joint intended to serve as breakfast. Whether it's hash or heroin, I have the same opinion concerning drugs: I loathe them. And I loathe those who love them.

"We've got some serious talking to do," I said. "Must you do that first thing in the morning?"

Raising his eyes from the joint he was rolling, he gave me a surprised and questioning look.

"You've been accused of murder! Do you want to be taken in for drugs, too?"

"This is just dope," he said.

In his book, dope was not a drug apparently.

Refik, who was perched on the other end of the sofa we were sharing, tensed at the tone and direction of my little exchange with Okan. Although sitting on a thorn, his silly smile as he looked at Okan was that of a man who has reached nirvana.

"Well, *he's* not butting in. And it's *his* home. What's it to you?"

Okan had revealed his true colors. Our boy with the hangdog look was a real rebel! He'd modeled himself on James Dean, most likely without even having a clue who that was. A misunderstood and undiscovered treasure, at least in his own mind, he was playing the rebellious and sulky Eternal Boy.

There was no point in antagonizing him right from the start. I still had so much to learn.

"You know best," I said. "It's your body and your brain. Destroy them however you like."

He gave me a hard stare, then a smile spread across his face as he got back to his rolling. His hands were quick and practiced.

"How did you meet Faruk Hanoğlu?" I asked.

"Who hasn't met him?" he said, without raising his head.

"Look, sweetie," I said, in my famous warning tone, "don't talk back to me! I came here to help you. And I don't think he killed your brother. Someone's trying to pin it on you. They'll put it down to revenge, case closed and completely forgotten about while you rot in prison. Do you understand me?"

He took a deep drag on his joint, the tip of which gave me a fiery wink. An acrid sweetness reached my nostrils. I kept my eyes on his face, waiting for an answer, a response of some kind. He held the smoke in his lungs for a moment, speaking as he exhaled.

"I'm not stupid. I get it."

"Good," I said. "Then tell me all you know. Right from the beginning."

Staring into space with an expression only he found meaning-ful, he was silent for as long as it took to take two more drags on his joint.

"I was staying with Volkan, my big brother . . ." he said. "Before he died."

That was the cue for Refik to produce a shrill shriek, followed by a fit of hiccups.

"He lives on, for all time, in the hearts of those who loved him," Refik whimpered. "He lives on . . . right here . . ."

Naturally, he closed his eyes and clasped his hands "right here."

Okan and I looked on, both equally nonplussed. The only dif-ference between us being that his eyes had begun fogging over.

"We were real tight," he continued. "He always looked after me, like a good big brother. He's the one who brought me to Istan-bul from the village, taught me how to dress, how to act."

Face soppy, eyes watery, Refik nodded and nodded. I had to look away to keep from bursting out laughing, but I couldn't ex-actly plug my ears to keep out the low keening.

"There's so much to learn . . . especially from someone like him."

None of this had anything to do with the matter at hand, nor was I interested in the slightest, but the "boy" had opened his mouth at last. I would have to hold my tongue and be civil. A few well-timed questions would get him back on track, if necessary.

The prelude lasted even longer than I'd feared. Refik even had to make another round of coffee. The Volkan being described to me now was nothing like the one in the other testimonials. He was a Henry Higgins, a Svengali, an angel, even. A good-natured, thoughtful, sensible, responsible, and tender older brother. He'd been generous to a fault with his little brother, showering him daily with tokens of affection, handing him pocket money, and even presenting him with a brand-new minibus.

"What's more," added Okan, waving the joint in the direction of my face, "he never fussed about this. He'd even ring me up, ask about my stash so he could keep me supplied."

Okan talked and talked, occasionally falling silent, spaced-out, head tilted back and eyes on the ceiling. Then he'd come to and keep talking. So far there had been no mention of the source of Volkan's money, his reputation as a gigolo, or his relationship to Faruk Hanoğlu. I waited patiently. He'd finished his first joint and was sprawled out on the sofa, shoulders slumped, eyes glazed and faraway.

"So, what's the story with Faruk Hanoğlu?" I finally asked, keeping my voice as soft and reassuring as possible.

"Oh yeah, that. It's kind of complicated."

"Do tell . . ."

"As you know, my brother helped them out now and again."

Actually, I knew no such thing. In fact, I'd planned to confess that I'd never even met Volkan. But I said nothing as I sat there, gazing benignly at him. Refik looked on, as curious as can be, forcing a smile as he listened to Okan. The expression on his face was that of a mother braced for the worst but ever hopeful as she consulted a teacher about her good-for-nothing child. His eyes were trained on

Okan's lips; it was obvious that they hadn't discussed any of this before. Depending on what Okan said, Refik would have to seriously
revise his personal history with Volkan.

"How exactly did he help them?" Refik asked.

Okan looked over at Refik as though trying to place him.

"He'd arrange girls and stuff when asked. For customers . . ."

Yet another dark chapter in the life of Volkan was unfolding: his
role as a pimp. It was anyone's guess who had been peddled to
whom. When I considered Faruk Hanoğlu's client portfolio, the
names just kept on coming.

"Sometimes he'd go over himself . . . to loaded broads and all
that . . ."

I was watching Refik out of the corner of my eye. He was
growing tenser by the minute. Was his new lover about to confirm
that the brother, his former lover, had been a gigolo?

"You mean he was a gigolo?" I asked, eyes still on Refik.

"I suppose so," said Okan.

Refik's face ran like a watercolor. I savored the sight.

"My brother wasn't into it, but the money was good. But lately,
when work came in, he'd try to get out of it. He had plenty of
money. Said it wasn't worth putting up with those rich bitches' bad
breath."

Refik sat up straight, eyes wide, biting his lower lip.

"Did you ever visit any of those ladies?"

Refik's eyes blazed at Okan, and he was no doubt furious with
me, too, for having dared ask such a thing.

"Nope," Okan said. "I got no time for that stuff . . . I'm a boy
lover. Through and through."

Lowering his eyes bashfully, he proudly smiled at Refik.

What a family, I thought to myself.

"What about your brother-in-law?" I asked. "Ziya . . ."

"He's all talk!" he said, grinning unpleasantly. "All talk and no
action."

"What if he killed your brother? They'd had a falling out. He tried to stab him once . . ."

"No way!" he said. "He hasn't got the balls."

"Faruk Hanoğlu and his men could well have killed Volkan," I said.

"Come on," he drawled. "If he'd had him killed, why'd they come looking for me later? Some dog-suckler pimp of a gypsy bitch knifed my brother. I'm sure of it. The pimp bastard probably wasn't happy with the money Volkan gave him. And if his whore told him she'd been to a five-star hotel, he'd have held out for even more. Then, when my brother didn't give it to him, he stabbed him. Volkan should never have gotten mixed up with those types. He was asking for it. And it was a big mistake to hold back the dough, of course. But how was he supposed to know? That's what I think. Why else would he have been in Belgrade forest?"

"Surely Volkan's clients wouldn't have asked him to arrange for some third-rate hooker."

"That's what you think! You wouldn't believe the types they're after. The lowest of the low. Straight from the whorehouse. Some big-mouthed, rough-talking bitch who'll do what their wives and mistresses won't. Different strokes for different folks, and we got all types in this country, my friend."

There was no point in getting into the sexology and sociology of our beloved homeland.

"What did you mean when you said Faruk Hanoğlu came looking for you? What did he want?"

"To help me, what do you think?" he said. "He was a real class act, that guy. When he was in jail, his lawyer came and asked me if there was anything I needed. They kept the press off my back, gave me some cash. They told me not to get the wrong idea about the money, said Volkan had been an employee, even if he hadn't had insurance or nothing. They're the ones who arranged the funeral, even said they'd have prayers read at the memorial service. When he got out of jail, he called me himself. His wife called, too. They invited me over to their house. They said Volkan was like a son to them, treated me real good. Faruk was a great guy. I'm sorry to hear he's dead."

Even if I hadn't visited the very same Faruk Hanoğlu just the previous night—and even if his treatment of me hadn't been so abhorrent—I would have found his special interest in Okan to be highly suspicious.

"Have you never wondered why Faruk was so good to you?"

"So I'd keep my mouth shut; you think I'm stupid, or what?"

"Keep your mouth shut about what, exactly?"

"The girls. All the pimping they did. We're talking high society here. 'They all do it, but it's always hush-hush,' Volkan would say. May he rest in peace . . ."

Refik jumped in with a heartfelt "amen."

"You've been to their house, haven't you!"

"Hang on! I said I didn't go last night. Not that I never went."

"But?" I stammered. "If you weren't there last night . . ."

This could only mean that Okan had been recorded by the camera on a different night. According to the police, last night's footage contained both Okan and me. The answer to the riddle was obvious. Someone had rigged the recordings. The camera was pointed at what was usually an empty garden or doorway. It would have been easy enough to splice in footage of Okan from another night. I wondered how I looked. The camera would have been positioned at an angle to capture faces.

"I think I know what happened," I said, and explained.

"That's pretty smart," Okan said. "That way they're fooling the police, too. Perfect."

"Yes, but you're the one taking the bullet," I reminded him. "Perfect!"

Refik made his presence known with a tiny high-pitched scream meant to express shock and horror.

"Nothing will happen to him?" he said. "Don't terrify us like that, I beg you. We're only just recovering from the deepest anguish."

He really was worried, but I couldn't decide if he was a total idiot or if he was just pretending to be one. I didn't deign to respond.

"What did you talk about with them, at their house?"

"Nothing much . . . They invited me to stay for dinner. Then we had cake and coffee . . . What a house, huh? More like a palace!"

"So they just invited you over for a social chat?"

"Yeah . . ." he said. "Oh, and they asked me to bring Volkan's address book and some other things with me."

Intriguing. My brain and teeth were set on edge.

"What 'things'?"

"Whatever I had. Bank books, business cards, videocassettes . . . That kind of stuff. They paid good money for it. In dollars, cash on the barrel."

"*Ayol*, a regular mopping up operation," I said. "Sounds like the CIA. They gathered up all the evidence and destroyed it. Without a trace. I still don't understand why they felt the need to be so thorough, though . . ."

"But what's going to happen to Okan now?" said Refik, sticking his nose into the conversation again. He'd adopted the arrogant and quarrelsome look of the parent who has decided to blame any bad news on the teacher.

"How am I supposed to know, *ayol!*" I said. "Things are mixed up enough as it is. I still think they were looking for a fall guy. And Okan's the chump who's going to get nailed for all of this. Once he's inside, there will be no one left to squeal. Cleanest job in the world!"

"Thank you ever so much, sister, for your encouraging words. *Ayol*, people don't talk like that to their worst enemies. Not that anyone needs enemies with friends like you. Here I am, trying to ask your advice, and what do you do? I hope you're pleased with yourself. And someone like you, with your record of sleuthing and snooping and crime solving . . . I really must deplore your insensitivity. I hope you know that."

That final sentence was punctuated with a ducking of the chin that only served to expand his jowls.

I ignored his pleas for help. There wasn't anything left to talk about. Even if Volkan's killer was still at large, it didn't matter anymore. How could anyone hope to get the better of such a well-organized and powerful racket? Everything was running like clockwork. Evidence of the slightest misstep or mistake was eliminated with the force of an atomic bomb.

"Cat got your tongue, sister? You're as quiet as a nightingale with a beak full of mulberries . . ."

"It's nothing," I said. "Everything's been set in motion. I was just trying to figure out if there's anything we can to do to stop it."

Okan turned to Refik with a giggle.

"Do you know why nightingales are so quiet after they eat mulberries?" he asked.

"What on earth are you talking about?" Refik scolded him. "You're a bit too happy-go-lucky for your own good. We're talking about you, and what's going to happen to you . . . and you just sit there grinning."

Slapping his knees, Okan had a fit of the giggles. I put it down to the strain, not the joints. Spluttering and giggling, he managed to choke out a few sentences.

"When the nightingale eats mulberries it gets the runs. With every squawk, it goes plop! So it shuts up and stops squawking . . . İsfendiyar Dayı told us that back in the village. It plopped into my head. Plop! The runs! A squawk . . . and a plop!"

He felt compelled to demonstrate with his hand just where the plop was produced.

Confronted by our icy faces, our little nightingale seemed astonished that we weren't laughing at his squawks and plops. He suddenly stopped his guffawing and presented us with a surprisingly serious expression, considering how stoned he was.

"I didn't say I handed over everything, did I? That would have meant drying up my money supply . . . What kind of patsy do you take me for, anyway? . . . Of course I kept a few things for my own protection."

Chapter 29

$\mathcal{E}$very time I thought I'd sorted things out, events took another unexpected turn. Everyone I came across turned out to be a double-dealing trickster of some kind, and I had no idea where their stories were leading me. As if the lies weren't bad enough, they all had something to conceal. Now I had Okan, who I'd taken for a junkie and a simpleton, declaring with glazed eyes that he, too, had something to hide.

It wouldn't be easy to get a straight story out of Okan, but it was definitely doable.

First, I would have to silence Refik's protests and lock him into the bathroom. His cries of "Please don't wreck my house!" and "Don't hit my face!" were getting on my nerves.

Ever merciful, I promised to spare his house and his face. Then I added, "If possible."

Okan was made of sterner stuff. All it had taken to put Refik out of action was a swift chop to the back of the neck, from which it would take him considerable time to regain consciousness. I intended to honor my promise to Refik, but had no choice but to empty a bucket of cold water over Okan's head, drenching a precious carpet in the process. Well, I *had* mentally crossed my fingers, and the living room had escaped *serious* damage.

When it came to Okan, now dripping wet, I'm afraid I had to resort to physical violence. As various bits of the boy's anatomy were twisted and wrenched, he became most cooperative, chatty even; backhanded slaps and flying kicks of medium severity were

less effective, as often as not provoking nothing but drugged slur-
ring, weeping, and snatches of village folk songs. All too often he'd
retract what he'd just said, contradict himself, or blurt out utter
nonsense.

By the time I'd extracted the information I required, it was getting dark.

Much of what I'd learned was confusing to the point of incom-
prehensibility. According to Okan, everyone from the money-lender
mafia to antiquities smugglers was in on the action. And as for our
brothers, they were smack dab in the middle of it all. Okan was not
the dolt he appeared to be. He had comprehended and deduced all
he needed to cover his own ass and remain a step ahead. Under
considerable duress, he'd kindly pulled the key to Volkan's safe-
deposit box out of his pocket and handed it over to me.

It was too late to go to the bank. In any case, I wasn't certain I'd
be able to access the safe-deposit box without being cross-examined.
I didn't even know if possession of a key was sufficient, or if identi-
fication of some kind had to be produced. Years ago, when I was a
child, my mother had taken me with her to the bank. All I could remember was that she kept her more valuable jewels in a box there,
believing it to be more secure than our home. When she visited the
bank to retrieve her special necklace and rings for the wedding of
my doe-eyed cousin, Seher Abla, she took me along. Every time we
ran into Seher Abla's fiancé, Oktay, he'd cry out, "What a cute kid,"
and spend the longest time hugging me, jiggling me on his lap,
sniffing at my neck and under my ears, and kissing my cheeks. At
the wedding, I was so jealous I refused to talk to anyone. Most of
the guests tactfully blamed it on too much rich food, but my mother
was embarrassed and my father furious.

However Volkan had reached the decision to stash away some
potentially explosive documents, he'd been wise to do so. The man
I'd considered to be nothing but a well-hung, handsome, part-time
gigolo deserved a second appraisal. Having the presence of mind,

right from the beginning, to store in a secure place all kinds of papers, private phone numbers, hotel invoices, and even documents
of a more official nature indicated a calculating intelligence and a
well-developed sense of organization, if nothing else. I was as curious as can be but would have to wait until tomorrow. And if it
turned out that Okan had been lying about the contents of the
safe-deposit box, he would live to regret it. The police were still
after him, and he had nowhere to go, couldn't even leave Refik's
flat. He was a wanted man. Unless the police got to him first, he
would be all mine.

I called Cihad2000 the moment I stepped out onto the street.

"I think I'm onto something important," he began.

"Tell me quick. I'm dying to know what it is."

"Have you arranged the hotel room?"

"Believe me, I haven't had a chance," I said.

"Forget it!" he said. "I've been here all day working like a don-
key for you and you couldn't find the time to reserve a hotel room.
Forget it."

"I think I've stumbled onto something important, too," I said.
"I won't know for sure until tomorrow morning. Come on, tell me
what you found out."

"It's not fair! I'm expected to tell you everything, but you
haven't got anything for me. You owe me big time. We'll talk later.
I'm fed up with the whole business. I mean it, I've had it. Get me
Pamir Hanım. Tonight. It'll be a good deed in God's eyes . . ."

"I'll call you back later," I said, hanging up. I was focused on a
case involving two murders, and all he could think about was
hanky-panky. If whatever he'd found out was so important, he
wouldn't have been able to keep it from me. It couldn't be all that
valuable.

I was stuck in commuter traffic. The taxi barely inched forward.
Once again, I considered and rejected the idea of getting out and
walking home.

I was tired. And confused. I imagined how nice it would be to arrange a house call by a masseur. How nice to be kneaded and pummeled, then to fall into a deep sleep.

But I had work to do. First I'd call Pamir and arrange a hotel, then I'd have to contact Ponpon to organize a visit to Faruk Bey's house, even if it was just to pay my respects along with hordes of others. Next on the list was a little chat with Ziya Göktaş. I'd hurt my hands beating up Okan. How amateurish, I thought. Or was I just getting old and careless? I immediately banished the thought. It was unthinkable!

As we drove past the Conrad Hotel, I remembered its wonderful views and cake shop, and decided to reserve the room myself, in person. Ignoring the grumblings of the driver, I insisted he turn around and drop me off in front of the hotel.

A room with a whirlpool looking out on the Bosphorus would cost a small fortune, but Cihad2000 could afford to splurge. It was better than making a donation to some frivolous charitable foundation.

I ordered a slice of the divine pear cake, along with a cup of weak tea.

As the smiling waitress served me, I began placing phone calls. Pamir was hard to reach. I had to call several times before I got through.

"*Ay*, I was dyeing my hair. That's why I couldn't answer," she said. "Red, just like the flag!"

I broke the news of her evening rendezvous with Cihad2000.

"But what if the dye doesn't take? I mean, what if it turns out bright orange or something? I'm not setting foot outside the house if that happens, I swear it!"

"He'll still want you," I said. "And even if he doesn't like it, so what? It's a favor after all."

"Don't say that. You're taking out all the passion."

"Look, darling Pamir. It's got nothing to do with passion. Just be yourself. And be strict with him!"

"Alright then. I'll wear leather."

"Good choice," I commended her. "I'll call you later to let you know the exact time."

I dug into my pear cake, light as a feather. As I raised my shoulders and tilted my head back to heighten the heavenly experience, I realized my eyes were half closed. I may even have moaned. It was that good.

Recharged, I called Cihad2000 to fill him in on Pamir. His breathing grew heavier as he listened.

"Now," he croaked.

"Don't be ridiculous, she's dyeing her hair. It'll take at least another couple of hours."

"Fine then," he said. I gave him the reservation number. He'd have to confirm his credit card by telephone or e-mail.

"Now tell me what you've found out," I said, leaning back and taking a swallow of warm tea.

"I forwarded it all to your computer," he said. "I thought it'd be a nice surprise when you got home. It'll take too long to explain now. A lot of bank account transfers. Lists of names from around the world, some of them familiar. Large sums, small sums . . . Nonstop money traffic. International accounts and local banks . . . I haven't deciphered all the information yet, but I've got more than enough to give us a good idea. You'll see."

"But what good will any of that do? What are we supposed to do with these Telekom lists?"

"We've got access to the private records of almost anyone you can think of. A long list of names. It'll be child's play to hack any bank."

"It already is," I said, lightly pressing the last forkful of pastry against my palate with my tongue.

"Good luck to you then, *bacı*."

"Since when have you addressed me as 'elder sister'?"

"God willing, you're now a big sister to me. No one has ever done me a favor like this. No one."

I still planned to call Ponpon, but I'd do it when I got home. Brother-in-law Ziya could wait, too. I'd been tired even before dessert; now I was about to be overcome with drowsiness. Even a massage seemed like too much trouble. I paid the cheerful waitress and got into a taxi waved over by the doorman, tall and well built in his cape and top hat. As he closed the door for me, he shot me a smile that, though courteous, let me know that he was on to me. I was too exhausted to flirt, and simply nodded my appreciation.

I nearly dozed off in the taxi. It was all I could do to stay awake.

When I got home, there in front of the apartment building was a police car waiting to take me to the station.

Chapter 30

*f*ortunately, the police were most polite. Once again, my friendship with Selçuk had done me no harm. It was "sir" this and "sir" that. Exhausted, I calmly did all they asked and produced perfectly plausible responses to all their questions.

There was the matter of my visit to Faruk Hanoğlu. Why had I gone to see him, and when? How long I had stayed? What was the exact nature of our relationship? How well I'd known him, and such . . . They were simply gathering as much information as possible, that was all. A routine interview. Nothing to be concerned about. Not yet, anyway.

Nothing was asked about Okan, and nothing volunteered. With Okan so terrified of the police, he'd have no choice but to spend a couple more days with Refik Altın, at their love nest. Within a couple of days, everything would be clear, in any case.

I was certain that they'd interpreted my fatigue as boredom, therefore assuming that all I told them was true. My testimony was typed up. After glancing over it, I signed a copy. I was thanked, and a policeman went so far as to accompany me to the exit, no doubt due to his respect for, and fear of, Commissioner Selçuk. Shaking my hand as we parted, he said, "Give my regards to the chief."

I was deposited in front of my building by the same car that had taken me off to the station an hour earlier.

At last, I could crawl into my inviting, empty bed, with particular emphasis on the word "empty." Were John Pruitt or even Haluk Pekerdem to come calling, I'd have politely turned them away. I was that tired. As I got undressed, I took the large safe-deposit box key out of my trouser pocket and placed it on the nightstand. I'm normally a tidy person, some would even say compulsive, but for tonight I simply tossed my clothes onto the low armchair near the bed.

It would take an alert mind to go through the lists forwarded to me by Cihad2000. That could wait until morning. It was nearly nine o'clock. Cihad2000 and Pamir would be going at it by now, I thought. Then I was out cold.

A blissfully deep sleep and delightful dreams were cut short by the endless ringing of the phone. Even worse, the call had been placed not to the line attached to the answering machine, but to my modem, the number of which even I didn't know. It seemed the ringing would never stop; I'd have to answer it.

Opening a single eye, I peered at the alarm clock. It was well after midnight.

I dragged myself into my home office and produced my grimmest "*Alo.*"

"I just called to thank you" came the voice of Cihad2000. "I haven't woken you?"

"I was sleeping. Anyway, I'm awake now."

"It was amazing, better than any of my fantasies. I couldn't get enough. It was so . . . punishing."

"I'm so happy for you," I said.

"Anyway, you'd better get back to bed. We'll talk tomorrow. I'm too wound up to sleep. Maybe I'll get some more work done. Oh, by the way, have you had a look at the lists I sent? Did you find anything useful?"

"You wouldn't believe how exhausted I was. I passed out the second I got home."

"Alright, alright. I can take a hint. Sorry. Tomorrow then . . ."

"Okay." I yawned.

He thanked me again before hanging up.

It had been a short call, but I was now fully awake. I went back to bed, hoping for the best. The covers were still warm. I pulled them up to my chin.

I started imagining what I'd find when I opened the safe-deposit box the next day. It'd be just like a film. I'd walk in and open the box with my key. The name of the bank, branch code, and box number were all engraved on the key, after all. In order to ensure that I'd be able to stride right past the lines of envious bank customers, with a curt nod directed at the deferential manager, I'd have to follow the example of my mother, chin high, eyes straight ahead, and dressed to genteel advantage. I could only guess at the dirty laundry that awaited me. It might lead me not only to Volkan's killer, but to that of loan shark Faruk as well. It's true that the police were on the case, but they now had me to contend with as well.

I turned over onto my other side, completely altering my train of thought. Volkan was just Volkan, and Faruk just Faruk. And both were dead. But then there was Haluk Pekerdem . . . Ah, that Haluk Pekerdem. I tried to picture him lying next to me. And failed. It just wasn't happening.

I was feeling sleepy again. But I thought I heard strange sounds in the flat. I froze and listened carefully. Yes, someone was in my flat. Perhaps even more than one person. Whoever they were, they hadn't turned on a light. It could only mean trouble.

I considered confronting them. I was half dressed and barefoot. It's true that shoes aren't necessarily required for Thai boxing, but this wasn't a question of fun and games. It could well be a question of life and death. As always, the right shoes were essential. And then there was the damage that might be caused to my flat, my home. Life and property both hung in the balance!

I was just sitting up when two shadows appeared before me. I'd have had to be blind not to notice the glinting barrel of a gun pointed right at me. Both of them wore ski masks. I guessed that they were male, strong, and young.

The one nearest me seemed somehow more alert and in charge. Indeed, he spoke first.

"Give me the key," he hissed, waving the gun at my nose.

I'd have to think carefully before springing to action. And springing out of a prone position would be no easy matter.

"What key?" I said, buying time.

"Don't play dumb. The first question is always 'who are you?' or 'what do you want?' I'd expected more of you. Don't drag this out. And don't try any tricks."

Well, at least he had a sense of humor. The voice was unfamiliar.

"That last line of yours was a bit hackneyed," I said, reaching for the lamp.

He rapped my hand with the gun.

"We won't be getting married or anything. There's no need for that light."

"But how I am supposed to see what I'm doing, sweetie?" I asked.

I'd hoped to be able to spring out of bed and onto my feet.

"Now if you'll just allow me to get up."

He pushed me back onto the bed with his gun.

"We know all about your special skills. It's better you stay like that. We don't want to hurt you. Just hand over the key . . ."

Good for Okan. So, he'd sent a pack of his dogs after me. Or he'd hired some. Well, he did have the backing of the Hanoğlu family.

"So," I said. "What am I supposed to do?"

"Just tell me where the key is. I'll get it myself."

"Who sent you? Okan?"

"You talk too much!"

He pressed the gun into me, just under my chin. So that's what's meant by "looking down the icy barrel . . ." It was freezing.

Actually, I was glad he hadn't switched on a light. For one thing, he would have noticed the key on the nightstand right next to me.

For another, he hadn't yet considered that I had the home-court advantage. I knew the exact location of every stick of furniture in my flat, as well as the positions of every potential weapon. Anything I got my hands on could be smashed into him or his partner.

With the gun sticking into my chin, I couldn't see the other intruder. But I sensed that he was close to the foot of the bed. Right around where my knees were.

I did a quick calculation.

"It's right next to me, by the table light."

As he reached toward the nightstand, he turned his head to look for the key. Big mistake! And mistakes are never handier than at moments like these.

The blow to his kidneys with my strong right hand surely cracked two ribs. The other man took a reverse kick to the face and was buckled over and bellowing.

By the time the gun was pointed at me again I was on my feet and standing right between them. It's my favorite position. Nothing's more fun than leaping into the air and smashing a leg into one assailant, a turned foot into the other. Throw a midair spin into the equation, and it's sheer joy.

I did it!

When I landed, there was now a gun in my hand.

We stood there, at the corners of a triangle. The partner, who hadn't yet spoken, was now unarmed and no doubt dumbstruck at the loss of his weapon.

"Enough already!" said the one in charge. "Put it down."

"You put yours down," I said. "My gun's as good as yours."

As I took a step back, I checked the safety catch. It wasn't on. They meant business. Still, it seemed a heavy weapon for a job like this. I'd have chosen something smaller, lighter, more elegant—chic shiny steel beats dull black any time. After all, they weren't on safari! They'd set out to break into a flat and shoot at close range, if necessary, a person—not a wild boar!

Stamping his foot like a petulant child, "Drop it!" said Mr. Take Charge.

My gun trained on him, his on me, I reached over and grabbed the key.

"Drop it!" he said.

"Hah, you're repeating yourself!" I scolded. Then I bluffed. "I recognize your voice."

He said nothing.

I shoved the key into my underwear. These days, I sleep in designer label boxers left over from my old lover. Not only are they manly, they're sexy as hell. I mean, if Madonna can get away with it, why can't I?

The key was cold. I tingled.

"Don't push us," he said in a low voice. "We don't want to hurt you. This has got nothing to do with you. Give me the key and we'll forget all about it."

The other one was still rubbing his nose. Not being in possession of a weapon, he concentrated on licking his wounds.

There would be that can of pepper spray on the dressing table, if I could reach it. It looked like an ordinary can of deodorant. I'd bought it when self-defense techniques became all the rage after the explosion in purse snatching. I'd never actually used it, though.

Actually, I had no idea whether it would do any good. After all, the three of us were breathing the same air, and in close proximity to each other. No, I'd have to rely, once again, on my skills in Thai boxing.

Chapter 31

When they came to, they had been stripped of their ski masks and were stretched out on the floor. Arms handcuffed behind their backs! It hadn't occurred to me that rabbit fur handcuffs could be used for such serious business, but *voilà*! It sure beat fussing with clothesline . . . And as for me, I was wrapped in an embroidered red kimono on loan from Ponpon, legs crossed as I sat directly in front of them. One of the guns was in my hand, the other resting nearby.

The first one to open his eyes was the partner. A supporting actor, I said to myself. An extra, even. He'd also been the first to pass out.

"Hello," I said. "Are you alright?"

He floundered for a bit, then stopped when he realized he'd been cuffed.

"Argh?"

"What a big baby. You keeled over at the first blow. You're just not built for this line of work."

He tried hopping to his feet. And failed, managing only to rock in place.

"Argh?"

Either he was a complete idiot or he simply didn't understand me. I'd kicked him in the head, but surely hadn't cause brain damage. No, I couldn't have!

"Speak up, *ayol*!"

Wide-eyed, he stared at me.

"He can't talk. Don't bother . . ." said the other one.

I hadn't noticed in the darkness, but now that they were open and the lights on, I saw that the one in charge had huge, dark blue eyes. Liquid eyes, as though he was on the verge of tears. His thin lips made him look suitably tough, however.

"He's a mute," he clarified.

"Well then, I guess you'll get to do all the talking," I said.

"What do you want me to say? You're in big trouble, and it's getting bigger all the time. There are only two of us. You polished us off. Bravo! But what about the next time? And the next? How much can you take? How many can you handle?"

"My, don't you talk pretty," I said. "I could listen to you all day."

"Go on, keep making fun. When you finally realize what you're up against, it'll be too late."

"I already know all about them. Now tell me who sent you."

He was smarter than the other one. Instead of simply writhing around, he was checking out his cuffs while trying to turn onto his side.

"I tested them out. They're sound," I said. "Strong enough, anyway . . ."

"That's enough. You've had your fun. And we can see that you're a good fighter. Now take off the cuffs and let us go."

"Go? Go where?" I asked. "We were just getting warmed up."

"Look," he said. "What are you going to do? You can't kill us, so you'll have to let us go. So don't push me. Take off the cuffs!"

The liquid eyes grew even larger, and filled with malice.

"Maybe I'll call the cops."

"You wouldn't dare. You're in trouble, too. And you lied to them." Bending his knees, he tried to sit up. From a seated position, it wouldn't be all that difficult to stand up. And if he stood up, I'd have to chase him around the flat. A light kick sent him sprawling. It was safer that way.

"First, you'll talk!" I said. "If you don't, I'll keep you here, like a dog or a cat. Both of you! It could go on for days or weeks. I wouldn't mind one bit."

"You wouldn't dare!"

"Just try me!"

Picking up the second gun, I went to the office. I immediately found what I'd come for: duct tape.

When I returned, the one with the functioning vocal cords was still babbling. I wasn't having it. I stuck two lengths of tape over his mouth. That shut him up. Then I wrapped tape around his ankles. His range of action had been severely curtailed, giving me the peace of mind to roam freely about the house.

I was just about to go when I decided that the fur cuffs weren't all that dependable, and I wrapped some tape around their wrists as well. I appraised my work: Yes, it was pleasing to the eye and completely secure.

The sun would be rising soon, and I was getting hungry. Not a single crumb of that scrumptious pear dessert remained in my stomach.

"Now, I want the two of you to lie there, nice and well-behaved. I'll be around if there's anything you want to tell me . . ."

Silly me. Their mouths were taped.

"Scratch that last bit. Anyway, I'll be around."

I'd finished off Ponpon's breakfast offerings. It was too early for vegetables cooked in olive oil, and there was no more cake, börek, or poğaca. I decided on a classic breakfast of toast, jam, and a two-egg cheese omelette . . . or would soft-boiled be better? Yes, definitely soft-boiled.

The bread toasted while the eggs boiled. I had to check on my guests from time to time. There was no telling what they might get up to. Back and forth I went, from the kitchen to the bedroom, where they lay side by side, like a couple of sacks of potatoes. What I needed was some music, low enough that it wouldn't disturb the neighbors but high enough to mask any grunting and groaning. Furthermore, music was an integral part of my morning routine. Nothing beats Handel, but melodious baroque harmonies would never camouflage the sound of me shouting at them, or perhaps, even, of furniture being shattered. My eye landed on Dusty Spring-field's double album *Something Special*. I hadn't listened to it for ever so long. I must have missed it, for it was playing a moment later.

This time I managed to rescue the bread from the minioven be-fore it burned. It smelled wonderful. Placing my eggs and tea on a huge tray, I carried it to the bedroom. No change, except that they seemed to be eyeing my tray a bit hungrily.

"Let me know when you're ready to talk," I said. "You'll get some chow and your freedom."

I get a pang every time I listen to "What Are You Doing the Rest of Your Life?" What a voice. Pure emotion, and no histrionics. It's my favorite Dusty piece, along with "The Windmills of Your Mind." Marmalade-slathered piece of toast in hand, I went off to play it again. No one writes a ballad like Michel Legrand, with the possible exceptions of Burt Bacharach and Michel Berger.

Once upon a time I'd presented someone with what I consid-ered a highly meaningful compilation cassette consisting entirely of different versions of this song. The lyrics "What are you doing the rest of your life? . . . I have only one request of your life, that you spend it all with me . . ." seemed to encapsulate perfectly all of my hopes and dreams. The idiot found the song too "heavy" and gave the cassette to someone else. Naturally, that was the end of our relationship.

My trip down memory lane ended with my breakfast. On the way to the kitchen with the tray, I gave the mute a good poke with my foot.

"I know you can't talk, but I can always get you a pen and paper. Your friend's too pigheaded. Think it over!"

I was dying to have a long shower, look over the files sent by

Cihad2000, and get to the bank promptly at the stroke of nine to see what was in that box. While I had plenty of time, I was too paranoid to turn my back on my guests. Yes, they were bound and gagged, but even so.

I needed someone to watch them for me. Ponpon would pop over in a jiffy. But she'd panic in a situation like this. I could call Hasan. He was a cool character. But he was having troubles of his own, and it wouldn't do to get him mixed up in all of this, too. I decided on İpekten. She was strong, dependable, and bold to the point of being a bit rash. What's more, she adored this kind of thing.

I didn't hesitate to call her on the spot, especially knowing that she'd still be up. She answered on the second ring. There was no need to go into details. I simply told her she was needed.

"At your service, my lord," she said. "Give me ten minutes to fly to your side, hubby!"

İpekten's a real scream. She always finds a way to make me laugh.

The prisoner with the voice had begun squirming.

"What's up?" I asked. "Ready to talk?"

He blinked.

Kneeling next to him, I ripped off the tape in one swift movement. It was something like a beard waxing. I had to muffle his shouts with my hand.

"I'm so sorry," I said. "I knew full well how much it would hurt . . ."

"I'll get you back one day," he hissed.

"Sure you will. We'll talk about that when it happens. Right now, you're all mine. So speak up."

"I haven't got anything to say," he said. "I have to pee."

I froze.

"What?"

"I need to get to the toilet. Or do you want me to go on the floor?"

I hadn't foreseen this. It never happens in films or books, so I had no clue how to proceed. I thought for a moment.

"I'm not freeing you."

"What do you expect me to do, pee right here?"

No, I didn't want him peeing in my bedroom, not right on my pale pink carpet.

"Look, just free my legs and you can walk me to the bathroom."

That didn't sound like a bad idea.

I went off to fetch one of the guns. I'd wrapped the tape around the cuffs of his trousers, not on his bare skin. I wouldn't get to wax his legs.

"Take it nice and slow. You can't imagine the consequences if you try anything funny . . ."

"I know what you're capable of . . ."

Ducking under his arm, I helped him to his feet. He leaned all his weight against me, and I nearly lost my balance. Despite the late hour and all the tussling, he still smelled faintly of aftershave.

Gun thrust into his back, I walked him to the bathroom.

"Well, I'll leave you to it!" I said.

With bruising coming out on one of his cheeks, the other one seemed strangely pale. "You'll have to help me," he smirked. "I can't get my pants down."

I hadn't thought about that one either.

With his arms cuffed behind his back, he was helpless. Not only would he expect me to lower his trousers, I'd have to point his willie at the toilet bowel, and even give it a good shake when he was done.

The doorbell rang just in the nick of time. It must be İpekten.

I hesitated for a moment. Then I hastily unfastened his belt and pulled his trousers and white briefs down to just below his knees.

"Aren't you going to hold it?" he asked, with a filthy grin. I smacked him full across his bruised cheek.

"Sit down to pee!" I shouted as I marched off to open the front door.

Chapter 32

Just as I'd expected, it was İpekten.

There she stood, grinning ear to ear, enormous eyes filled with curiosity.

"Here I am to the rescue!"

A toss of her Wonder Woman mane of hair was enough to re-store calm. The girls all imagine themselves to be up on the latest fashions. Some of them model themselves on my idol, Audrey; others are still stuck in their seventies Bearded Barbie phase. But İpekten is something else. She slavishly follows *Harper's Bazaar*'s picks of the month, from hairstyle and color, skirt length and matching accessories, right through to scent, makeup, and length of nails and shade of polish. Even the shampoo and soap in her bathroom gets a monthly update!

I summarized things for her as we went inside.

"I'll shit in their mouths! Break in, did they? And in the middle of the night, no less. And you still nursing a broken heart. Well, I never!"

"What's that got to do with it? . . ." I began.

"Maybe it's irrelevant, maybe it's not! That's not the point. The point is, they're clearly deranged. It's a wound in the social fabric, it is. Completely sociological. Did I say logical? Well, there's not a trace of that, honey! That's the problem. I'll knock some sense into them. They're all mine now. Dr. Mengele has nothing on me."

"Sweetie," I pleaded, "please don't ramble on. I'm just not up to it. I don't think I can take it."

"Well, alright then, hubby . . . You're in a deep depression, after all. You think you're over it, but you're not, of course. Who can snap out of something like that in just a couple of days? Don't you agree? I mean, look what happened to Virginia Woolf. You've seen *The Hours*. And there are other films, too . . . This is serious stuff. No one pulls through just like that. No, it always leaves a scar. Deep down . . ."

"İpekten!"

"Alright, alright!" she pouted. "If you invited me over just to shut me up . . ."

I handed her one of the guns.

"Do you know how to use this?" I asked.

"*Ayol*, I did my military service, same as everyone else. And I never miss. Don't worry, hubby."

I let her know that the body on the floor was a mute.

"I'll have him singing like a pressure cooker," she trilled. "That tongue'll be wagging in no time! . . ."

Purple Cheek had come out of the bathroom, trousers down around his ankles, and taken penguin steps as far as the door to the bedroom.

"I'm afraid I couldn't flush it," he apologized sardonically.

İpekten turned her head to look at the newcomer.

"Ah! Sarp? What are you doing here?"

For several moments, three pair of eyes traveled from face to face. There was deadly silence.

"Who on earth is Sarp?" I finally asked, surprised and a bit panicked.

İpekten eyes's shifted from me, to Sarp, down to his limp manhood, and then back to me again.

"You see . . ."

"You slept with him?" I interrupted.

"You could say that . . ."

Either they had or they hadn't.

"So you did . . ." I said, pointing the gun at the floor. It suddenly seemed heavy.

"Uh-huh . . ." she said, feigning embarrassment. The shameless hussy.

Now we all avoided each other's eyes. What an unpleasant development. The person I'd called for help turned out to be my assailant's lover.

We both turned to look at Sarp, who was speaking.

"Would one of you mind pulling up my underwear?"

İpekten sprang to his side, seizing the opportunity to plant a small kiss just where his waistband snapped into place.

"İpekten! Really!"

"Oh, come on, he's a good kid, actually."

She was standing right next to him, one of the guns in her hand. It was like one of those scenes where the heroine switches sides, goes over to the forces of evil.

"But he broke into my house. Assault and battery with a deadly weapon," I protested, getting a firmer grip on my gun and waving it about a bit. "And he won't even tell me who put him up to it."

İpekten took two steps in my direction, glancing now and again at me, then back at Sarp. Nothing's worse than doubting an old friend. But once you've got a man in the picture, friendship goes out the window. She made up her mind.

"Who hired you? You'll tell us, won't you?" she said to him.

"Don't be stupid!" Sarp muttered out of the corner of his mouth.

"What kind of an answer is that?" asked İpekten, running her fingers through his hair. It wasn't a good sign, but it was still too early to take action. "Talking like that to me of all people. And in front of my best friend, no less . . . Well, I won't stand for it!"

"You just don't get it!" shouted Sarp. "You're a couple of clueless shitheads!"

"Look, lion boy, watch who you're calling 'shithead.' When I blow my top, I blow it big time. I'll shit in your mouth, I will. I'll wipe that sneer right off your face. That tackle you're so proud of won't do you any good when I get through with it. Do I make my- self clear?"

She dug the gun into Sarp's crotch and opened the safety with a click chillingly audible to us all.

This was getting interesting.

Sarp had no intention of talking. Even worse, he was insolent about it. A crooked smile on his face, he even threatened us with a long list of likely retributions.

We had no choice but to wrap more tape around his ankles and turn our attention to the mute.

"If you don't talk, we'll torture you," said İpekten.

She was serious. Even I believed her.

Eyes wide with fright, the mute stared at us.

Of course, meddlesome Sarp did all he could to discourage him.

"What's his name?" I asked.

"None of your business. It's not like you're going to get married."

Sarp seemed to think that a formal introduction inevitably leads to nuptials. It was the second time tonight he'd said that. Either he had an extremely limited vocabulary and utter lack of imagination, or he was obsessed with the wedding ceremony.

"Sorry, İpekten," I said, giving Sarp a good kick to the ribs. He'd begun to irritate me.

"Look, shake your head if you have something to say!"

İpekten was kneeling next to the mute.

"If you write a single word, you're dead. No one'll be able to save your ass. You can count on it!"

Clearly, Sarp hadn't been satisfied with a single kick. And İpekten wasn't helping me reprimand him.

Then she motioned with her head for me to follow her. The two of us went off to the kitchen, shutting the door behind us.

"I've got a plan," she whispered.

It was simple. First, we put them in separate rooms. We also had to muzzle Sarp. He was quite the chatty Cathy. And he'd gone as far as calling us "a couple of stupid fags." I have zero tolerance for the word "stupid."

We filled a hypodermic needle with the saline solution I use to clean the colored lenses I sometimes wear.

Brandishing the needle, İpekten went up to Sarp.

"It's truth serum, honey. Rohypnol. Once we inject you with this, you'll be singing like there's no tomorrow. We'll find out even more than we'd care to," she said, holding the needle in front of his nose.

The lens solution would, of course, have no physiological effect of any kind, but as a placebo we might get results. Anyway, it wasn't entirely unscientific and certainly worth a try. We'd try it out on both Sarp and the mute. It would be enough that they believed us.

"Where should we stick it in?" I asked.

"Where would it hurt most?"

"Down there, I suppose . . ." I fairly cackled.

Sarp was trembling. The cords in his neck had come out and his eyes had grown into dinner plates. I stifled a giggle.

"Pull down his pants. I'll do it," said İpekten.

Sarp struggled to move, but failed. We'd made a tidy little package out of him, nicely gagged and bound. I managed to get his trousers and underwear down and grabbed his hips so he couldn't move.

"Look here," said İpekten, "if you shake like that the tip of the needle will break off in your dick. So lie still, darling. Or talk . . ."

He was a big, strong boy, our Sarp. A regular commando. But when the needle pricked his privates he was out cold. I could have roused him with cold water but decided a good slap would work just as well.

"Open your eyes, you big lug!" I shouted. "We haven't even done it yet! You'll miss the show!"

I could only guess at the curses and threats building up inside him, but his mouth was taped shut. Those liquid eyes were petrified, glassy. It seemed we were finally getting through.

"I'm asking you for the last time," said İpekten, giving his pee-pee a poke with the needle. "Are you ready to talk?"

Sarp nodded.

I took great delight in tearing the tape off his mouth, once again uprooting mustache and beard hair in the process. His eyes flashed fire.

Gritting his teeth, he gave us our name.

"Nimet Hanım."

And he passed out again.

Chapter 33

The wife of our newly departed loan shark, Faruk Hanoğlu, came from an old family of good stock and enjoyed a reputation as a traditional lady of impeccably conservative credentials. Her name was none other than Nimet Hanoğlu! Life's full of surprises, and this one was a real doozy. Gracious wife and mother Nimet Hanoğlu had sent a pair of thugs after me. There I was, hard at work salvaging my own reputation and the good name of her husband, and she'd arranged for a couple of shantytown roughs to break into my flat! Great favors are so often repaid with ingratitude.

It was now morning. I had things to do, places to go, people to meet—and two thugs bound and gagged on my bedroom floor. I felt like a busy executive with no time to pick his teeth.

Full of energy, I took a shower, shaved quickly (twice), and applied a light coat of makeup. Meanwhile, İpekten sat in front of the TV with an enormous cup of milky coffee, a gun, and a can of pepper spray, watching a *Queer as Folk* episode she'd selected from my extensive DVD collection.

Sarp and the mute had been dragged out of the way but were still in plain view. Sarp hadn't yet regained consciousness. The mute was still trembling.

The day was sunny and my spirits high. I decided on pastels. I was thrilled at the prospect of finally getting to the bottom of this murder case. Slipping into the sweetest little beige pantsuit, I knotted a pink and yellow Hermès scarf just above the Mao collar, around which I draped a faux gold chain that hung nearly to my waist. The seventies had sprung to life. With a wide-brimmed hat I would be the spitting image of Faye Dunaway in the original 1968 version of *The Thomas Crown Affair*. A hint of Chanel No. 5 and I was set to go.

Every time I pick up a bottle of Chanel I think of the magnificently icy demeanor of Catherine Deneuve in that old ad, then I remember Marilyn Monroe replying "two drops of Chanel No. 5" when asked what she wore in bed.

I suddenly felt like Monroe, Deneuve, Dunaway, and Audrey all rolled into one. It was a bit unsettling. Such a rare cocktail of beauty and elegance could prove overly potent. I decided to remove the hat.

"Hey hubby, why'd you ditch that tray on your head?"

"*Ayol*, İpekten, just keep watching your DVD. There are some real cuties in it," I said.

"I can't concentrate. I'm keeping an eye on them . . ."

With her big toe, she pointed to Sarp and the mute.

I'd have a look at Cihad2000's e-mail when I got back home. I was determined to get into the safe-deposit box the moment the bank opened.

Under İpekten's hawklike eye, I checked my pocket any number of times to ensure that I'd remembered the key to the box. She didn't say a word, just watched. There are times when a steely eye is far more unsettling than a river of well-chosen words.

I cautioned İpekten, making her promise to keep the door bolted and not to let in any strangers until I got back.

"Don't worry, hubby," she called out after I'd closed the door behind me, deviant smile no doubt in place.

I'd been so excited I'd forgotten to call a taxi. I'd have to walk down to the main street and hail one.

Volkan's safe-deposit box was at a huge bank branch in Şişli. It was always packed. I'd been there a few times before and went straight to the assistant manager. I realized now that despite my best intentions I was a bit overdressed, but I had enough faith in my Chanel No. 5 to take a seat right across from her.

Full cheeked and under the mistaken impression that minimal makeup and unkempt hair would make her look younger, she smiled at me expectantly. In dignified, ladylike tones I explained my business, adding that I was in something of a hurry.

"Just a moment, madam," she said.

I'd expected her to ask for ID, but she dialed a number instead. The other party must have answered immediately.

"The guest we've been expecting has arrived," she said.

"What do you mean?" I thought to myself. Expected guest? Me? Who was expecting me? I'd found out about the key just the day before. Crazy Okan wouldn't have dared to tell anyone. He couldn't have. It was impossible.

I must have gone white as sheet, and hoped I'd applied enough makeup to conceal it. I held my breath and waited. Or was I simply unable to breathe? In a word, I froze. I ran through every worst-case scenario, but still couldn't imagine who had been the recipient of that phone call.

The assistant manager continued smiling at me sweetly. I studied her eyes and expression. No curiosity, excitement, or concern . . . Nothing. She faced me wearing the same pleasant mask of a few moments earlier.

Soon, in would walk the general manager, chairman of the board, or worse, and I would be discreetly led away. The police might even come. Or agents from MİT, the National Intelligence Agency. Flanked and handcuffed, I'd be asked for my name, the male name I'd been given at birth. I'd be thoroughly disgraced. Audrey Hepburn would abandon me in disgust, never to return.

Perhaps I could fight back? That depended on who came to confront me. I wouldn't hesitate to resist ordinary bank guards . . . But the police, MİT?

I could run away right now, make it out to the pavement in record time. If anyone tried to stop me, and someone surely would, I'd fight for dear life: aikido, Thai boxing, a flurry of desperate punches, kicks, and slaps.

My brain was working, but my body had frozen. I couldn't move a finger. Not a finger! I tried . . . I tried to move the hand I'd placed on the desk. Nothing. There was no response to the signals my brain was sending. I was petrified. Or paralyzed, perhaps.

I couldn't hear anything, not a sound. The clocks had frozen; time stood still. Surely no one could remain motionless and not breathing for such a long time. But I was doing just that. The woman sitting opposite me wasn't breathing either.

The telephone was ringing, ringing endlessly. Why was no one picking up?

I tested myself to see if I could remember Selçuk's phone number. I could. If worst came to worst, I could rely on him again. Anyway, it wasn't like they'd lock me up or torture me just for being in possession of a key.

"Please follow me, madam," she said as she stood up. Her silk shirt and designer scarf confirmed her position as assistant manager. She walked round the desk, stopping directly in front of me.

I followed her out of the door. I seemed to have forgotten how to walk like a lady, had adopted the springy lope my big brother taught me when I was a boy. The manager's office seemed miles away. We walked forever. The other customers all stopped and stared, eyes filled with fear, curiosity, surprise, and even a little pity.

The general manager's office was suitably spacious and decorated in cool, modern colors. There were no policemen or bodyguards. I relaxed, breathing normally. But I was convinced that my face was waxen.

Rising from behind his desk, the general manager came over to shake my hand. He must have had a background as a bank inspector. Chin thrust forward, he was overbearing, and the hand he reached out was held higher than necessary.

"Would you be the decedent's next of kin?" he asked, obviously more out of a sense of duty than of genuine interest or sympathy.

"Uh, no," I said. "I'm a friend . . ."

"As you no doubt realize, an application form for the release of safe-deposit box contents must be completed by an executor, the attorney for the estate, or the decedent's next of kin . . ."

He looked at me as though he were unraveling all the secrets of the universe for my benefit.

"You must also realize that here we face a highly unusual situation. The key holder of the box did not die as a result of what we would normally deem . . . natural causes."

"So?" I asked.

"However, if you can prove that you are an executor or next of kin, we might be able to make special arrangements. Otherwise, I'm afraid there's nothing we can do."

The beaming assistant shut her eyes and nodded her approval.

"Furthermore, we're aware that a criminal investigation is currently underway."

"Well then, the police should come and have a look. Wouldn't you agree?" I asked.

"Unless you possess documentation demonstrating your relationship . . ."

"I don't," I said. "I wasn't his wife or anything like that."

"Yes, we can see that" was his dry response.

Normally I would have been mortified, but at that moment I couldn't have cared less.

"So then," I said, "you have, of course, informed the police?"

"Not yet . . ."

"Why not?" I persisted. "As far as I understand, the police are to be notified immediately in these circumstances."

"There are certain . . . sensitivities involved," he continued, carefully choosing his words. "We make every effort, whatever the circumstances, to protect the interests of our customers . . ."

"Hmmm," I said. I raised my left eyebrow as high as it could go. "But I've got the key."

"I'm afraid that's irrelevant."

The cheery assistant was there to rubberstamp her boss's every remark. Once again, she shut her eyes and nodded affirmation. She probably had a limited set of facial expressions, smiles, and head movements, each of them appropriate to a particular situation.

We eyed one another. I looked them up and down; they did the same to me. All three of us were perfectly calm. We were still in the early stages of sizing up and assessing.

I was too close now to back down. I'd never forgive myself. I compiled a list of multiple choices:

(a) Give up and go home.
(b) Try bargaining. That's what they seemed to expect, after all.
(c) Get the police involved; that is, ask Selçuk for his help in accessing the box.
(d) Wait for them to make the first move. Only then decide on a course of action.

Neither "all of the above" nor "none of the above" were options. None of the choices satisfied me, but I decided on D before switching to B at the last second.

My self-confidence had returned, along with my sense of style. I sat down and crossed my legs.

"So, what should I do?" I asked.

Playing a dumb blonde often does the trick, but, thanks to his background as an inspector, the manager was proving to be a tough nut indeed.

"Allow me to offer you something to drink," he said. "Please take a seat . . ."

I was already sitting. I just looked at him.

Ms. Cheery sat down in the armchair opposite; the manager settled into the high-backed leather chair behind his desk.

"What would you like? A cup of Turkish coffee?"

"Unsweetened, please," I said.

The assistant had dialed the number of the beverage service already.

"I'll have one as well, Gülben Hanım."

So that was the name of the assistant now ordering herself a medium-sweet Turkish coffee.

The weather was discussed in the short time it took for the coffee to arrive.

The moment the office boy left the room with his empty tray, the manager got down to business.

"You're not the only one interested in Volkan Bey's safe-deposit box."

"Do you mean the police?"

Eyes closed, Gülben Hanım shook her head from side to side this time.

"The person in question," he continued, slurping his first sip of coffee and establishing beyond doubt his class, or lack thereof, "is one of our most valued customers."

I'd grown impatient and tossed off the first name that came to mind.

"Nimet Hanoğlu?"

Dear Gülben's eyes had narrowed, but her head remained stationary. It was either a halfhearted endorsement, or she had withheld automatic approbation at the last moment.

"You've made her acquaintance?"

"In a sense," I said, remembering what she'd sent me. No doubt, they were still sprawled out on my floor.

"What do you propose?" I suddenly asked.

They hadn't expected me to be so direct but didn't react in the least, except for exchanging glances. It didn't take a genius to see that they were in on this together, whatever it was.

"We could invite her here . . ."

"What difference would her coming here make?" I said, stubbornly playing dumb. "Is she the executor?"

They exchanged glances again as they plotted the best response. I had to hand it to them: Without a word, a sound, or even much facial movement they were able to communicate with each other perfectly.

They'd reached agreement. A sympathetic expression on his face, the manager turned to me.

"Maybe we could be of service. Provided that Nimet Hanım is allowed access first . . ."

"But that would be fraud . . ." I said.

He continued smiling. He was a cool character indeed. Good for him.

"Special clients deserve special treatment. I hope that you appreciate that."

"Of course I do, *efendim*." I smiled. "And I, too, will soon be joining the ranks of the 'special'?"

His smile widened.

"Naturally. Had you doubted it?"

"Well, what if I decide to file a complaint? I could inform the police, or ask them to open the box."

"You could, certainly," he said. "But it might not be in your best interests. We all know about . . . certain developments. You may wish to reconsider."

So, that pillar of respectability, Nimet Hanım, was acting as a kind of benefactress for the manager and his assistant. They were eating out of the palm of her hand. In a bid to get the key, not only had she sent her thugs after me, she'd also ensured that I'd be thwarted once I arrived at the bank, if I ever did.

I had no idea if Selçuk would be able to protect me if the police got involved. I couldn't risk it. What's more, for all my success in previous cases, in this one I was now a suspect—or under suspicion, at least.

If Nimet Hanım came, the box would at last be opened, and I, too, would be permitted access. But I had no way of knowing how much Nimet and her banker flunkies would actually allow me to see. I was all alone and felt quite sorry for myself. If only I had someone to support me, to encourage me and give me strength. But there was no one!

The manager broke the silence.

"So, *efendim*, what it is to be? You do realize that you're not the rightful owner of that key."

I ignored the veiled threat. It's not like they'd be able to wrest it away from me. Not here, in a bank full of customers.

"It doesn't belong to Nimet Hanım, either," I said.

He pretended to smile. But his eyes continued to bore into me.

Chapter 34

Sometimes my recklessness scares me. What was I thinking when I agreed to wait for Nimet Hanoğlu to open the safe-deposit box?

The great lady was phoned, and her presence politely requested. I was offered another cup of Turkish coffee. Gülben even went so far as to suggest that Necla Hanım, over in operations, be permitted to read my cup, assuring me that her fortune-telling was always spot on. Clearly, Nimet Hanım wouldn't be arriving any time soon.

A second cup of coffee would be too much for my stomach, but I liked the idea of having my fortune read.

"Perhaps a bit later," I said.

The manager and I waited tensely in our respective seats. Gülben flitted in and out of the office, no doubt imagining herself to be "on top of things." Peering at the computer screen on his desk, the manager was the picture of industry. I wasn't fooled. The waiting game must have been equally excruciating for him.

I thought it best to amuse myself with pleasant thoughts. I ran through Audrey Hepburn's filmography from start to finish, and back again. Then I busied myself with choosing a favorite from among her leading men. Even though he was well past his prime, and so nervous about playing opposite the young Audrey that he'd had a last-minute face-lift before shooting began, the legendary Gary Cooper deserved top spot. After all, he'd received the Tallulah Bankhead stamp of approval when she'd declared, "The only reason I went to Hollywood was to fuck that divine Gary Cooper, and

to make the odd film." All of his leading ladies, from Ingrid Bergman to Patricia Neal, had fallen for him. Who was I to turn up my
nose? Yes, top of the list definitely went to Gary Cooper.

Then there was Burt Lancaster in the woefully miscast *The Unforgiven*. His athletic physique and tough guy image, along with
those mouth-watering nude photos making the rounds on the Internet, earned Burt second billing.

Instantly relegated to bottom of the list were Rex Harrison in
My Fair Lady, Alan Arkin in *Wait Until Dark*, and Albert Finney in
Two For the Road.

Now I would have to choose from among Gregory Peck, Cary
Grant, Peter O'Toole, and William Holden, who costarred twice,
first as a young man and then in middle age. George Peppard wasn't
bad in *Breakfast at Tiffany's*, but he was too bland for my taste. Ditto
for husband Mel Ferrer in *War and Peace* and Anthony Perkins in
Green Mansions.

What was taking Nimet Hanoğlu? How much longer would we
have to wait?

"Are you sure you won't have another cup of coffee?" asked the
manager.

I decided fortune-telling would be the very best way to pass the
time.

"Without sugar, right?" he confirmed

So, despite appearances, he had a memory for detail.

Nimet Hanoğlu arrived at the same time as my coffee. It was
the first time I'd seen in her person. She was exactly as she'd been
described: A self-assured woman of middle years who holds herself
fully erect and looks one unflinchingly in the eye. It becomes in-
creasingly difficult to pinpoint a woman's age as she matures: I
guessed that she was about fifty. Although she wore no makeup,
her graying hair had been swept up into a spectacular bun. Her
jewelry consisted only of a ring and a single pendant. But what a
ring, what a pendant. While her tailored suit appeared deceptively

simple at first glance, it was beautifully cut of exceptional fabric. She could have been a not too distant relative arriving for tea with the queen of the England.

After a quick glance at me, she shook hands with the manager and Gülben. We were then formally introduced.

"*Merhaba*, Nimet Hanoğlu. I'm Faruk Bey's wife."

Even her handshake demonstrated force of character.

She sat down in the chair opposite, appraising me. I did the same. She had a flawless pink-and-white complexion.

I offered her my coffee. The fortune-telling could wait for another time. Anyway, it infuriates me when things don't turn out as promised, and they usually don't.

"I understand that you have the key to Volkan Bey's safe-deposit box . . ." she began.

She had a deep voice, and there was something barely perceptible about her intonation that suggested she'd been educated at a foreign school and had roots somewhere in Anatolia.

"I do." I smiled.

"I have no knowledge of your exact relationship to Volkan Bey, but I suspect that the contents of the safe-deposit box could shed light on the suspicious circumstances surrounding my husband's death, as well as the accusations he faced concerning the murder of Volkan Bey. That's why I would like to see the box first. This is the first time my family has experienced something like this, and we'd like to resolve this question immediately."

That wasn't at all what I'd expected.

She must have sensed my surprise. And continued.

"Look, I don't know you. But there's something I'd like you to know: My husband would never have become mixed up in these kinds of unsavory activities. He may have had dubious dealings, but they were always of a financial nature. Not anything like this. My family and I will not . . . cannot . . . allow our names to be dragged through the mud. Everything must be made known, however disagreeable it may be. I need to know. No matter what. No matter how painful it may be. I am prepared for the worst."

"The police," I said, playing dumb, "are working on it. In a day or two, they'll have solved the case."

She smiled bitterly.

"Don't forget, this is Turkey," she said. "The murderers of Uğur Mumcu, Abdi İpekçi, and Bahriye Üçok are still at large. Our family will not permit my husband's murder to be relegated to the third page of the gutter press. That is not our way."

"Well, what if the contents of the box implicate your husband and your family? What will you do then?"

This time, the smile was fierce.

"You don't know me, so your misgivings are perfectly understandable. I've already explained everything, here at the bank, but I'll do it again for your benefit. My family is from Kilis and of some prominence there. My marriage to Faruk was arranged while we were still children. I was raised to become his spouse, sent to the best Swiss schools, and trained to be the perfect wife. I have a strong sense of justice. I don't mince words. I have nothing to hide, and nothing I can't account for. That has always been the case, and always will be . . . I once feared God, and only God. No longer. If He wishes, He can take my soul. End of story."

I couldn't help smiling as I listened.

"I loved Faruk. And respected him. He reciprocated. We were married for twenty-four years. Couples always imagine that they know their partners. I believe I knew Faruk . . . No, not 'believe,' I *know* I knew him. Yes, I knew him through and through, what he was capable of, and what he was incapable of. Those malicious rumors in the press insinuating relations with a man of the lowest character were untrue. Fabrications of the worst kind. He'd need to be quite an actor to have fooled me all these years, and he was no actor. But if I am wrong, and if he has been deceiving me and my family for all these years, I need to know. And to act accordingly."

"You're right," I said.

"I've been so preoccupied with these questions, I haven't even had the opportunity to mourn him. I haven't shed a tear. The man I've known since I was a child, the man I've shared a bed with for twenty-four years, the man who has always been at my side just couldn't be the man they say he is. It can't be true. I knew him too well."

Her eyes had grown misty. We all looked on silently.

She didn't cry, just closed her eyes and raised her eyebrows for a moment, as though she was merely stretching her facial muscles. When her eyes reopened, she was back in iron lady mode.

"I knew him well," she repeated. "Perhaps you'll understand better if I tell you we were friends. The best friend I ever had. That's important. Without a sense of companionship, marriages wither and die. Ours had never been a love match, but we grew up together and respected each other. Some things may have remained unspoken and unsaid, I don't remember right now. But I can tell you honestly and straight from the heart that we shared so much. I've lost a friend, a treasured friend. Can you understand what that means?"

I wanted to assure her that I could. She had affected me deeply. Her choice of words may have been conventional, but it was her intensity and sincerity that got to me.

"I think I can," I said.

"He wasn't the type of man who would commit suicide. He was full of life. He wasn't an outgoing person, but he was, in his own way, full of life. And those crimes they wrongly accused him of, they were beneath him. Like I said, I knew him well, as well as I know myself. And I trusted him completely."

"And what about them?" I said, waving at the bankers.

"I found out about the box from Volkan Bey's brother. I've known Nejat Bey for years. He kindly agreed to help me."

Nejat Bey proudly stirred in his seat at the mention of his name.

"Don't mention it," he murmured.

"Faruk Bey and I have known Nejat Bey for some years. We've done each other favors. Of a financial nature, of course. There are some people one can count on. Nejat Bey is one of them."

More murmuring from Nejat Bey.

She was somehow appealing. Her large, honey-colored eyes were candid. She seemed honest. She commanded respect. She may even have resembled Ingrid Bergman in her later years. The Bergman in a tailored suit who seduces Yves Montand and Anthony Quinn . . .

"I need to know who's behind this, how Faruk died, why he was accused of murder, and who has been slandering him. He had as many friends as enemies, but these . . . accusations of murder . . . are going too far. I can't take it anymore . . ."

"So you do really want to get to the bottom of all this?" I asked.

"Certainly," she said, eyes widening.

"Then why did you send two armed men to break into my house? In the middle of the night?"

Arching her eyebrows, she looked in turn at me, the manager, and the cheery assistant. Finally, her eyes came to rest on me again.

Now she was steely. "Look, I still doubt your true intentions. Just as I doubted those of Volkan Bey's brother."

One of the arched eyebrows settled into place, the left one remained raised as she looked at me inquisitively.

If she was acting, she was a real star.

"Who do you think I am?" I asked.

"I have no idea," she said. "I'm meeting you for the first time.

But Okan Bey tried to blackmail us, and it was you who took the key from him. What conclusion was I to draw?"

So that's what Okan meant when he claimed they had "helped out." And he assumed I was trying to get in on the action, too. What a dope. I laughed aloud.

The three of them stared uncomprehendingly.

"That's not it at all," I said, and explained why and how I had obtained the key. Naturally, I said as little as possible about why I'd been drawn to the case and my hacking job with Cihad2000.

"Well then, let's open it together," she said.

"As long as nothing falls into the wrong hands, I have no objections," I concurred.

Nejat and Gülben led the way to the vault, followed by Nimet Hanım and me. I hadn't forgotten about the thugs tied up in my bedroom. I'd have to reach İpekten and let her know. In fact, it'd be a good idea to arrange a little chat between Sarp and Nimet Hanım.

Having dispensed with the formalities of signing in and producing ID, we soon found ourselves standing in front of a full-size safe-deposit box, number 170. Gülben was more brisk and businesslike than ever as she inserted the first of the dual keys. Now it was our turn; that is, my turn.

Like an amateur actor taking up her role, I glanced meaningfully over my shoulder at them.

Nimet Hanoğlu had the presence of mind to request that Nejat and Gülben leave us alone.

They were so in awe of their own dedication to service that they left without a word, to wait outside the entrance to the vault. I'd have been unable to resist peeking inside from time to time.

Nimet's eyes met mine. In them, I read hauteur, supplication, curiosity, compassion, even a slight helplessness—that is, the full gamut of her emotions. She had the most amazing eyes! Any suspicions we'd had of each other evaporated with that look. I opened my handbag and withdrew the key.

I tried to get excited about opening a safe-deposit box for the first time in my life. But I felt nothing.

Inserting the key carefully, I turned it. I tugged on the box. It wouldn't open. I tried again.

Nimet calmly reached over to turn the second key provided by the bank. The box opened.

Eyes on the contents of the box, we both hesitated to make the first move.

Chapter 35

As I got to know Nimet better, my respect and admiration for her grew. I found myself liking her immensely. She had a soothing presence, she looked me directly in the eye when she spoke, and everything she said was measured and eminently reasonable. It helped, of course, that Nihal Hanım, my beloved elementary school teacher, had also looked a bit like Ingrid Bergman.

We'd quickly glanced over everything that came out of Volkan Sarıdoğan's box, taking it all with us for later inspection.

We were being driven in Nimet's car. Not wishing to take any chances, I'd suggested we go directly to my place. In any case, the Hanoğlu household was still in mourning. There would be a lot of visitors. I was also anxious to rid myself of Sarp and the mute, and to relieve İpekten of her duties. It would also be a good idea to look over the files Cihad2000 had sent me.

"All right, we'll stop by your home, and I'll have a word with Sarp. But I've already caused you so much trouble. Let's look over the documents at my house. I'll arrange tea and coffee, and something to eat."

When I pondered the state of my refrigerator, no doubt completely cleaned out by now by İpekten, I saw her point. She had a houseful of servants. And I'd love to see that amazing view in the daytime.

"But what about your visitors?" I asked.

"Everyone who matters has already expressed their condolences. The rest can stay away. At times like this, you learn who your true friends are. Some avoid you, some suddenly fall ill, others find they have urgent business overseas . . . Scandals are contagious, you see!"

She laughed bitterly, turning her face toward the window for a moment.

"I'm sorry. I'm not feeling well," she said, in a voice treading that thin line between hysterical laughter and tears.

I gave her a moment to collect herself.

"Have you got a computer?" I asked.

"Certainly," she said. "The house is full of them . . ."

"I've got some computer files I'll need to take with us."

I didn't tell her that the files concerned her husband's business dealings, but I did suggest that they might be of use.

"Of course, of course . . . Certainly."

The word "certainly" was her trademark response, uttered on every possible occasion.

When we stepped into my flat, everyone was in for a shock.

İpekten was still in front of the TV, but *Queer as Folk* had been replaced by porn. Two hairy musclemen were going for the "money shot."

Sitting on the floor in the lotus position—naked!—she was flanked by her captives, whose underwear had been pulled down to their knees. Her hands were full, and busily at work.

Things went from bad to ludicrous. When the two men saw Nimet and me walk in, they hastily assumed prone positions to hide their privates, their white bottoms bobbing in the air. İpekten launched into a stammering explanation.

"I just . . . for fun . . . The film did it."

Nimet stood stock still and silent, surveying the scene before her. Trying to conceal her groin with one hand, her breasts with the other, İpekten managed a *"merhaba"* and a weak grin that only made her look more ridiculous.

"I'm so sorry," I said, leaping in front of Nimet.

"Think nothing of it."

"Let me introduce you. This is my friend, İpekten. She's been guarding your boys. And this is Nimet Hanım. Nimet Hanoğlu."

Without rising, İpekten extended her right arm, the one that had been covering her breasts.

"Pleased to meet you."

That was a lie. Even İpekten would have been embarrassed by the antics we'd seen. There was nothing to be pleased about. If nothing else, she'd failed to discharge her duties as a guard.

They shook hands.

"Could you give me that robe, hubby?"

The robe was Ponpon's kimono; hubby was, of course, me. I handed it over.

"Come with me," I said, taking Nimet by the arm and leading her to the office. I have no idea if she turned around for another look. I was in front. I turned on the computer.

"It'll take about five minutes," I said.

"Fine, no problem."

"Can I get you anything?"

"No, thank you."

Excusing myself for a moment, I raced back to the living room. İpekten had put on the kimono and was busily pulling up the prisoners' underwear, no easy task, as they were bound and gagged grown men.

I helped, heaving Sarp up to his feet while she tugged at his briefs.

"I'm sorry, hubby . . . When you took so long I thought I'd watch a new film . . . And then I got into the mood . . . all those men . . . And these two were here, right at hand . . . I thought it'd be fun . . ."

"I see," I said. "Never mind. Forget about it."

"I just hope you don't get the wrong idea. That's why . . ."

"Like I said, forget it. What happened, happened."

"Tell me you forgive me. I couldn't bear it if you didn't. I'd lose sleep for at least three nights."

"Alright, *ayol*," I nearly shouted. "There's nothing to forgive. It's just that it was a bit embarrassing."

She threw her arms around me and gave me a big kiss.

"I was embarrassed, too," she said. "Let's make this our little secret. Don't tell anyone!"

"It's a deal," I agreed. Then I put an end to the subject by adding, "And even if I did, who'd believe it?"

She paused, then smiled when the truth of what I'd said sank in.

"Come on," I said, pointing to the mute, "let's get him dressed, too."

"Right away, hubby!" she said, getting to it.

Sarp was staring daggers at me.

I went over to him and whispered in his ear.

"As you saw, Nimet Hanım is here. Your work's done. Finished! If you breathe a word of this, I'll tell everyone how I beat you up, and that'll be the end of your career. And if I have to, I'll tear your impressive tackle right off and stuff it down your throat."

To illustrate my threat, I reached down and grabbed him.

"So wipe that scowl off your face and give me a sweet smile."

His forehead seemed to twitch. He was probably trying to smile. I ripped off the bandage covering his mouth, removing any hairs that had grown out during the day.

"Bitch!" he exploded.

His hands and feet were still bound. I grabbed him again, squeezing harder this time.

"I don't think you get it . . ."

He was in pain. And he did get it now, or he wouldn't have gritted his teeth without a word.

"Good," I said. "That's a good boy."

Before returning to Nimet, I instructed İpekten to free his legs, but to leave him handcuffed.

"I'm so sorry," I said to Nimet, as I entered the office. "We caught them unawares."

"No matter," she said, polite to the end. I wasn't sure what she meant, but it was clear that she was anxious to close the subject.

Sitting in front of my computer, I began copying Cihad2000's files onto a disc. A huge bouquet of virtual flowers appeared with each file. Red carnations, yellow and white gladioli, a huge basket filled with purple, pink, and crimson anemones. With the last file appeared a bunch of red roses, upon which were written the words: "Thank you, Kemal." I was touched.

"All done," I said, trying to smile as though that scene in the bedroom had never taken place. "We can leave whenever you like."

While Nimet had a word with Sarp and his accomplice, I wiped any fingerprints off the guns. I wouldn't have put it past Sarp to shoot someone with that gun and then try to pin it on me. One can never be too careful.

The boys were dismissed. İpekten came in to say good-bye, a fashion plate once more. Clasping Nimet's hand between her own, she apologized again.

"Sarp and I go way back, you see . . ." was her unnecessary explanation. I suspected Sarp would no longer be on Nimet's payroll, whatever İpekten's explanations.

"Not a problem. Really. Forget it." She blushed.

Her chauffeured car was waiting in front of the building, the passenger doors flung open as we approached. After winding through the steep narrow streets of Cihangir to drop off İpekten, we headed for the coast road to Yeniköy.

On the way we studied the contents of the box. Volkan seemed to have obsessively squirreled away everything he got his hands on.

There were also separate envelopes for each of his clients, containing telephone numbers, parking stubs, hotel invoices, an outline of sexual preferences and kinks, and even a few photographs. For some reason, Nimet quickly passed over the photos, focusing mainly on various documents. Some of the envelopes contained nothing but a business card, others were stuffed with bank draft vouchers. I had no idea what we were looking for, so I busied myself with the photos, especially those of the rich and famous in compromising poses. Nimet seemed to know what she was after. Passing over some envelopes, she reviewed every line of every document found in others. It was only natural that some names would mean more to her than they did to me.

I observed that Nimet's eyes had narrowed, as with pursed lips she sorted through the documents more and more quickly. Whatever she was looking for, she obviously hadn't found it.

Chapter 36

The upstairs room of the Hanoğlu *yalı* I was led to was even more spectacular than the one in which Faruk Bey had received me. The view and the antiques were equally magnificent. I felt like I was in a château in the Loire Valley. But then again, nothing in the Loire Valley looks out on the Bosphorus, today a deep blue and at arm's length. A white *vapur* glided past. I fought the urge to wave to the passengers in childlike delight.

"Here's your computer!"

Nimet had placed a laptop on the tiny writing desk in front of the window. The legs of the desk appeared too delicate to support the weight of the laptop.

"Now," she said briskly, "while you do whatever it is you need to do, I'll continue examining the things from the safe-deposit box. Faruk's account books are here as well. If necessary, we'll look them over, too."

"Nimet, I'd love you to address me as *sen*," I said. I'd deliberately used only her first name, along with the more formal *siz*. She didn't need to know that it was a privilege enjoyed by few.

The smile she bestowed on me was warm and somehow heartbreaking, perfectly encapsulating the current state of her heart, mind, and soul.

"Naturally," she said. "But use *sen* with me as well, would you . . ."

The cupboard she opened was filled with notebooks, labeled and leather-bound.

"As you can imagine, these are strictly confidential. But I no longer have the luxury of privacy. We'll look through them together and destroy what we must."

I turned on the computer, hesitantly flipping through one of the notebooks while I waited. It comprised a meticulously penned list of names, sums, and dates. There were also explanatory notes next to some of the names: identities, references, questions.

Nimet had settled onto a "Josephine" sofa at the other end of the room. I'd always wanted one, upholstered in Bordeaux velvet, like hers. Behind her, a *mille fleurs tapisserie*, fine as a Botticelli, hung from the high ceiling. Standing among thousands of wildflowers in the clearing of a dark forest was a maiden, in a pale blue gown and conical hat, and three hunters, the faces of whom were obscured. Cinnamon-colored game birds with huge wings drooped gracefully from the mouths of long-eared hunting dogs. In the background, a fairy-tale hilltop castle and nearly transparent white unicorn, its head peeping out from behind a tree, its eyes on the maiden.

The computer was ready to go, and so was I. Sitting on the spindly Gobelin tapestry chair, I uploaded my CDs. The chair was more comfortable than it looked. I was soon absorbed in my work.

"Would you like something to eat?"

I often forget to eat when I'm concentrating. Many hours had passed since breakfast, and I didn't feel hungry. But I liked the idea.

"Please," I said.

"I'll see what we have," she said as she left the room.

We were soon being served by Esra Hanım, a rotund woman in her fifties with ample breasts. On one side of the enormous platter she carried were rows of cold cuts; on the other side, my favorite delicacy of all time, Circassian shredded and dressed chicken. The middle of the platter was heaped with stuffed cabbage and vine leaves drizzled with olive oil, and a generous helping of *kuru mantı*.

The question came as we were enjoying our late lunch. In fact, I was, at that moment, once again totally absorbed by the Bosphorus; I was skimming the waters as I flew all the way to the Asian shore.

"Why do you dress like that?"

I paused for a long moment, eyes fixed on the view. Then I turned to look at her. I deliberately chewed a piece of chicken, and swallowed hard.

"You're obviously a man; why do you wear women's clothing?"

I chewed it over some more. Then I reached for my glass of water, taking care to smile.

Something was missing. Yes, we would need some music. Light strings would do, or a chamber orchestra. Or even some soft crooning. Dean Martin, perhaps.

"I like it," I said.

She wasn't satisfied. She continued looking at me with questioning eyes.

"Do you feel like a woman?"

Alright, we had a couple of murders to solve and needed to work together, but I wondered if that gave her the right to delve quite so deeply and abruptly into my private life.

"Sometimes . . ." I said.

"How long have you been like this?"

"A transvestite, you mean?"

"Yes . . ."

"For quite some time, I suppose. I also dress as a man at times."

What was I saying? That last part sounded almost defensive.

"If you'd rather not talk about it, let's not. I just wondered . . ."

She'd returned to her plate and was avoiding my eyes. She toyed with a piece of warm *kuru mantı*.

"I haven't met many people like you, that's all . . ." she said.

I could have gone into the philosophy and history of cross-dressing, expounding my own views and feelings on the subject, bringing up the fact that not a few straight men get a kick out of wearing silky panties, heels, and nail polish, not to mention that some women, too, choose to dress in masculine clothing on occasion, among them Marlene Dietrich and George Sand . . . But I couldn't be bothered.

The fiery reflection of the setting sun was captured in the tens of thousands of windows on the Asian shore, the deepening shadows bringing into stunning relief each detail of the view I watched in silence.

Cihad2000 had worked hard. When combined with Volkan's papers and Faruk's notebooks, we would get a clearer picture. Nimet was one of those compulsive note takers. Color-coded pens were used to mark dossiers laid on the floor.

"Mind mapping," she said. "I was taught in Switzerland. It's a highly effective aid in study, organization, and problem solving."

She was right. We'd made significant progress in sorting through a complex web of relationships. But we hadn't yet found the killer or the motive.

The servants were told to turn away visitors and not to put through phone calls.

During a break, I called Ponpon, to tell her where I was and not to worry, as well as Kemal Barutçu and Hasan. I kept it short. I'd have plenty of time to share details later.

"I'd like some cognac," Nimet announced as she stretched out on the Josephine. "It's getting chilly. A spot of cognac would warm us up. Would you like one?"

"Certainly," I told her.

"You know," she said, "this reminds me of my school days. Boarding school . . . just us girls and a bottle of cognac . . ."

I wanted to hug her. I'd decided to love her, and it didn't matter what she said or did.

Crystal balloons of cognac cupped in our hands, we sat on the floor, looking over the mapped-out and labeled files and papers. We switched a few of them over. New links were established. It was getting dark outside. Lights twinkled, one by one, on the opposite shore; ships began to glow.

I was pacing around the room. We'd taken nearly all of the notebooks out of Faruk's rosewood cupboard. The palatial carpet was obscured by papers and notes.

"Why don't we play some music?" I suggested. "It always does the trick with me. It's inspiring."

I suddenly remembered that the house was still in mourning. "Would music be disrespectful?"

"Of course it won't." She smiled. "What shall we listen to?"

There was no point in asking what she had. It'd take too long to run through a whole list of selections.

"Something soft," I said.

"I've got just the thing. Wait a moment. I'll go and fetch it from my bedroom. This is—was—Faruk's sitting room. He listened mostly to Turkish music, along with the occasional French chanteuse."

She raced out of the room. I returned to the rows of papers, each of them numbered and affixed with notes in the precise handwriting that is a hallmark of Central European culture.

Nimet was back in a flash.

"What do you think?" she asked, eagerly handing me Pergolesi's *Stabat Mater*. It was my favorite version, featuring Teresa Berganza and Mirella Freni.

"It seemed appropriate," she said. " 'The mourning mother was standing . . .' Neither of us is a mother, but I am in mourning, like the Virgin Mary as she stood beside the cross . . ."

"Certainly," I said. "You know, it's one of my favorite pieces. Especially this particular recording."

"Really?" She beamed. She looked ten years younger at that

moment. "I first heard it in Switzerland. I played the record so often I wore it out. Then I looked everywhere for a CD. The other versions just aren't the same. Anyway, I only recently found this. I was so thrilled."

I silently sang along: "*Stabat mater dolorosa juxta crucem lacrimosa dum pendebat filius . . .*"

Cognac, Pergolesi, the ever-deepening dusk . . . And after switching around a couple of pieces of paper I cried out, "Look! Here it is!"

Chapter 37

It was nearly nine at night, and all of our guests had assembled in the enormous drawing room of the waterfront mansion. That it would be a finale straight out of an Agatha Christie novel, I had no doubt. For that was our intention.

As the guests arrived, we were on the floor above completing our preparations. Preparations that were both physical and mental. It was critical that we planned exactly what would we say, as well as when and how, and that each and every allegation be backed up by the appropriate source or document.

And, of course, we had our costumes to consider. After our quick, separate showers, Nimet and I began rummaging through her wardrobe. That is to say, by opening up her wardrobe to me, as well as her heart, Nimet confirmed beyond a doubt that all of my intuitions on the subject of her generous nature had been spot on. She chose a simple, dark blue dress. No sleeves, no collar. A perfect fit. When it was my turn, she instinctively gestured to the area of the capacious wardrobe reserved for frills and embroidered evening gowns. While it's true that my eyes had involuntarily strayed to the sequins and ostrich feathers, tonight was different. And what's more, Haluk Pekerdem would be coming. I'd have to rein it in a bit. I selected an ensemble every bit as sober as hers: white, high-waisted YSL trousers and a white silk blouse. They were, of course, rather too big, so I accessorized with a wide belt. Perfect.

The guest list was long and varied, compiled in a process not unlike that of a wedding, with "yours" and "mine." I'd insisted on

my commissioner friend, Selçuk, Cihad2000, who was also in it up
to his ears, and Ponpon, who would be enraged if uninvited. Nimet
chose her attorney, Haluk Pekerdem—how could I say no?—Canan,
who was his wife and Faruk's sister; Hikmet, who is not only
Nimet's brother but could also apparently be counted upon to
maintain order if things got out of hand; and, finally, Faruk's assistant, Sami Bey, whom I hadn't yet met. Nimet told me he was a
prominent member of the Jewish community and summed him up
as taciturn, tense, and trustworthy.

On our joint list were: Volkan's brother-in-law, Ziya Göktaş, who
was to be picked up by Nimet's chauffeur; and Okan, who would
be escorted to the house by the always dependable Selçuk. And, of
course, where Okan goes, the great poet Refik Altın also goes.

It was exactly nine o'clock when Nimet and I descended to the
drawing room. Everyone was present and accounted for. We'd
planned an impressive entrance, but Ponpon spoiled it by running
up the moment she saw me.

"Sweetie!" she said. "What on earth's going on here? Tell me
quick. I dropped everything and came straight over. I'm dying of
curiosity. Don't do this to me! Come on, tell me everything this
instant!"

"All in good time," I said coolly.

"What do you mean, *ayol*?" she snapped. "I'm not like *them*. I've
got to work for a living. I have a show to put on." Ponpon's words
were accompanied by a sweeping wave of the arm that condemned
those present who had not found gainful nocturnal employment.

"It won't take long. Take a seat, if you like," I said in my calm-
est voice.

"And if I don't *like*?"

Hands on her hips, Ponpon had thrown back her head. She'd
neglected to apply foundation under her chin. I even spotted some
shadowy stubble.

Leaning forward, I whispered in her ear. Her hands and chin shot down to a more appropriate level. Cupping her chin, she shot me a wink. She looked slightly embarrassed.

"And stop screeching," I added. "Everything's on track. I only invited you because I thought you'd want to see for yourself. And it'd take too long to tell you all about it later . . ."

Flashing me a look of sisterly solidarity, she trotted off to her chair.

Cihad2000 was the only person none of the other guests had met. He was sitting in his wheelchair, of course. I introduced him to Nimet, and then to the others, not explaining why he was there. Then I shook hands with all present, saving Haluk for last.

Hikmet looked nothing like his younger sister, Nimet. He was dark, with searching, intelligent eyes and a firm handshake. On his cheek was a lesion of the sort we call an "Eastern Boil." He spoke in a deep, reassuring baritone. I could see why Nimet had insisted he come. With Selçuk and Hikmet both present, one in an official capacity and the other in an informal one, we'd be safe. Still, those eyes of his missed nothing, and I felt like I was under constant observation.

Wearing a Prince de Galles jacket, Sami was tiny, thin, and totally bald. His blue eyes looked even smaller behind the thick lenses of his rimless glasses. His hands were small, too. And hot. We exchanged "good evenings." His lips were thin to the point of nonexistence. He looked like a real hothead to me.

"It'd be nice to meet privately for a change," said Selçuk, who was in a dark suit for the occasion. To his mind, he was among the crème de la crème, and he'd dressed appropriately. He gave me a friendly hug. I introduced him using only his first name, with no mention of his title. For obvious reasons, it was too early to mention the presence of a commissioner in our midst.

"Now remember your promise," I said to him softly. "No interference without a sign from me."

"I've exceeded my jurisdiction just by being here. We could all be taken in for aiding and abetting. This isn't right. You should have let me bring a colleague. You know this isn't my department," he whispered.

"You're enough for me," I said, giving his arm a squeeze. "You're the only one I trust."

Holding Refik's hand, Okan was cowering in either fear or embarrassment. In an exaggerated show of respect, he kissed Nimet's hand and touched the hand to his bowed head. He didn't even shake mine, settling for an arid *merhaba*. So, I hadn't been forgiven for the thrashing of the day before.

Refik looked at me timidly.

"I hope you're not up to no good," he said as he shook my hand. "You'll save my Okan, won't you? I couldn't take it if you didn't . . ."

What could I say? He'd have to take it, or else what?

"I trust you . . ." he threw in as I moved along to the next guest.

I produced my most refined, most English smile. This was an Agatha Christie moment, after all. I'd been transformed into a Wendy Hiller, a Vanessa Redgrave, a Diana Rigg, a Jane Birkin!

Ziya, who was looking around furtively through narrowed eyes, was smaller than I remembered. By hunkering down in an armchair at the very back, as far away as possible from the others, he only emphasized how out of place he was. I introduced him to Nimet. I can't say the look he shot her was a friendly one.

"You're up to something," he told me. "Let's see what happens."

Gone was the fawning rascal I'd met at the wake, replaced by someone with hunched shoulders, gaunt cheeks, and sunken eyes.

"What's that mongrel looking for here?" he said, pointing to Okan.

"Patience please, *beyefendi*," interjected Nimet. "We'll explain in a moment. We have our reasons for inviting you."

Unaccustomed to being addressed so formally, Ziya hung his head and said nothing.

Next in line was Canan Hanoğlu Pekerdem. Ever chic; ever elegant. Still smelling sexily of Vera Wang. In short, as irritating as the night I'd met her. We made a show of briefly clasping frosty hands. I was cold to her out of jealousy; but what was her problem with me?

Finally, there was Haluk. I clung to his hand for as long as possible. After all, physical contact is physical contact. It was perfectly clear that he affected me; equally clear that I affected him not at all.

"I'm so happy to see you again," I said.

"Yes" was his terse reply. Even worse, his eyes were blank. Did the man have no feelings, no soul?

Nimet and I took our places. Placed in the middle of the huge room were two high-backed chairs. A fire had been lit, its reflection refracted into ruby and topaz droplets by the heavy crystal chandelier hanging overhead.

We exchanged glances. Yes, everything was ready. We could begin. The lady of the house, Nimet Hanım, would start.

"The reason we have so suddenly requested that you all join us here this evening is that we have an important announcement to make. As you know, Faruk was accused of having murdered Volkan Bey. He was then found dead, under suspicious circumstances, in front of the pier."

At the mention of Volkan's name, Ziya moaned softly. Refik squeezed Okan's hand. Otherwise, there was dead silence, disturbed only by the crackling of the fire. Everyone held their breath, all eyes were on me and Nimet.

It was my turn.

"Nimet and I met just today, but it has been a long and eventful day. We exchanged all we knew. We thought long and hard. And we believe we have made a terrible discovery."

Temperatures were rising. Sami, who was sitting on a sofa next to Hikmet, pulled a large white handkerchief out of his pocket and wiped his forehead.

Cihad2000 looked slightly indignant, so I quickly mentioned him, and outlined our adventure with Türk Telekom. A voice told me to tell them all about his hotel fling with Pamir the previous night. I ignored it.

"*Ayol*, you said it would be over in a minute and you're still getting warmed up," Ponpon burst out. "Look, I'll spell it out for you. I've got to clear out in twenty minutes, at the latest. I've got a show to get to. You can't keep an audience waiting. It'd be the end of my career. I've still got to get ready. I hate rushing."

"Getting ready" would consist of little more than repowdering her jowls. Some of the girls fall apart at the slightest sign of facial hair. It had been a mistake to invite Ponpon. It didn't matter that she'd read all the English murder mysteries in the world, she'd never get the knack of behaving like a cold-blooded aristocrat. Impatient, testy, and determined to be the center of attention—that was Ponpon. Perhaps that's what's meant by "star quality": the burning desire to hog the floor no matter what!

"A little patience, dear Ponpon!" I said.

"I'm trying to go along with you, sweetie, but you just don't seem to get it. I've got a show. No one cares! I've still got makeup and costume to get through . . . Don't you get it!"

She anxiously rubbed her chin, confirming my suspicions.

"Now, now, dear," I said.

I turned to Nimet to make it clear that she was up next.

She sat up straight and turned an appraising glance on each of the guests. That was a critical part of the plan. As her eyes met those of each guest, I carefully did my own appraisal of their reactions.

"We found some important papers among Faruk's documents. At first we didn't know what they were. Then, a note in Volkan

Bey's safe-deposit box and a detail found among the phone and computer records compiled by Kemal Bey helped us connect the dots. We'd overlooked a certain detail for quite some time. But now we're sure."

Silence!

She turned to me. We were both certain now.

"Someone had been extorting money from Faruk Bey for a considerable time," I said.

It was important here to note the reaction of each and every guest. We'd decided beforehand who would observe who.

Impatient Ponpon jumped straight in, of course: "Gigolo Volkan!"

"No, not him," I said. "He was an intermediary. In fact, he was just a tool."

"What?" reacted Sami Bey, wiping his misty eyes with his handkerchief. "That couldn't have happened without my knowledge. We kept meticulous accounts."

"Correct, Sami Bey," said Nimet. "It happened without your knowledge. You, too, were used."

Sami waved his large handkerchief, avoiding eye contact.

"Well I never, *hanımefendi*!" he objected.

"But why?" insisted Nimet Hanım. "You knew Volkan better than anyone. You may have availed yourself of his services more than anyone else . . . Which is why you're sweating now."

Nimet fixed her honey eyes on his. "I had no knowledge of your preferences. Nor was I interested in them. That is, until today. The bedroom is private. I don't care who does what. Nor do I have the right to . . . But someone turned your head."

"Those are baseless insinuations!" Sami shouted.

So he was a hothead, just as I'd thought. I'm never wrong when it comes to men.

Now it was Refik's turn to kick up a fuss. The suggestion of a relationship between Sami and Volkan had been too much for him.

"Slandering the dead like this! How dare you . . ." he began, before Okan deliberately cut him off.

"Leave my brother out of this!"

"No one knew him or loved him like me. Don't you see?" mumbled Ziya from the back. Then came the sound of choked sobbing.

"The murder of Volkan Bey is another matter entirely," Nimet said evenly and calmly. "Everyone had a motive for killing him. Wouldn't you all agree?"

I picked up where she'd left off.

"Ziya Bey, you were in love with him," I began. "You'd do anything to keep him with you always. When he left you, you threatened him with a knife. How are we to believe that you didn't kill him?"

"How could I bring myself to harm someone I loved? Could this hand have stabbed him? I swear, I'd cut it off first!" he sobbed.

"But you were the one who got him mixed up in all this. Admit it. It was you!" cried Okan, beginning to lunge at Ziya. Refik and Selçuk forced him down into his chair.

"What about you, Okan?" I asked. "You adored your brother, but he couldn't keep up with your demands for drugs and cash. After he died, you went through his things, hoping to find someone to shake down. Why did you come here before the body was even cold? It wasn't over grief for your brother; it was to demand money from Faruk and Nimet."

"That's a lie!" he snarled.

"I'm still here," Nimet quietened him. "You said you had damaging evidence and tried to bargain with us. Don't deny it. There's no point."

Selçuk winked at me to indicate that he was ready to step in. I winked back, as we'd agreed beforehand, to let him know that it was still too early and that everything was going as planned.

Ziya was dumbfounded. He'd even stopped crying, and was staring at Okan.

"You bloodsucking leech!" he said. "You did it. It'd be just like you . . ."

For some reason Refik was the most affected. Tears streamed down his cheeks. I wondered why. What was it to him?

Nimet continued playing her role to perfection in a flat voice devoid of emotion, hands folded in her lap. She'd pause from time to time to look over our guests, then look directly into the eyes of the person concerned as she resumed her speech. There wasn't a hint of malice, hatred, pity, or condemnation in her voice or words. She was enviably austere and unpretentious. She turned to Okan.

"It was through you that we learned about the blackmail of your brother's clients, the money that was extorted. His death would have meant a new life for you. Only your brother stood between you and what you would have considered to be a fortune."

"And your income from the minibus wasn't half bad either," I added.

"What do you mean? Are you accusing *me* now?" asked Okan, in a panic.

Refik had frozen. Mouth open, jaw slack, tears halted midway down his cheeks, he stared at Nimet.

"No," said Nimet. "We're not accusing you. We only point out that you had motives of your own. That doesn't necessarily mean you did it. And it would also, in a sense, have meant killing the goose that lays the golden egg. You're too smart for that."

"It wasn't him then, was it?" asked Refik. At a sign from me, he contentedly returned to loud sniffing and crying.

"This thing is dragging on longer and longer. And the longer it goes on, the more disagreeable and messy it's becoming," said Ponpon.

"Shut up and listen," said Hikmet, surprising everyone with his beautiful baritone. He had huge fingers and big hands. Turning to Nimet, he added, "Please, go on."

Nimet looked at me. It was my turn.

"If I may continue," I said, clearing my throat. "It gets a little confusing at this point, because we haven't yet put all the pieces together. But it involves Canan Hanım."

There was no special reason for my voice to crack when I mentioned her name. I wasn't used to sitting near an open fire. Or it may have been the smoke, those fumes.

Canan Hanoğlu Pekerdem's cold eyes latched onto mine like a lethal weapon.

"Nonsense," she said, tossing her head. "You can't prove a thing."

Reaching into her jeweled evening bag, she pulled out a cigarette. Her hands didn't tremble once as she lit it with a Dupont lighter. Crossing her legs, she looked at Nimet. What perfect legs!

"We can prove it," said Nimet, sounding a bit excited for the first time. "The telephone records tell us a lot. You arranged everything. You had your eye on your brother's—my husband's—money. Faruk had to bail you out after all your failed business schemes. Just to protect the family name, our name. The slightest whiff of scandal and it would have been over for us all. You were always the darling of the family, and Faruk may have had a soft spot for you, too. I don't know. You tell me. Faruk gave you free rein. Never held you to account. But you kept sinking one business after another. You took on too much, more than you could handle. And it always ended in catastrophe. It's all been recorded in Faruk's ledgers and notebooks. Hard facts and cold sums. How much Faruk spent to bail you out . . . I've got it all upstairs."

Unfolding before my eyes was a regular family feud, one that had probably been brewing for years.

"Like you said, we're a family and he bore responsibility for the family name. Of course he backed me up," said Canan.

"But then things changed," said Nimet, who was now looking directly at Canan. "Sami, in his capacity as junior partner, noticed what was going on. Capital that could have been bringing in high returns was being used to bankroll you. Someone had to stop it. He confronted you. But you knew all about his weakness for gambling and for strapping young men! You set him up by arranging gambling partners, and drove him into debt. He couldn't play openly because he had a reputation and a business to protect. And as he got in deeper and deeper, he became your plaything. As for the young men, we don't know how you met Volkan, or who slept with him first. But we have receipts for the hotel rooms you both shared with him."

I needed more than one pair of eyes at that moment. I wanted to see the reactions of Ziya, Refik, Sami, Canan, and Haluk all at once.

Gritting her teeth, Canan listened. Her face had tensed to the point where she looked like a plastic surgery victim: slitty eyes, a projecting forehead, elevated eyebrows, lips stretched thin, and a squared-off chin! She didn't say a word. And if she had, her clenched lower jaw might have shattered into a thousand pieces.

Poor Haluk Pekerdem looked stunned. I wanted to fold him into my arms and comfort him. A man like him, cheated on! And with a gigolo, no less. But then again, this was no ordinary gigolo . . .

"Canan introduced me to Volkan!" cried Sami, springing to his feet and playing the victim. Hikmet pressed him back down into his seat.

Canan produced an artificial burst of laughter. It was so forced!

"So what if I did?" she exclaimed brazenly. "Sami needed a strong man in his life, and Volkan was certainly that. A real pro. They were the perfect match . . . So what?"

She shot out a cloud of smoke. She was visibly shaken. Her crossed leg swung to and fro irritably.

"I warned him. I told him to stay away from you society types. I took him in, gave him everything he wanted. But he didn't listen. If he'd just listened," bawled Ziya.

"That's an important point," I said. "But, in fact, there was no harm in Sami seeing Volkan. Excuse me, Refik, I don't say this to break your heart. But it's the truth. The problem was Sami's fear and self-loathing. He was ashamed. Just as he is now."

I stopped and looked at him. He was industriously wiping his glasses.

"That's enough. Stop sweating and stop wiping your glasses!" I said. "I'm losing my temper, mister . . . And as for you, Canan Hanım, you turned his shame to your advantage. You forced Sami to send Volkan to some of your most important clients, on the house. A sweetener! And you also used him to gather information about those same clients . . . for blackmail purposes. If anyone had found out what you were up to, that would have been the end of Faruk. No one wants a loan shark—sorry, Nimet—who knows too much and may blackmail them one day. And as for Volkan, he was no dummy. He kept records on all his clients, shaking them down for whatever he needed. It wasn't long before Faruk Bey found out . . ."

". . . and intervened," continued Nimet. "At first, he didn't understand exactly what was happening. Some clients were making extra payments for no apparent reason. It was only much later, when Okan Bey came to visit, that we found out why. Faruk learned that some of these funds were being channeled directly into Canan's personal account. I vividly remember the night Canan and Haluk also visited. While I was in the parlor, playing bezique with Haluk, you, Canan, shut yourself away in the office with Sami and Faruk."

Bezique? Haluk and Nimet playing bezique in the parlor, like a couple of old maids? I could just imagine the green baize, and Haluk keeping score. I immediately banished him from the scene.

"That's enough," said Haluk, reacting for the first time. He sounded like a criminal lawyer making a final objection in a losing case. He stood up. "What's all this nonsense? How can you accuse Canan?"

"Because she's guilty!" I cried.

Haluk's eyes widened in shock. He seemed unable to breathe for a moment. Then he turned and looked at Canan. She just shrugged a shoulder. My Haluk collapsed onto his chair.

"But why?" he groaned.

Expressed in that "why" were a multitude of anguished questions: Why was I cheated on? Where did I go wrong? How could a wife like mine tire of a man like me? What could a gigolo give her that I couldn't?

"Money," I answered. "Clearly, she needed more cash. She was playing a foolish and dangerous game. Blackmailing her own brother, poisoning his business relations. It was easy enough to raise money while it worked. At first, Sami was putty in her hands. Volkan made sure of that. In fact, we have letters showing how infatuated Sami Bey became with Volkan. He was even jealous. Jealous of a gigolo!"

I occasionally glanced at Ponpon out of the corner of my eye. Face a picture of astonishment, her head swiveled from one speaker to another.

"I loved him," mumbled Sami. "More than any of you will ever know . . . What we had was special."

"Not like me, you didn't. I loved him. Understand?" Ziya said, softly sobbing at the back. "I'd have died for him! Gone to hell and back!" He sounded wretched and looked miserable. And he knew no one was listening to him.

"Well, he was my lover at the end . . . We dreamed of a new life together. Together for always . . ." Refik chimed in. "We were going to travel abroad."

Sami's sweaty face flushed angrily. "You! Where'd you spring from?"

Kemal, who had been sitting quietly in his wheelchair all night long, let out a low whistle and the words "This is getting complicated!"

Here we had three men, all of whom claimed to have been the love of Volkan's life. The three of them looked at one another with tear-filled eyes. Fortunately, Refik had Volkan's brother, Okan, for comfort. And as for Ziya, he just sobbed away quietly.

"You may well have loved him, Sami Bey, but that didn't stop you from peddling him to others," I said. "And it was also Sami who arranged the transfer of funds—with or without the knowledge of Faruk—to Canan's London bank accounts. Volkan was starting to get greedy. He'd realized just how rich and powerful his customers were, and he wanted a piece of the action. Somehow, Faruk found out. And pulled the plug. Both on Sami and on Canan . . . Right?"

"Not really," said Sami.

"Well, anyway," I continued, "on that night, Sami and Canan put their plan into action. Maybe they'd cooked it up earlier. We don't know for sure. They telephoned Volkan using Faruk Bey's cell phone. One of them may even have taken his cell phone with them. All we know is that calls were placed to Volkan late one night. Volkan had gotten out of hand. He was threatening Sami. And Sami met with him that fateful night!"

"No, it wasn't me!"

If he kept sweating like that he was in danger of dehydration.

"Well then, who was it?" asked Nimet. "It couldn't have been Canan. She was at the nightclub that night. There are witnesses."

"Oh, you mean *that* night?" said Ponpon, finally realizing what night we were talking about. "Of course, you came to watch my show."

"Even I was there," I added.

"We hired someone . . ." whispered Sami. A public confession. "An ex-con. We keep a few around. Sometimes they come in handy."

Ziya, Okan, and Refik were all glaring at Sami.

"And you claim to love him . . ." Refik said reproachfully.

"You're in deep shit, four-eyes! You're gonna have to deal with me now," Ziya growled, unleashing a series of threats outlining in some detail the agonies Sami would suffer at his hands.

Selçuk was squirming in his chair.

"Have you got any hard evidence?" he inquired.

"We've got a heap of documents and papers, but you'll have to sort through them and decide what you can use," I said.

"Let's continue," said Nimet, taking the floor.

"Sami killed Volkan, even if he wasn't directly responsible. But all of the evidence pointed to Faruk. If he'd been imprisoned and out of circulation, they would have taken over the business."

"But then Haluk Bey saved the day," I said.

Haluk was still looking utterly crushed. And gorgeous in a new way.

"That idiot," spat Canan. How could anyone look at a man like that with so much hatred?

Nimet and I talked rapidly in turn.

"That's right, Haluk did all he could to defend Faruk," said Nimet. "The case against him was full of inconsistencies. I think he may even have confided his suspicions to Haluk."

"Yes, I did find out one thing," Haluk said, his head bowed. "Canan was heavily overdrawn."

"And," I said, "that's when we came into the picture: me and Kemal! But who hired us? Haluk! Why? To rescue both his wife and Faruk. He paid us good money. And he got what he paid for. But he cast the net too wide. If he'd simply settled for deleting a few phone records, Kemal and I wouldn't have suspected much. But the international dimension caught our attention."

"The funds were always transferred via the Island of Jersey and London. I had to wipe out those records . . ." Haluk muttered.

Canan looked at him in disgust.

"Canan naturally realized that things were going to blow up in her face," I said. "Faruk had become too dangerous. She laid all her cards on the table, but he hadn't even been arrested at that point."

"That brings us to the night Faruk died . . ." said Nimet. She was speaking more precisely than ever. With her right hand she toyed with her necklace. "When Faruk was released, many people came to wish him well. I was too ashamed and upset to leave my room. But I do know that the last three visitors were Sami, Canan, and Haluk!"

"The three prime suspects," I said. I hoped Haluk hadn't done it. Canan could go to prison, and then he'd be mine. I'd be there to console him. "A person or persons persuaded Faruk to go out on the pier that night. And then into the sea . . ."

"First he was clubbed on the head!" Cihad2000 provided that critical detail. "With a blunt instrument. I was listening in on the police radio."

I silently congratulated him. Sometimes his obsessive snooping was useful.

No one spoke. You could have sliced the tension with a knife.

"If we consider Sami's diminutive physique . . ." said Nimet, breaking the silence. "Faruk was a big man, even a bit stout in his latter days."

Everyone was staring at Canan and Haluk.

"*Ay*, alright already. I got it," said Ponpon, shooting to her feet. "I'm late. You can tell me later who did it. I'm confused enough as it is. You're driving the lyrics right out of my head."

As she shook Nimet's hand and prepared to leave, "Thanks so much for inviting me. Your house is so nice. I hope to come again another time," she remarked.

"Certainly," Nimet managed in reply.

Selçuk kept things moving.

"I'll call in the squad . . ." he said.

"Please . . ." said Canan tearfully. She wiped her eye with a recently manicured finger. "Haluk, do something . . . Please don't call the police . . ."

Even Ponpon looked back, spellbound.

"*Ayol*, you mean you did it?" she cried, finally grasping the seriousness of the situation.

Canan broke down. None of us had expected that. She was sobbing hysterically, oblivious to her ruined makeup. Gone was the Nişantaşı girl who'd looked down her nose at everyone, most of all me. I almost felt sorry for her.

"He turned on me . . . He wouldn't even listen . . . What was I to do? . . . Everything was falling apart . . . What else could I do?"

Haluk embraced her. I found that unnecessary. It should have been me.

"Can you leave us alone until the police come?" he asked.

Chapter 38

Everything happened that night just as Nimet and I had planned, like an Agatha Christie novel, or even better, the star-studded finale of a film adaptation: *Murder on the Orient Express*, *Death on the Nile*, *The Mirror Crack'd*, and *Evil Under the Sun* had nothing on us, even with cameos by Sean Connery, Ingrid Bergman, Bette Davis, Maggie Smith, Lauren Bacall, Jacqueline Bisset, Diana Rigg, Elizabeth Taylor, Jane Birkin, Mia Farrow, and Anthony Perkins.

Canan and Sami were led away in handcuffs. That business with the Telekom records was kindly swept under the carpet, thanks to Selçuk. After all, Cihad2000 and I had helped solve two murders.

With the mystery of her husband's murder cleared up, Nimet began the painful mourning process. We hope to visit each other regularly. We even talked about taking a short holiday together. She's always wanted to visit the coast of Croatia. "Dalmatia is supposed to be wonderful," she says. We haven't yet had a chance to make definite travel plans. I hope we become friends. And if we do, she'll certainly be a novel addition to my little circle.

Ali was terrified when he found out what a close call we'd had. I expect he'll steer clear of shady contracts, at least for a while. I also expect a resulting drop in the company's fortunes—and mine.

Kemal, alias Cihad2000, meets regularly with Pamir. As far as I know, he no longer rents five-star suites, settling instead for more modestly priced hotels. "I only have eyes for her," he claims. Pamir retorts, "I'm a professional, *ayol.*"

No one's seen Refik around for a while, at the club or anywhere else. They say he and his lover have taken a long holiday, either in Tunisia or in a village down south. Rumor has it that he's working on his latest masterpiece.

Sami is in jail, of course. If he does get out, Ziya Göktaş may honor his oath to avenge Volkan's death.

We've still got to take care of the scum in Hasan's neighborhood. I don't want to bother Selçuk about it. Perhaps I can find another way. I'm thinking it over.

Haluk Pekerdem is still in jail. I can't imagine him there. I hope nothing bad happens, that he doesn't get droopy shoulders and sad eyes, gain or lose too much weight, or otherwise allow his amazing good looks to deteriorate in any way. He's being charged only with being an accessory to a crime and with concealment of evidence. In any case, he'll be out long before his wife, Canan. I'm still hopeful. Who knows?

Acknowledgments

J have always watched awards ceremonies—especially the Oscars—with a sense of amazement and good-natured envy. The award winners invariably present a long list of those believed to have contributed in some way to their general development. It is a fascinating life survey, embracing everyone from parents and teachers, to those well-known sources of inspiration, neighbors and pets.

Presented with the opportunity to compile my own list, I have decided to milk it for all it's worth. If I have overlooked anyone, I apologize for the oversight of my editor and consultant.

First of all, I would naturally like to thank my family: My mother, dearest Meloş; my late father, even if he is unable to read this; my brother, who I believe has always taken life much more seriously than I have; his spouse, the happy result of my skills as a matchmaker; my late grandmother on my mother's side, who was always a source of joy and panic in the house where I grew up; that pillar of dignified calm, my late great-grandmother on my father's side; various other relatives, some living, others no longer with us, including my aunts, uncles, maternal uncles, first- and second-generation cousins—those passed over know who they are—and, finally, because anything but a specific mention would be a disgrace, my "special" cousin, Yeşim Toduk; my aunts' husbands, and my aunts-in-law.

Next come the friends I would like to thank: Naim Faik Dilmener, who patiently read my manuscript, guiding and encouraging me, and who is himself a keen reader of detective stories and an authority on golden oldie 45s, as well as his son, but in particular his wife, "Belinda"; Berran Tözer, who set out with me when this project was a five-book miniseries, but threw in the towel by the time we reached page 27; my esteemed partners and fellow consultants with whom I make a respectable living—for it would be impossible for me to survive on my earnings from writing books— Işıl Dayıoğlu Aslan and A. Ateş Akansel and their spouses Burçak and Suada (who is also my Reiki master), as well as Işıl and Burçak's daughter, Zeynep; and Ateş and Suada's dogs.

Despite their not really know what exactly was going on, I would like to thank, for their unfailing emotional support, Mehmet "Serdar" Omay; Murathan Mungan; Füsun Akatlı and her daughter, Zeynep, though we haven't seen each other in a long time; and Zeynep Zeytinoğlu; Yıldırım Türker; Nejat Ulusay; Nilgün Abisel; Levent Suner; Nilüfer Kavalalı; Mete Özgencil, whose painting, in which I lose myself from time to time, hangs on the wall of my study; and Barbaros Altuğ, who somehow managed to motivate me without making his intentions obvious, and who is now my agent and imagines that he will somehow emerge unblemished from all of this.

Miraç Atuna, who constantly reinvents herself and, like me, wakes up before dawn, therefore making it possible for me to have a phone conversation with someone before 7 AM.

My business colleagues Kezban Eren, Derya Babuç, and—yes, her surname is real—Pelin Burmabıyıklıoğlu; the ever-smiling Remzi Demircan and Meral Emeksiz, who are the most positive people I've ever met; everyone I've met and encountered at offices anywhere, especially the sometimes capricious secretaries for enduring all kinds of cruelty; all of my eccentric former managers and bosses—I have somehow never been able to locate the normal ones, with the exception of Ergin Bener, who, of that group, is the only one completely at peace with his inner child.

And as far as those responsible for my technical development: naturally, all of "our" girls, if for no other reason than their courage and their very existence. My encounters with each and every one of them has enabled me, consciously or unconsciously, to make use of their many impersonations, gestures, styles, and sometimes the revealing detail of a single word.

The publishing house that will print this book, my editor or editors, copy editor, proofreader, binder, cover designer, and all those involved in promoting, distributing, and selling the book.

The many who through their works have inspired me over the years, including Honoré de Balzac, Patricia Highsmith, Saki, Truman Capote, Christopher Isherwood, Reşat Ekrem Koçu, André Gide, Marquis de Sade, Pierre Choderlos de Laclos, Yusuf Atılgan, Hüseyin Rahmi Gürpınar, Gore Vidal, Serdar Turgut, and many others.

Those whose music has enabled me to find inner peace: G. F. Handel, Gustave Mahler, Schubert, V. Bellini's *Norma* in particular, Tchaikovsky, Eric Satie, Philip Glass, Cole Porter, Eleni Karaindrou, Michel Berger, and all composers everywhere.

And all the artists who give voice to these works, but especially the opera singers—I treasure their presence: Maria Callas; Lucia Popp; Leyla Gencer; Anna Moffo; Teresa Berganza; Montserrat Caballe; Inessa Galante; Gülgez Altındağ; Yıldız Tumbul; Aylin Ateş; Franco Corelli, for both his voice and physique; Thomas Hampson, whose portrait hangs in my bedroom, next to Maria Callas's, for his Mahler *lieder*; Jose Cura; Tito Schipa; Fritz Wunderlich; Suat Arıkan for making me feel to the marrow each time I watch or listen to him, and for the joy of performance; and for the same reason, composer Leonard Bernstein; Yekta Kara, whose wonderful productions restored the visual pleasures of opera; and finally, on another level, the worst soprano of all time: Florence Foster Jenkins.

For similar reasons Mina, whose albums I would rush to buy if they recorded no more than a belch; Barbra Streisand, back before she transformed every three-minute song into a five-curtain opera (that is to say, pre-1980s); Yorgo Dallaras; Hildegard Knef; Sylvie Vartan; Veronique Sanson; Jane Birkin; Patty Pravo; Michael Franks; Lee Oscar; Manhattan Transfer; Supertramp; Juliette Greco; and, again pre-1988—for better or worse—Ajda Pekkan; Hümeyra, for all she is; Nükhet Duru, who manages to inject a dramatic meaning into all of her songs, even when they are rubbish; Gönül Turgut, whose decision to leave music I have never understood and whose absence I continue to lament; Ayla Dikmen, for her costumes alone; and Madonna, whose songs I'm not wild about, but whose presence seems to me to be a good thing.

Those geniuses of cinema, whose numbers seem without end, but whom I'll try to reel off: Visconti; John Waters; Joseph Losey; Almadovar, for his "marginal" films, in particular *La ley del deseo*; Bertrand Blier, before he went too far; Fassbinder, for *Querelle* alone; John Huston; Truffaut; Salvatore Samperi for *Scandalo* alone; Mauro Bolognini; Ernest Lubitsch; George Cukor; Billy Wilder; Alain Tanner for *Dans la Ville Blanche*, the film I have watched most frequently; Audrey Hepburn, of course; Jeanne Moreau; Elizabeth Taylor, especially for her voice; Lilian Gish and Bette Davis for *The Whales of August*; Catherine Deneuve, who, even if she does age, ages beautifully; Faye Dunaway, before she became a caricature of herself; Giulietta Masina; Cate Blanchett; Tilda Swinton; Emma Thompson; Divine, the ultimate simulation; Bruno Ganz; Rupert Everett; Alain Delon, when he was fresh; Patrick Dewaere, whom I'm actually cross with for his early departure; Dirk Bogarde, despite his having denied everything in his autobiographies; Montgomery Clift; Gary Cooper at all times; Terence Stamp, during his *The Collector*, *Teorema*, and *Priscilla* periods; Franco Nero, for whose sake I sat through dozens of rotten movies; Steve Martin; Den Hopper; John Cleese and all of Monty Python and *Fawlty Towers*; Hülya Koçyiğit; Müjde Ar; Serra Yılmaz; and—why not—Alkan; Güngör Bayrak for her legs and determination; Kadir before he gained weight and became thick; Metin Erksan; Atıf Yılmaz; Barış Pirhasan for the screenplays he has written; and Sevin Okyay for her translations, critiques, and articles.

Just for being men, John Pruitt; Tony Ganz; Jason Branch; Mike Timber; Taylor Burbank; Aidan Shaw; and the late—I was so sorry when I heard—Al Parker, as well as dozens of others whose names I don't even know.

Pierre and Gilles, for scaling the peaks of kitsch; Tom of Finland; Jerome Bosch; the Bruegels father and son; Edward Hopper; Tamara Lempicka; Botero; El Greco; Modigliani; Andrea Vizzini; Jack Vettriano; Pablo Picasso before his cubist phase; Leonardo and Michelangelo, for being both masters and members of "the family"; Caravaggio; Latif Demirci, who was the reason for my eagerly awaiting Sundays; the Zümrüt photograph studio, whose front window overwhelms me every time I pass it on Siraselviler.

For reminding me, with their sparkling intelligence and wit of the pleasures to be had from life, Mae West, Tallulah Bankhead, and Bedia Muvahhit; Gencay Gürün for, in a word, *embodying* nobility and graciousness; and Truman Capote again.

Finally, and most important, Derya Tolga Uysal, for his unstinting support in all things, for sharing with me for seven years the ood and the bad, and for his unbelievably affectionate response to y flare-ups, outbursts, depressions, fatigue, mood swings, and alice.

Thank you very much.
salute you all.

arch 2003
müşsuyu, Istanbul

Thank you very much.
I salute you all.

March 2003
Gümüşsuyu, Istanbul